Like many authors, Lesley s

actor, model, cabin crew and nightclub DJ,
feature writing for publications including *Business Matters*,
Which? and *Farmers Weekly*.

She progressed to short stories for the vibrant women's
magazine market and, following a master's degree where
she met her publisher, she turned to her first literary love of
traditional British mysteries. The Libby Sarjeant series is
still going strong, and has been joined by The Alexandrians,
an Edwardian mystery series.

Praise for Lesley Cookman:

'With fascinating characters and an intriguing plot, this is a
real page turner' Katie Fforde

'Intrigue, romance and a touch of murder in a picturesque
village setting' Liz Young

'A compelling series where each book leaves you satisfied but
also eagerly waiting for the next one' Bernardine Kennedy

'Nicely staged drama and a memorable and strangely
likeable characters' Trisha Ashley

'A quaint, British cozy, complete with characters who are
both likeable and quirky' Rosalee Richland, author of the
Darla King series

MURDER
REPEATED

LESLEY COOKMAN

HEADLINE PUBLISHING GROUP
An Hachette UK Company
Carmelite House
50 Victoria Embankment

ACCENT

Headline's p ... lable
products a ... her
controlled s ... cted
to confor ... .

For Hazel Cushion

Acknowledgements

Thank you, again, to my son Miles for the setting of this story, to the rest of my family, Louise, Phillipa and Leo for their unflagging support, to everyone at Accent Press, and with apologies, as usual, to all police forces everywhere. And for information on Bat and Trap, thanks to Carole and Ian. Sorry I never got to come to one!

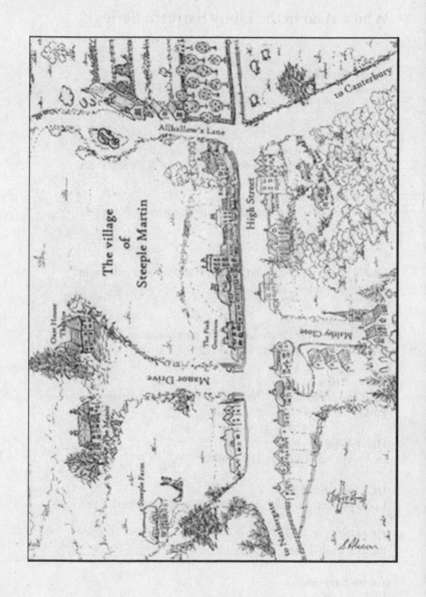

The village
of
Steeple Martin

Allhallow's Lane

to Canterbury

High Street

Manor Drive

Maltby Close

The Park Gardens

Oast House

Steeple Farm

to Nethergate

Who's Who in the Libby Sarjeant Series

Libby Sarjeant
Former actor, sometime artist, resident of 17, Allhallow's
Lane, Steeple Martin. Owner of Sidney the cat.

Fran Wolfe
Also former actor, occasional psychic, resident of
Coastguard Cottage, Nethergate. Owner of Balzac the cat.

Ben Wilde
Libby's significant other. Owner of The Manor Farm and
the Oast House Theatre.

Guy Wolfe
Fran's husband. Artist and owner of a shop and gallery in
Harbour Street, Nethergate.

Peter Parker
Ben's cousin. Freelance journalist, part owner of The Pink
Geranium restaurant and life partner of Harry Price.

Harry Price
Chef and co-owner of The Pink Geranium and Peter
Parker's life partner.

Hetty Wilde
Ben's mother. Lives at The Manor.

DCI Ian Connell
Local policeman and friend. Former suitor of Fran's.

DI Maiden
DCI Connell's forger sergeant.

Adam Sarjeant
Libby's son.

Belinda Sarjeant
Libby's daughter. Lives and works in London.

Dominic Sarjeant
Libby's elder son. Lives and works in London.

Sophie Wolfe
Guy's daughter.

Flo Carpenter
Hetty's oldest friend.

Lenny Fisher
Hetty's brother. Lives with Flo Carpenter.

Jane Baker
Chief reporter for the *Nethergate Mercury*. Mother to Imogen.

Reverend Patti Pearson
Vicar of St Aldeberge's.

Anne Douglas
Librarian, friend of Revered Patti.

Dr Nigel Peasegood
Village doctor.

Chapter One

'I don't like it here,' said Libby Sarjeant, looking round at
the bare walls, crumbling plaster, and broken window
frames. 'I think we should go.'

'Oh, no, there's loads to explore yet!' Fiona Darling
pushed her thick fair hair back off her face and beamed
back at Libby.

'I wouldn't fancy trying to get up those stairs,' said
Libby darkly. 'They look as though they might collapse
any moment.'

'Oh, I'm sure Ted said they were solid enough,' said
Fiona. 'Anyway, I'm going through here. Kitchen, was it?'

'I don't really know. I only came here a couple of times,
and that must have been at least twenty years ago.'

Fiona stopped and looked back over her shoulder.
'Wasn't that a long way to go for a meal from where you
lived?'

Libby shrugged. 'A lot of people came over here. We
didn't have quite so many up-market restaurants in the area
then. Now we've got television chefs and all sorts, but back
then, no. So the Garden Hotel got a lot of trade. And it was
pretty.' She looked around sadly. 'All pink and green and
light wood, it was. I expect they would have changed it

when those colours went out of fashion, though.'

'And when did it close?'

'Not long before I moved here – or just after. I know there was never any suggestion of competition with Harry's Pink Geranium. I think the owner died.'

Fiona nodded. 'That's what Ted said. The son took over or something, but didn't want to carry on with the hotel.'

'I've not heard much about it, which is surprising,' said Libby. 'Although I expect some of the older residents know. I shall have to ask.' She peered at what looked like burning on the floor. 'I think there've been kids in here having bonfires.'

'Really?' Fiona came back and looked down. 'That's dangerous.'

'Certainly is.' Libby frowned. 'Just who is your Ted? I don't think I've ever heard of him, either.'

'Oh, local builder,' said Fiona carelessly. 'He did some work for us when we moved into the barn.'

'I see.' Libby put her head on one side. 'And was it Ted who told you about this place?'

'Well, yes.' Fiona's gaze slid away.

Libby stayed silent for a moment. 'And who had the idea about the community centre?'

'Oh, me!' Fiona turned back enthusiastically. 'I thought I told you?'

'Well, you did when we met at Harry's, but -'

'Oh, I know – I didn't have time to tell you properly! But everyone said you were the right person to talk to...' Her gaze slid away again.

'Well, I was surprised.' Libby perched on the unstable

windowsill. 'After all, we have the theatre, the village hall, and Carpenter's Hall, and each of those has groups that meet in them. I wasn't sure we needed another one.'

'We could have a craft centre,' said Fiona, 'and a women's networking centre -'

'Networking centre?'

'Well, you know, to exchange ideas. That sort of thing.'

'Oh, well,' said Libby with a sigh, 'if you want to waste your money…'

'My money?' Fiona looked shocked. 'Oh, I was thinking more of a public subscription.'

'Round here?' Libby was amused. 'Not a lot of landed gentry with deep pockets in Steeple Martin, Fiona. I doubt if you'd get anyone wanting to invest. Maybe if you intended to turn it back into a top quality hotel and restaurant…'

'Well, no…' Fiona turned back towards the once imposing staircase. 'I'm sure it would work, you know.'

'Maybe, but you've had a look now. Can't we go? I must say I'm not impressed.'

'No, I can see that. But Ted says, with a bit of plasterboard and new skirting boards and window frames – well, he said -'

'I think it would need more than that,' said Libby. 'Anyway, you hang on if you like, but I've got a few things to do, so I'll shoot off, if you don't mind.'

'Oh, OK.' Fiona looked despondent for a moment. 'I'll just take another quick look round the ground floor, then I'll go.'

'Right. I'll see you then,' said Libby vaguely, and slid

3

carefully out of the front door. She hesitated, then turned to her right and began walking down Steeple Martin's high street towards the doctor's surgery and Maltby Close, where she crossed over and waved through the window of the Pink Geranium restaurant at Harry.

She couldn't quite put her finger on the atmosphere inside the former Garden Hotel, but it had made her most uncomfortable. She assumed once refreshed and refurbished it would be fine but now, she didn't really want to go near it again, and could not understand Fiona Darling's aspirations for the place. Still, she'd done her duty and taken the woman round there, although why she should have done so she had no idea. Now she could wash her hands of it and go off to do her supermarket shop in Canterbury.

Nearly three hours later, as she drove back into the village, she was aware of blue lights flashing at the other end of the high street as she drove across into Allhallow's Lane from the Canterbury Road. Sighing, she wondered which of Maltby Close's elderly residents had needed the ambulance this time, and hoped it wasn't Flo Carpenter or Lenny, Flo's long time partner.

She had barely had time to get inside number seventeen with the shopping when there was a knock on the door.

'Constable – er -' she began in surprise.

The young woman on the doorstep smiled a little sheepishly. 'Trent, Mrs Sarjeant. Except it's Sergeant, now. Detective Sergeant.'

'Oh, congratulations, DS Trent. What can I do for you?'

'Er – could I come in for a moment?'

4

Libby frowned, but stood back. 'Let me just put this frozen food away and I'm all yours,' she said, turning back to the kitchen. She heard DS Trent shut the front door behind her and frowned again. She looked over her shoulder.

'Now – what's up?'

'I believe you were with a Mrs. Fiona Darling this morning?' DS Trent said, a little diffidently.

'Yes?' Libby felt the first stirrings of alarm.

'Can you confirm where you were?'

'The Garden Hotel – why?'

DS Trent looked puzzled. 'The Garden Hotel?'

'Yes. Why – where did she say we were?'

'You weren't at a derelict building in the high street here?'

Libby's brow cleared. 'Oh, I see! Yes, that's what it's called. Was called. It was the Garden Hotel for years. And yes, we were there. I left her there.' She stopped. 'What's happened? Is she all right?'

'Could we sit down, Mrs Sarjeant?' DS Trent waved at the armchair beside the empty fireplace, looking weary.

Libby nodded and perched on the edge of the sofa. 'Come on, tell me what's happened. And for goodness' sake, call me Libby.'

DS Trent relaxed back into the armchair and smiled. 'I'm Rachel,' she said, 'thank you. Well, you see, Mrs Darling says she found a body.'

'*What*?'

'You weren't there at the time?'

'No, I was *not*!'

5

'She did say you'd already gone.' Rachel Trent sighed. 'She was looking in the kitchen at the time. Or what had been the kitchen.'

'Yes, she said she was going in there.' Libby shook her head. 'I didn't want to go there in the first place, and I got out as quickly as I could.'

'So why did she want to go there?' asked Rachel. 'She wasn't very clear about it.'

'Do you want to take notes?' asked Libby, eyeing her guest's unencumbered hands.

'No, this is an informal interview.'

'Tea, then? Have you time?'

Rachel looked over her shoulder, as though expecting to see a large superior officer loom up behind her. 'Oh, I suppose so.'

'Come into the kitchen while I make it,' said Libby. 'That'll save time.'

'Now,' she went on, having switched on the electric kettle and fished teabags out of a box. 'Fiona and the Garden Hotel. Didn't she tell you anything about why she was there?'

'I'm afraid she was hysterical.' Rachel sat down at the kitchen table and rested her chin in her hands. 'She was out in the road when the officers who answered the 999 call arrived, and apparently they couldn't get any sense out of her. Then I arrived with SOCOS and Sergeant Davies, then the inspector, and they got her into a police car. So the Inspector sent me to see you to see if you could make it any clearer for us.'

'Inspector? DCI Connell?'

6

Rachel shook her head. 'No, Inspector Maiden's SIO on this one.'

'Oh?' Libby's eyebrows rose.

Rachel tried to suppress a grin. 'Well, Deputy SIO. The top brass don't think DCI Connell should be taking quite such an active part in the investigations, so he's now heading up an MIT at headquarters. He's overall SIO – office-based.'

'MIT?' asked Libby.

'Murder Investigation Team. They're theoretically in charge of all murders on their patch. How it'll work in practice, I'm not sure. Especially keeping the DCI out of the front line.' The grin finally broke out.

'Ah.' Libby grinned back. 'And how long do you think he'll be able to resist it?'

'Not long.' Rachel accepted a mug. 'Thanks. So why was Mrs Darling there?'

Libby repeated the story Fiona had given her that morning.

'Why, though? You've already got community spaces in the village, haven't you? That hall where we've had the incident rooms, and that other one in the same little lane, as well as the theatre...'

'I said that to her, but she's got some new-fangled idea for a craft centre and a cake shop, or something.'

Rachel considered. 'A tea shop might work, perhaps for the older people in the village.'

'It might, but Harry opens at lunchtime and stays open as long as anyone wants him to in the afternoon. And he does wonderful cakes.'

'Harry?'

'The owner of the Pink Geranium.'

'Oh!' Light dawned. 'He does that lovely Mexican street food.'

'That's him. Although it was just a Mexican restaurant when he started. Street food's become a buzz word in the last few years. Anyway, back to Fiona…'

'Sorry, yes. So what did she tell you about this builder? Or the owner of the building?'

'Very little. The builder did some work when she and her husband moved in to the barn at Steeple Well.'

'Where's that?'

'It's just a lane, really. There was an old well there once, and I suppose people just built houses round it. There are only a few, and they're very expensive. Anyway, Fiona started getting involved in everything going on in the village.' Libby gave an amused grunt. 'Only there wasn't much to get involved with.'

'So she thought she'd start something herself?'

'Maybe.' Libby shrugged. 'Anyway, this builder, Ted, had been asked to do some refurbishment on the Garden Hotel building, I presume with a view to selling it on. Why Fiona thought she could get hold of it I've no idea, and why he thought it was all right to just hand over the keys…'

Rachel nodded. 'It is a bit odd. And you don't know what this builder's other name is? Or the owner?'

'Sorry, no. But you can find that out easily, can't you?'

Rachel smiled and stood up. 'Of course. Thank you so much for your help, Libby – and for the tea. I didn't think

I'd be seeing you quite so soon after all that Shakespeare business.'

'No problem.' Libby stood up and saw her to the door. 'Give my regards to Inspector Maiden, won't you?'

'Of course. I expect he might want to talk to you himself at some point – and if I want to know anything else, can I ask you?'

'Course you can. If I don't know the answer, I'll know someone else who does.'

She closed the door thoughtfully after Rachel's disappearing back, and went back to the kitchen to put the rest of the shopping away, before sitting down on the sofa again and picking up the phone.

'Wolfe's Gallery,' came the familiar voice on the end of the line.

'Fran, it's me. I remembered you said you were working today. Guess what? We've got another body!'

Chapter Two

There was a charged silence and Libby imagined Fran standing stock still with her eyes shut, possibly breathing deeply.

Eventually, she let out her breath in a gust and said 'Go on, then. Tell me.'

So Libby told her.

'Do I know the Garden Hotel?' asked Fran. 'It doesn't ring any bells.'

'Long before your time,' said Libby. 'The Ex and I used to come over for dinner occasionally. I don't think I knew the family who owned it.'

'And there's a body. How long has it been there?'

'Oh!' Libby stopped in surprise. 'I don't know. I didn't ask.'

'Well, is it a recent body, or an old one?'

'I've said, I don't know. I don't suppose Rachel knew, either. It was only found a couple of hours ago. There won't be much in the way of forensics, yet, will there?'

'No. So why do you say WE've got a body? It's nothing to do with us.'

'Fiona told them I was with her. Oh, not when she found the body, but I suppose to explain why she was there.'

'But you aren't the reason she was there. That Ted the builder was.'

'Only because he told her about the building. The idea of this community centre seemed to be entirely hers.'

'Will it cost a lot to get the building back to life?'

'Hey!' said Libby. 'I don't care about that! It's the body I'm interested in.'

'You don't think the community centre or Ted the builder have anything to do with why it's there?'

'Good heavens, Fran! How do you work that out? No, I don't! Fiona is brand new to the village – well, almost – and Ted the builder has simply been given the keys to the building. Which I find very odd.'

'It is odd,' said Fran. 'One does wonder why.'

'To tart it up, Fiona said. I assume by whoever's left of the family who owned it. I'm going to ask around to see if anyone in the village remembers anything about it.'

'Leave it to the police.'

'Ah!' said Libby. 'But that nice Rachel Trent has asked if she can come and ask me if she wants to know anything.'

'She means about the village.'

'Well – yes...'

'And Inspector Maiden won't want you poking your nose in.'

Libby sighed. 'No, all right. I just thought you ought to know. Anyway, you're coming over tomorrow for Edward's party, aren't you?'

'Wouldn't miss it!' said Fran, and ended the call.

Edward Hall, historian, lecturer, and friend, had moved into the area just before Christmas, and although that was now some months ago, he had only just got around to having a house-warming event. Libby was looking forward to it, especially as she would be able to catch up with friends she hadn't seen for some time.

'Because,' said Ben Wilde, her significant other, later, 'you haven't been delving into any murders recently.'

Libby began to be indignant and changed her mind. 'Yes,' she said thoughtfully. 'That's really sad, isn't it?'

'It's really only Fran and Guy and Ian, I suppose,' said Ben.

'And I do see Fran,' said Libby. 'Just not as often.'

'Well, tomorrow she and Guy will be staying here, so we'll see as much of them as we want.' Ben gave her a hug. 'And now I want my dinner, woman.'

To Libby's frustration, Rachel Trent did not appear to ask her any questions the following day. Nor did Fiona Darling answer her phone call, letting it go to voicemail, so she had nothing to tell Fran when she and Guy arrived in the evening.

'Well, in that case, you'll just have to let it be an ordinary police case, won't you?' said Fran with a grin. 'Especially if even Ian isn't going to be involved.'

'Maybe Ian'll be there tonight,' Libby began.

'And you will NOT bring it up!' said Guy. 'Leave it, for goodness' sake.'

Libby sighed and gave in.

At a quarter to eight, the four of them walked down to the Pink Geranium to meet Peter Parker, Ben's cousin, and Harry Price, his partner, who had closed the restaurant for the evening. They had delivered food to Edward earlier in

12

the day and now they were more or less off-duty. The people carrier Ben had booked for the Steeple Martin contingent was picking up his mother, Hetty, at The Manor and coming on to The Pink Geranium before taking them all to Grove House, near the village of Shott a couple of miles away.

'Who else is coming?' Fran asked, when they were settled and on their way.

'Don't know,' said Libby. 'I expect he's invited Andrew.' Andrew Wylie was another historian, whom Edward had met during a previous adventure of Fran and Libby's.

'And Ian, of course,' said Guy, with a sly glance at Ben.

'But I expect it will mostly be colleagues from work,' said Ben. 'He doesn't know many people except us locally.'

'Philip Jacobs,' said Harry. 'They both belong to the chess club at the pub, and they have a meal in the caff on occasion.'

'Who's Philip Jacobs?' asked Guy.

'Barrister bloke we met last year when *Twelfth Night* was on,' said Libby. 'I didn't know they were friends.'

'He doesn't have to tell you everything, Lib!' said Peter.

When they arrived at Grove House, a perfect small Georgian manor house set back from the road, they found several cars already on the gravelled forecourt. The big front door stood open and light spilled out into the dusk.

'Hello, everyone!' Edward suddenly appeared, sporting his famous wide grin. 'Lovely to see you all.'

He greeted Hetty, Libby, and Fran with kisses, and the

men with manly hugs. 'Come inside! Hetty, Fran, you've not been here before have you? I'll give you the tour in a bit.'

Inside in the long drawing room, Edward hurried them towards the long table set with drinks.

'Pushed the boat out, haven't you?' said Libby. 'This is lovely.'

'You have a way of putting things, Libby,' said a voice behind them.

'Ian!' Libby turned round with a delighted smile.

'Hello, mate,' said Ben, holding out a hand. 'Haven't seen you for a bit.'

Detective Chief Inspector Ian Connell greeted them all in a similar, but slightly more restrained, way as Edward.

'And you know Philip, don't you?' said Edward, waving forward a rotund, dapper man in a tweed waistcoat.

While greetings were being exchanged, and Edward went off to meet more new arrivals, Libby took the opportunity to have a quiet word with Ian.

'No, Libby,' he said with a smile, before she'd got started. 'I can't tell you anything about the body you nearly found yesterday. A – I don't know very much myself, and B – I'm currently confined to the office.'

'Yes, Rachel told me that.'

'Rachel? Oh, yes, DS Trent. You're busy getting her on side, are you?'

'Well, she was asking about the village, and -'

'She's very sensibly getting a little local background knowledge and went to the most qualified person she knows.' Ian patted her shoulder. 'And if you don't know,

14

you'll know someone who does, won't you?'

'That's what I told her,' said Libby. 'It'll probably be the Steeple Martin Mafia again.'

'Mafia?'

'You know – you've used them,' said Libby with a grin. 'Hetty and Flo and their cohorts.'

'So we have. But what would they know about a boy – I gather the body is of a young male – hiding in a derelict hotel?'

'But what if he was hidden before it became derelict?'

Ian shook his head. 'No, the body is comparatively recent. Well, within the last six months, the pathologist thinks.'

'So really, looking back into the history of either the village or the hotel is pretty useless?'

'Oh, I wouldn't say that.' Ian smiled down at her again. 'Cheer up, Libby. You can have a lovely time ferreting about on the outskirts of the investigation for a change.'

Disgruntled, Libby turned back to her friends, who had been joined by Professor Andrew Wylie, small and dapper, with a neat white beard. She asked after his health and that of Talbot, his adopted cat.

'I gather you found another body?' he said, taking a sip of his red wine.

'No, I didn't – I just *nearly* did,' said Libby. 'I had been with the woman who did find it, though.'

'I used to know the Garden Hotel,' said Andrew, smiling reminiscently. 'Very pretty it was.'

'Yes, I used to go there for the odd dinner,' said Libby. 'Pink and green decor. Very "in" back then.'

Andrew nodded. 'Such a shame what happened.'

Libby's ears pricked up. 'Why? What happened?'

Ben groaned. 'Oh, don't, Andrew, you know what she's like.'

'Oh, it's nothing awful – just that the owner died and his wife couldn't keep it up on her own. The son didn't want it, either, so it was closed up and more or less left to rot.'

'Why didn't they sell it?' asked Fran. 'From what you and Libby have said it was a thriving going concern.'

'I've no idea.' Andrew shrugged. 'You'll have to ask one of those remarkable village ladies of yours. One of them will know.'

'That's what I was thinking,' said Libby. 'What Ian calls ferreting about on the outskirts.'

'Ah.' Andrew turned to look at Ian, who was now deep in conversation with someone on the other side of the room. 'Is he in charge again?'

'Confined to headquarters, apparently,' said Ben. 'His superiors obviously think he spends too much time out of the office.'

'They've tried to do that before,' said Fran. 'It never works for long.'

'Will they set up an incident room again?' asked Guy.

'I don't know,' said Libby. 'Perhaps not, as it isn't a recent body.'

'I thought I heard Ian say it was recent – within six months,' said Fran.

'What I meant was, it hadn't been killed in the last week or so.' Libby turned a bright smile on to their host who was approaching with a tray of canapés.

16

'Harry's best bites,' he announced. 'Have one, do. Have two!'

A little later, when darkness had fallen, and the terrace outside the french windows was subtly lit and inviting, Edward took them on a tour of his new home. Apart from the large drawing room, there was a smart kitchen with room for a small table.

'For proper dinner parties, there's a big Victorian gateleg in the drawing room,' said Edward, and two en suite bedrooms.

'What about upstairs?' asked Hetty.

The staircase to the upper floor went straight up from the Georgian porch, while the door to Edward's flat was to one side of it.

'Has it finally been sold?' asked Ben. 'You weren't sure last time I came over.'

Ben had got into the habit of helping Edward with small DIY jobs – something at which the academic was notoriously bad.

'Yes, it has.' Edward nodded. 'Come on and I'll take you to see the new owner.'

'Oh, no,' said Fran, hanging back. 'We can't be that intrusive.'

'Oh, don't worry,' said Edward carelessly, 'I wasn't going to gatecrash the flat. He'll be somewhere in mine.'

'It's a he, then,' muttered Libby to Fran, as they followed the others back into the drawing room.

'Could be a they,' said Fran. 'A couple? Those two over there. They look likely.'

She indicated a couple chatting animatedly to Philip

17

Jacobs. 'Or them?' She pointed to a slightly older-looking couple and Libby gasped.

'Not them!' whispered Libby, turning her back.

'Why, what is it?' Fran frowned down at her.

'That's Fiona Darling – the woman who found the body!'

'Oh!' Fran surveyed the slender, well-preserved blonde with interest. 'And her husband?'

'I suppose so,' said Libby, 'I've never met him.'

'She looks a bit anxious. She's shying like a nervous horse.'

'I expect she's still getting over the shock.' She turned round slowly. 'Oh, look – Edward's coming back.'

'Now,' he said, 'Fran didn't want to intrude on my new neighbour.' He beamed. 'It's all right, isn't it, Ian?'

Chapter Three

'Ian?' Fran gasped.

'Really?' Libby's voice went up into a squeak.

Everyone else was expressing varying degrees of delight.

'Won't be stayin' so much then,' said Hetty gruffly. 'Neither of you.'

Ian put an arm round her shoulders. 'But we'll both be around for more Sunday lunches.'

Libby sniffed. Ben scowled at her.

'Are we going to get the grand tour of yours, now?' asked Fran. 'I can't believe we're actually going to see where you live.'

'I haven't moved in yet,' said Ian apologetically, 'so it's not really where I live. But yes, of course we can go up.'

Libby held back as the party moved back towards the hall, and went to greet Fiona.

'Hi, Fiona.' She smiled, sympathetically, she hoped. 'I'm sorry you had to face that on your own. Although I can't say I wish I'd stayed.'

'Oh, hi.' Fiona was unenthusiastic.

'Is this Mr Darling?' Libby turned to the man standing silently at Fiona's side.

'Er – no.' A faint colour came up under Fiona's cheeks.

'This is Ted – Ted Sachs. My builder.'

'Oh! The man who had the keys?' Libby gave him a friendly smile and jumped as she felt a hand on her shoulder.

'Come on Libby, you'll miss the tour.' Ian smiled impartially at all three and firmly ushered Libby away.

'This is not a fishing trip, Libby,' he said, once they were out of earshot. 'Yes, I do know she was the person who discovered the body, but it isn't up to me – or you – to question her. At the moment,' he added as she opened her mouth to protest.

'But why is that builder here with her?' Libby wanted to know. 'Why not her husband?'

'That builder happens to be doing some work for Edward and me. Edward invited him. If he and Mrs Darling chose to come together, that's their business.'

'Oh.' Libby mused on this as they climbed the shallow stairs to the first floor apartment. 'But -'

'No buts, Libby. Look here's my impenetrable fortress at last.'

Ian's flat was similar in layout to Edward's, but with the added advantage of a staircase to the attic space, which had been converted into a spacious bedroom suite. Libby and Fran were able to surmise nothing of Ian's taste, as the whole place was still empty, but they both approved of its appurtenances. Large airy rooms, a modern kitchen and bathrooms, and a beautifully solid balcony leading out from the main room, which looked out over the garden and the countryside beyond.

'It's quite similar to my present flat,' said Ian coming

up behind them, 'but bigger. I can use one of the bedrooms here as an office.'

'It's lovely, Ian,' said Fran. 'Perfect. And is it closer to Steeple Martin and Nethergate than where you are now?'

Ian grinned at her. 'Still trying to find out, Fran?'

Fran went slightly pink. 'No need to, now, is there? And it was always Libby -'

'Oi!' said Libby. 'You were always as curious as I was. Especially when you took to coming by on a Wednesday evening to join us at the pub on your way home, Ian.'

'Well, to put your minds at rest, I was further over on the Sussex side. It's just as easy to come down here and cut across.'

Libby frowned. 'Quite a long way. Is this quicker?'

'Yes, and I can even walk into Steeple Martin if necessary.' Ian laughed. 'Although I don't plan to.'

'You've got your own pub, here,' said Fran. 'The Poacher's really nice.'

'I know – I remember it,' said Ian. 'And your cousin's not far in her nursery, isn't she, Libby?'

'Cassandra – yes. And her Mike. Yes – I suppose you would remember the whole area.' Libby stared into the distance.

'What are you thinking about now?' asked Fran suspiciously.

'Just old cases.' Libby turned and smiled at her friends. 'I wasn't plotting. Honest.'

Ian and Fran looked at each other and sighed.

'It's rather romantic, isn't it?' Libby murmured to Fran as they returned to Edward's domain.

21

'What is?' said Fran, startled.

'That flat. With that view. The perfect seduction site.'

'Oh, Libby, honestly! Do you really think that's why Ian's bought it?'

'Well, no. But I can't quite work out *why* he's bought it.'

'It's nearer to Canterbury and nearer to all of us.'

'But,' Libby turned puzzled eyes on her friend, 'surely we aren't that important in his life? After all, he's never let us in, has he? He must have a whole other life. We know he's got relatives in Scotland...'

'Look,' said Fran with a sigh, helping herself to a refill of Prosecco from the bar set up in the corner, 'he's an exceptionally busy man. I don't suppose he has time to have a varied social life. He just happened to find us all congenial, and so it makes sense to live near enough to spend whatever time he has got with us – or some of us. And he and Edward get on, and they're both single, slightly older men.'

'Slightly older?' Libby grinned. 'Middle-aged!'

'Ian, maybe – he must be in his fifties by now - but Edward can't be more than early forties. Still a young man.'

'Funny how one's point of view on age changes as we get older ourselves.' Libby turned back to the crowded room. 'I suppose we ought to circulate.'

To Libby's chagrin she was unable to find Fiona Darling and Ted Sachs during the rest of the evening, neither did Edward have any information about the builder, other than the fact that he was repairing a small

22

summerhouse in the garden.

'I gather it's a bit beneath him, actually,' he said with a grin. 'He normally works on larger projects and restorations.'

'He was with Fiona Darling this evening,' said Libby, 'he's doing work for her, too. How do you know her?'

'Oh, Ted introduced us,' said Edward looking slightly surprised. 'He said she was lonely, with her husband working away a lot.'

'She's got herself involved in a lot of the village activities,' said Libby. 'And she wants to convert the Garden Hotel into a community space.'

'Oh, that's where the body was found.' Edward nodded. 'And she found it. How did she know about the hotel?'

'Ted told her.' Libby shook her head. 'It's all a bit mysterious, really.'

Edward looked at her with a dubious frown. 'Libby, you're not -?'

Libby sighed. 'No. I've been warned off. Although I think it's a bit thick. After all, if I hadn't left five minutes before, I'd have found the body with her.'

'With her? You were there?'

Libby nodded mournfully. 'Just my luck.'

Edward shook his head. 'Honestly, Libby, you take the biscuit.'

'I know, I'm just not a nice womanly woman, am I?'

'But no one should regret *not* finding a body, man or woman,' said Edward.

Libby nodded, a little shamefaced. 'I'm not natural, am I?'

23

Edward laughed, put his arm round her shoulders and gave her a squeeze. 'Just normally nosy.'

It was late by the time the Steeple Martin contingent was collected by their people carrier and ferried home.

'Nightcap?' asked Ben, as Fran, Guy, and Libby trailed into the cottage.

'Should we?' Fran looked doubtfully at the bottle of whisky Ben was flourishing.

'Go on, then,' said Guy gleefully.

'I will,' said Libby. 'Fran, would you prefer wine?'

'I'd actually prefer tea,' said Fran. 'Sorry!'

Libby went into the kitchen to make Fran's tea while Ben poured three generous whiskies.

'So, what do you think of Edward's flat?' asked Guy when they were all settled. 'And what about Ian? That was a surprise.'

'Did you really not know, Ben?' asked Libby. 'You've been over there often enough.'

'Not a word,' said Ben. 'It's a lovely building, though, isn't it? And so well divided.'

'Who did that, do you know?' asked Fran.

'What, the dividing? No idea. It was already done when Edward bought the ground floor.'

'It wasn't Ted Sachs, then?' said Libby.

Ben frowned. 'Not as far as I know. Look, Lib, I don't think there's anything suspicious about the man.'

'It's just that he gave Fiona the keys to that place. I wonder why he did that?'

The other three looked at her in puzzlement.

'To get in with her?' suggested Guy.

'I think he'd already done that,' said Libby.

'Well, let's face it,' said Ben, 'he wouldn't have let her have the keys if he knew anything about the body.'

'That's true, Lib,' said Fran. 'Come on – not our problem. Let Rachel and DI Maiden get on with it.'

'Yes, you're right.' Libby nodded and beamed at them over the rim of her glass. They all heard Ben's sotto voce comment: 'Where've I heard that before?'

Despite Libby's avowed intention to stay clear of the Garden Hotel case, it seemed this worthy ambition was doomed, as DI Maiden appeared on the doorstep of number seventeen Allhallow's Lane the following morning.

'I'm sorry, Libby – Mrs Sarjeant,' he said, sending Ben an apologetic glance. 'I know you weren't actually with Mrs Darling at the time she – er – found…'

'The body,' supplied Libby. 'Come in, DI Maiden.'

'I don't suppose you could bring yourselves to call me Rob, could you?' he said, hesitating by the table. 'This is fairly informal.'

Libby beamed. 'Of course!' she said. 'Is it Robert? Robin?'

'Robert,' he supplied with a grateful smile. 'But only my mother ever calls me that.'

'When she's annoyed with you,' said Ben. 'I know. Would you like coffee? Tea? As this is informal.'

'Coffee would be great.' Rob Maiden sat down in the chair by the table and looked round the room. Sidney the silver tabby stared back disdainfully from the hearthrug. 'I've always liked this room.'

'I quite like it, too,' said Libby, sitting down in a corner of the sofa. 'Now, what's up? I told Rachel – DS Trent – she could come to me if she needed anything.'

'And she said I might need a word, didn't she? Well, although I've worked on several cases around here, I haven't got the detailed knowledge that DCI Connell has, so I thought you might give me some background.'

'Is Ian not in charge at head office?' Ben came in holding mugs of coffee.

'Nominally he's SIO,' said Rob. 'But I'm Deputy SIO. He's just supposed to direct operations from on high.'

'Some hopes,' muttered Libby. 'But he actually warned me off this case yesterday evening.'

'He did?' Rob's eyebrows rose. 'But surely he can't object if I ask you for information?'

'Oh, no, I don't suppose so. I'm just not supposed to go nosing around on my own.'

Rob laughed. 'As you said yourself, some hopes!'

Libby grinned. 'OK, then, what do you want to know?'

'What do you know about Fiona Darling, and, if anything, this builder Ted Sachs?'

Ben and Libby exchanged glances.

'What?' said Rob.

'We met him last night,' said Libby, trying and failing to suppress another grin. 'At DCI Connell's new flat.'

'Wh-aat?' Rob Maiden almost choked on his coffee.

'I'll explain,' said Ben. 'We were all at our friend Edward's house-warming party, and Ted Sachs was also there. He's doing some work for Edward. Ian – DCI Connell - was also there.' Ben didn't enlarge on Libby's statement about Ian's new flat.

'And so was Fiona Darling. She and Sachs came together.' She paused to consider the euphemism. 'Sachs has been doing work for her and her husband on their barn. She must have told you this.'

'She has,' said Rob. 'What I can't get over is why Sachs should just hand over a bunch of keys for a building neither he nor she owns. It's just plain irresponsible. And we haven't been able to track Sachs down, either.'

Chapter Four

'Is Sachs local?' Ben asked. 'I've never heard of him.'

'Neither have I.' Libby frowned. 'How did Edward get hold of him?'

'Didn't you ask him?' Ben looked surprised.

'No – I asked how he knew Fiona, and he said Ted introduced her.' Libby looked up. 'That's rather odd, isn't it?'

'We gather Sachs set up as an independent builder a few months ago, based near Felling,' said Rob. 'He appears to work from home – at least we can't trace any actual premises.'

'Well,' said Ben slowly, 'he could have done a leafleting campaign, which would be how he picked up Fiona Darling and Edward, both new to the district, who wouldn't know any builders themselves -'

'But Edward could have asked us,' Libby interrupted.

'I expect he didn't want to bother us,' said Ben reprovingly. 'Was that how it was, Inspector?'

'Please call me Rob,' said Rob, 'and yes, we assume that's how it was with Mrs Darling. But what we can't understand is why he had the keys to the Garden Hotel.'

'The owner picked him up from a leaflet?' said Libby.

'I doubt it.' Rob shook his head. 'He doesn't live in the

village.'

'Who is the owner?' asked Ben. 'I don't remember who owned it when I lived here before.'

'It's registered to a Colin Hardcastle of Hardcastle Holdings.' Rob consulted his notebook. 'And they're based in London, so I doubt if that was a leaflet.'

'Hmm.' Ben was frowning. 'Shall we ask around, Rob? See if anyone remembers anything about who owned it?'

'You can do.'

'More likely to do with the current owner,' said Libby.

'I doubt it,' said Rob. 'He never comes down.'

'And if Sachs the builder isn't local, it can't be anything to do with him, either,' said Ben.

'Well,' said Rob, 'he did have the keys, remember.'

'But he'd never have let Fiona have them if he knew there was a body there,' said Libby.

'It was concealed,' said Rob doubtfully.

'Not very well, if Fiona found it.'

'It was behind a blocked cellar door,' said Rob. 'Only don't you dare say I told you.'

'How did she find it, then?' asked Ben.

'The door had warped, and she just picked away at it until it fell in.' Rob tried to hide a smirk. 'And so did she.'

'Oh, poor Fiona,' giggled Libby. 'Sorry, I shouldn't really, should I?'

'So what do you know about her?' asked Rob, getting back to the subject of his original enquiry.

'Only what I told Rachel the other day. She and her husband moved into a converted barn in Steeple Well. Her husband's in the City, or something, and she gets lonely, so she's managed to get herself involved in all sorts of village activities.'

'And now she wants this Garden Hotel as a – what? Community project?'

'So she said. But I'm not really sure why. She seemed to think she could get funding for it, although where from I've no idea.'

'And what exactly is it?'

Libby shrugged. "A community café, she said. And craft centre? Honestly, I'm not sure.'

'We haven't been able track down her husband, either,' said Rob, standing up. 'He's away, apparently. Well, thanks for the coffee, Ben. I'd better be getting on. If you do hear anything...'

'I know, we'll be in touch,' said Libby. 'By the way, what about the body? Do you know who that is yet?'

'Not definitely, but house to house has picked up that some lads used to get in and use it for – well, who knows? Nothing reputable, that's certain.'

'I noticed signs that a fire had been lit on the floor,' said Libby.

Rob nodded. 'So did we. Well, keep your ears open.'

When Inspector Maiden had gone, Ben and Libby began to get ready for lunch with Hetty at the Manor, a Sunday ritual. Had Fran and Guy stayed, rather than going back to open Guy's gallery and shop in Nethergate, they would have accompanied them.

'Never mind,' said Libby. 'Flo and Lenny will be there. We can ask Flo and Hetty if they remember anything about the Garden Hotel.'

Flo Carpenter was Hetty's oldest friend. They had come down from London in their youth for the annual hop-picking harvest. Now living with Hetty's brother Lenny in their comfortable bungalow in Maltby Close near the church, Flo was a good source of old gossip from the village, as well as a provider of extremely good wines, with an expertise learned from her late husband.

'Don't go poking around too much,' said Ben.

'They've asked us to,' said Libby. 'Carte blanche.'

However, to Libby's annoyance, when they arrived at the Manor, they found not only Flo and Lenny already ensconced at the big kitchen table, but Edward and Ian too.

'I thought you'd be working today as you've got a murder,' said Libby accusingly to Ian.

'I have DI Maiden and DS Trent on the ground, Libby,' said Ian, amused, 'and actually, I *am* working, in a sense. Information-gathering.' He indicated Flo and Hetty.

'Oh.' Libby eyed him with disfavour.

'And we was just going to tell 'im all about the Hardcastles,' said Flo. 'Do you know about them?'

'We know about Colin Hardcastle and Hardcastle Holdings,' said Libby, sitting down and accepting a glass of red wine from Edward. 'Are there more of them?'

'It was them that owned the Garden,' said Hetty, emerging from the Aga with a huge leg of lamb. 'Colin was their son.'

'When was this?' asked Ian.

'Oh, years ago, wasn't it, Het?' said Flo. 'When would it have been?'

'Bin closed nigh on fifteen years,' said Hetty. 'When Lil

31

died.'

'At least,' said Flo. 'She closed it after Bert died.' She turned to Ian. 'See, when Bert died, Lil couldn't carry on and she wanted young Colin to come back and help her run it. But he weren't interested, and in the end she shut up shop. He ain't been there since, far as I know.'

'Where had he gone? Colin, I mean,' asked Libby.

'London, didn't he, Het? Made money.' Flo nodded portentously.

'Hence Hardcastle Holdings,' said Ben. 'What was it, property?'

'We haven't found out yet,' said Ian, 'but I wouldn't be surprised.'

'If it is property, why hasn't he capitalised on the Garden Hotel?' asked Libby.

'That's what I was going to say,' said Edward. 'Apartments, surely, if he didn't want to run a hotel.'

'Planning permission,' said Ben.

'I wouldn't have thought that would be a problem,' said Ian.

'Bat and Trap,' said Hetty suddenly.

'What?' said Edward and Ian together.

'Bat and trap! Of course,' said Ben, laughing. 'It's an old pub game – being revived now, I believe – and the Garden ran a team, didn't they, Mum?'

'What – like shove ha'penny?' said Edward.

'No, no,' said Libby excitedly. 'It's an outdoor game – you have to have a proper pitch and everything. Mainly played in Kent, isn't it, Hetty?'

Hetty nodded. 'Greg used to play.'

32

'So did I when I was young,' said Ben. 'The pitch is still there, but completely overgrown.'

'Wouldn't it be great to revive it,' said Libby.

'You'd have to get permission from this Colin Hardcastle,' said Ian. 'And if he hasn't done anything about the building except let it fall into disrepair, he's hardly likely to be interested in reviving a pub game.'

'But,' said Libby, thinking hard, 'he'd given the keys to a builder, so perhaps he *was* thinking about doing it up at last.'

They all looked at her in surprise.

'Of course!' said Edward. 'There, Ian. It's not a mystery, after all.'

Ian looked doubtful, but as the roast potatoes arrived at the table just then, the subject was dropped.

They had reached the apple pie when Hetty said, 'Old Mrs Mardle. She'd know.'

'Eh?'

'What?'

'Who?'

Hetty nodded. 'Your next door neighbour, gal. Jinny Mardle.'

'Mrs Mardle?' Libby looked surprised. 'But I don't really know her.'

'Has meals on wheels, don't she?' said Flo.'

'Yes. I pop in if she needs a lightbulb changed or something like that,' said Ben.

'And we put her bins out,' said Libby.

'So you do know her.' Hetty offered more pie.

'Well, yes...' said Libby.

'Why do you think she'd know? Do you mean about the Hardcastles?' asked Ian.

'Used to clean up at the Garden,' said Flo.

'But she would have known the parents, not the son,' said Ben.

'Very thick with Lil, she was.' Hetty looked at Libby. 'Lil Hardcastle.'

'Wouldn't hurt to ask, would it, Ian?' Libby raised questioning eyebrows.

'I suppose not, but I'm inclined to agree with Ben,' said Ian. 'Lovely pie, Hetty.'

Shortly after this, again following tradition, Hetty retired to her sitting room, Flo and Lenny to Maltby Close, and Ben and Libby were left to do the clearing up, this time with Edward's help. Ian had excused himself to go back to work.

'So, how are you getting on with Ian?' asked Libby, as Edward handed her another pile of plates for the dishwasher.

'Fine – why?'

'Well, we were all so surprised when we found out that he'd bought your upstairs flat. You never said a word.'

'It wasn't my place to tell.' Edward grinned at her. 'And anyway, he only decided a month or so ago. I happened to tell him that the original buyer had fallen through, so...'

'But he didn't tell us he wanted to move,' said Libby.

'He doesn't have to tell you everything, Lib,' said Ben. 'You've always been so nosy as far as he was concerned.'

'Just interested.' Libby was defensive. 'Anyway, I didn't know he and Edward were such friends.'

'We weren't particularly.' Edward plunged his hands into the sink and began scrubbing at a roasting tin. 'But we met up for a drink occasionally in Canterbury. Don't look like that, Libby. We weren't excluding you, it was just if I happened to be at the Canterbury campus. And we've been to The Poacher a couple of times.'

Ben laughed. 'But she does look as if she's been slighted, Edward, doesn't she?'

Libby sniffed. 'I don't know what you mean.'

'Are you coming down to Pete and Harry's with us?' Ben asked Edward.

'No, I'll get off home if you don't mind,' said Edward. 'I've got work to do before tomorrow.'

It was Ben and Libby's habit to drop in on Peter and Harry on Sunday afternoons, and after saying goodbye to Edward, they strolled down the drive towards the high street. Peter and Harry's cottage stood just next to the drive, and as they arrived, Harry, still in his chef's whites, was letting himself in.

'Was that Edward I waved at just now?' he asked. 'Or a handsome stranger?'

'You know it was Edward. He and Ian were both at lunch.'

'Oh? Hetty trying to pull them into the family circle?' Harry flung himself into a corner of the deep sofa. Peter appeared in the kitchen doorway.

'Drink?' he asked.

'Yes, please,' said Libby. 'My *amour propre*, or whatever it is, needs soothing.'

'Edward and Ian have had the temerity to become
35

friends without Libby's say-so,' said Ben.

'God help either of them if they want to get married,' said Harry.

'Oi! I'm not that bad!' protested Libby.

'So what about this murder, then?' asked Peter, once they were settled with drinks. 'Ian have any more to say about it?'

'Rob Maiden's in charge,' said Ben. 'Or Inspector Maiden, as we should call him.'

'He of the carroty hair and very blue eyes?' said Harry. 'Quite liked him.'

'Yes, him. Ian was there today, information-gathering apparently, to see if either Mum or Flo could remember anything about the Hardcastles who used to own the hotel. The son is apparently being hard to track down.'

'And Hetty suggested my next-door neighbour,' said Libby. 'Mrs Mardle. Do you know her, Pete?'

'Mardle?' Peter frowned. 'Can't say... Oh! Hold on – Jinny Mardle?'

'That was it, wasn't it, Ben? We only know her to say hello to, really.'

'She used to clean at the Garden Hotel,' said Peter. 'Did a bit of waitressing, too, if I remember rightly. Very fond of the boy.'

'Ah! That's why Hetty thought we might ask her,' said Ben. 'I don't remember that.'

'That's because you're such an old man,' said Peter, and ducked the cushion thrown at him. 'He's nearer my age. What happened to him?'

'That's what we're trying to find out,' said Libby.

'Well, the police are.'

'That's easy enough, surely?' said Harry. 'Land registry will tell them who the owner is.'

'Yes, it has. Hardcastle Holdings. But they want to speak to Colin Hardcastle, and he's proving hard to track down. Sorry – no pun intended.' Libby made a face.

'But it sounds like a company – so why aren't there other people in the offices?' asked Peter.

'Don't ask me.' Libby shrugged. 'They want to find out why he gave the keys to Ted Sachs the builder, and then why *he* gave them to Fiona Darling.'

'All a bit peculiar, don't you think?' Harry swung his feet up onto Peter's lap. 'Not businesslike.'

'Oh, the police will get to the bottom of it,' said Ben. 'They always do in the end, especially when it's a matter of public record.'

'But,' said Libby, 'I want to know. And I'm going to find out.'

Chapter Five

Three male faces stared at her gloomily.

'Please, Lib -' began Ben.

'Look, coz,' said Peter, 'you know perfectly well that she'll carry on poking her nose into things regardless of what anyone says. Including Ian.'

Harry swung his feet down on to the floor and leant forward, elbows on knees. 'Why do you do it, Lib?'

Libby started back in surprise. 'Why…?'

'Yes. Why do you insist on trying to find out things?'

'Habit?' suggested Peter.

'Everyone wants to know, don't they?' Libby was floundering. 'You all join in…'

'But we'd be quite happy doing nothing,' said Peter. 'We don't start these things.'

Libby stared for a moment. Then, pulling herself together, 'You do sometimes. Harry did with those friends of his…'

'That was because of a direct attack on friends,' said Harry.

'But lots of things happen that involve us, don't they? The beer festival, for instance -'

'No, that didn't involve us. Except for you finding the body,' said Ben.

'Well, you don't get much more involved than that!' said Libby indignantly.

'She'll never change,' said Peter. 'Just make up your mind on that.'

'I don't see what the problem is,' grumbled Libby. 'Especially as Rob Maiden and Rachel Trent both asked what we knew about the village. All I'm doing is trying to find out for them.'

The three men exchanged glances.

'Unassailably right,' said Peter, standing up. 'Anyone want another drink?'

On Monday morning, Libby called Fran to tell her about Maiden's visit and ask if there was anything she should be doing.

'What do you mean?' asked Fran warily.

'Well, you know. Should I be asking questions?'

'Why?'

'To find out…'

'Find out what?'

'Oh, Fran!' said Libby, exasperated. 'You know what! What happened? Who was the body? Why did Fiona have those keys?'

'Look, all the police wanted to know was who might know about the history of the hotel. Give them the names you've got. That's all you need to do.'

'But don't you want to *know*?' Libby's voice rose.

'I don't know.' Fran's voice suddenly wavered. Libby caught her breath.

'Fran?' she said softly. After a silent pause, she said again, 'Fran? What is it?'

Fran's shaky laugh floated out of the telephone. 'I thought... I saw... Oh, Lib, I don't know.'

'This is a "moment", isn't it?' said Libby. 'Right. I'm coming over. Put the kettle on.'

Fran's 'moments' had, in recent years, become fewer and fewer, due, in Libby's opinion, to her settled and comfortable lifestyle. When Libby had first met her, she had been employed by an upmarket and exclusive estate agency to go into properties on behalf of new clients, to find out if anything unpleasant had happened in those properties. On one occasion a body had been discovered as a result, apparently, of Fran standing still and listening. Over the years, she had been of help to the police in several murder cases, although DCI Connell had learnt to keep her involvement as quiet as possible. But these days almost nothing floated through the ether towards her, so this was exceptional.

Ben was already happily ensconced in his micro-brewery behind the Manor, which had been gaining a reputation in the year it had been operating, so Libby told Sidney to be good, locked up, and climbed into her car. It was a straight run between Steeple Martin and Nethergate, and these days took only about twenty minutes from door to door, as long as the traffic in Nethergate wasn't backed up right to the top of the high street, which tended to happen in summer.

Today, however, traffic was flowing normally, although Libby couldn't find anywhere to park along Harbour Street and had to drive into the car park behind The Sloop, the pub on the arm of the jetty, at the foot of the cliffs.

She found Fran at home in Coastguard Cottage, the front door standing open and Balzac the cat sitting in the doorway, eyes screwed up against the sunlight.

'Come on, then,' she said, accepting a mug of tea and sitting down on the window seat. 'What is it?'

Fran frowned at her. 'I wasn't going to tell you,' she said. 'I wanted to think about it. I knew you'd jump to conclusions.'

'About what?'

'Murder.'

Libby looked at her friend in silence for a moment.

'Well, you'd better tell me about it and let me decide,' she said at last.

Fran sighed and sat back in her chair. Balzac, noticing the increased lap size, jumped up and began turning round preparatory to going to sleep. Fran absent-mindedly stroked his head.

'It was last night,' she began. 'Guy took me to The Sloop for dinner. We'd had a good day in the shop and Sophie was out somewhere with Adam.'

Guy's daughter Sophie and Libby's youngest son Adam were an occasional couple.

'And of all the inappropriate moments for it to happen, it was just as Guy was served his jam roly-poly.'

Libby grinned. 'Gosh! Do they do that? I shall have to take Ben there. So what were you having?'

Fran grinned back. 'Nothing! Well – the last glass of wine in the bottle, actually.'

'OK – so Guy gets his roly-poly. What happened?'

'I haven't got a clue. It was just like it used to be.

41

Remember when my old Aunt Eleanor died? And the Willoughby Oak?'

Libby remembered. In both cases, Fran had had visions – or experiences – that proved to be some kind of actual reflection of what was happening. At other times, she would just know a fact that no one had told her. Which always proved to be correct.

'Well, I saw a sort of improvised hearth. A circle of bricks on what looked like a wooden floor. And scorch marks. And a boy.'

Libby frowned. 'Do you think it was our hotel? With the fires I told you about? It looked as though there'd been fires on the floors.'

'I don't know. Your fires didn't have bricks round them, did they?'

'No. Terribly dangerous, with or without bricks – it's all wooden floors in that building.'

'Well, there we are.' Fran leant back with a sigh. 'Not much to go on, but it was so vivid. Oh – and there was a chair.'

'A chair?'

'Yes. Just one. A spindly sort of chair, a bit like a wrought iron garden chair.'

'Well,' said Libby after a pause, 'it doesn't exactly shout "Murder", does it? What made you think it was?'

'It was so vivid. And the boy.' Fran shook her head. 'I wish I could tell you what he was like, but I can't. Just like being there, you know?'

Libby did. Not from personal experience, of course, but from having worked with Fran in the past. How she knew

42

things as if they were solid fact. Something that several people in the past had been unwilling to accept, although Ian Connell always had.

'Is it worth passing on?' Libby asked, after a moment. 'To Rachel Trent, I mean.'

'Not to Inspector Maiden? Isn't he SIO?'

'He's Deputy SIO. Ian's Senior SIO, but office-based. It looks as though he's now heading up an MIT from headquarters.'

'MIT?'

'Murder Investigation Team. Rachel tells me he's chafing against being office-based.'

Fran laughed. 'He won't stay there.'

'No. Anyway, what do we do about this "moment" of yours?'

'It doesn't seem worth passing on, really, does it? After all, we know that a murder was committed – Fiona found the body.'

'Where was the chair?' asked Libby.

Fran was surprised. 'Where? I told you – in an empty room. Might have been a cellar?'

'No one's mentioned finding a chair.' Libby turned to stare out of the window.

'In that case, not worth mentioning,' said Fran. 'I feel better now.' She pushed Balzac off her lap and stood up briskly. Balzac stalked off in a huff. 'Let's go and have lunch at Mavis's.'

Mavis owned The Blue Anchor cafe at the end of Harbour Street, next to The Sloop.

'All right.' Libby stood up and picked up her basket.

'Now you've got it off your chest you can tell me what I ought to be doing.'

'Libby!' Fran turned an exasperated face to her friend. 'Nothing! There's no room for enthusiastic amateurs any more. We provide the team with any knowledge we might have of the history and that sort of thing, and that's it. We're simply witnesses, if that. I'm not even that in this case.'

'Neither am I, really,' said Libby regretfully. 'If only I'd stayed with Fiona…'

'You're such a ghoul!' Fran ushered her out of the door and slammed it behind them. 'Come on. Let's have a sandwich.'

After Mavis herself had come out to take their order, and bang down a tin ashtray beside Libby, despite the fact that she no longer – or only very rarely – smoked, Fran returned to the subject.

'I would like to know about those keys, though.'

'Keys?'

'Yes. The keys Ted Sachs had. Why did he have them?'

'I suppose the owner gave them to him. Fiona didn't seem to be interested. Ted had told her the place could be tarted up, although I told her it would take a bit more than a tin of paint and a bit of plasterboard. She seemed to think she could get funding for her community project. It all sounded a bit airy-fairy to me.'

'Strange, isn't it?' Fran squinted out over the jetty to where The Dolphin and The Sparkler bobbed quietly at anchor, waiting to take the next load of tourists out round little Dragon Island in the bay, or round the point to the

44

bathing cove. 'Who's the owner?'

'Son of the previous owners. He didn't want to carry on the business after his father died, apparently. Hetty told us to ask Mrs Mardle-next-door because she used to work for the Hardcastles – the owners – and was very fond of the son, so Pete seems to remember.'

'And this son gave the builder Sachs the keys?'

'Yes. You know all about that. And Edward using him to repair his summerhouse.'

'Where did he get him from?'

'A leaflet, we think. I expect Ian's asked.'

'Where's he based?'

'Felling, I think. Nearer to Shott than we are, anyway.'

'Not really,' said Fran. 'Just further away from Steeple Martin, which makes it even odder. If the owner is local himself, why not use a local builder?'

'Don't ask me. The whole affair's suspicious. I mean – why did the Darlings use Ted Sachs? They were new to the area; you'd think they would have asked for local recommendations, wouldn't you?'

Mavis arrived with their sandwiches and departed without a word.

'What do you know about Mr Darling?' asked Fran, before taking a bite of chicken and mayonnaise.

'Nothing except that he works in the city and is often away. I've never even seen him. That's why I thought Ted Sachs was him on Saturday. It's all odd, isn't it?'

Fran concentrated on her sandwich for a moment. 'And why did Sachs feel it was all right to let Fiona look round the property on her own?'

45

'And give her the impression that it would be perfectly in order to turn the place into a community centre?'

'Do you think the owner even knew about Fiona and the community centre?' said Fran thoughtfully.

'Come to think of it, probably not,' said Libby. 'The tuna and cucumber's lush.'

'Lush?' Fran raised her eyebrows. 'How old are you, exactly?'

Chapter Six

Allhallow's Lane drowsed in the afternoon sun. Libby turned off the engine and sat appreciating her surroundings. Her gaze moved from her own front door to Mrs Mardle's, painted bright yellow. She remembered the large young man who had arrived to paint it and the window frames. He had beamed and blushed when spoken to, but who he was and where he had come from, she had no idea. However, now he was giving her a hint. She got out of the car.

Mrs Mardle, small, slightly bent, and wispy-haired, opened her door.

'Libby! Hello, dear. All right?'

'Hello, Mrs Mardle – yes, I'm fine. I was just wondering... that young man who came to paint your woodwork. Is he a regular painter?'

Mrs Mardle smiled gently. 'Oh, yes, dear. That's what he does – paints. Bit of woodwork. You know the sort of thing. Did you want some work done?'

'We may do,' said Libby, passing her home swiftly under review. 'You'd recommend him, then?'

'Oh, yes, dear! He's my grandson.'

'Oh!' Libby, her grand idea collapsing. 'Does he always work on his own?' she asked, rallying.

'Oh, no, dear. Lots of other people. If ever you need

anything done – you know, plumbing or something, Gary'll know the right person.'

'Much better to have a personal recommendation, isn't it?' said Libby brightly.

Mrs Mardle nodded, then peered round Libby as if looking for someone else. Startled, Libby, too, looked over her shoulder.

'I heard about that body found up at the old Garden.' Mrs Mardle was leaning forward and whispering. 'Flo was telling me.'

Flo stealing a march on her, thought Libby with amusement. Still, it paved the way.

'Yes, she and Hetty said you used to work there,' she said. 'It must have been a shock.'

'Oh, it was, dear, it was.' Looking up and down the road again, Mrs Mardle held the door wide and stepped back. 'Why don't you come in for a minute – if you've got time?'

Well, that was easy, thought Libby, following her hostess into a miniature version of Hetty's sitting room up at the Manor. Despite the warmth of the day outside, the electric fire in the hearth was glowing brightly. Mrs Mardle sat primly on the edge of the armchair to one side of it, and motioned Libby to the other.

'I was going to ask you, dear,' she said after a long pause. 'Were you there when they – erm, when they...'

'Found the body?' supplied Libby. 'No, I wasn't. I'd gone home and left Mrs Darling there.'

'Ah. This Mrs Darling... Who is she?'

'She's new to the village, Steeple Well, you know. Just up the road. Her husband works in the City.'

'Canterbury?'

'No, London. The City of London.'

'Oh.' Mrs Mardle looked none the wiser. 'So why was she at the Garden?'

'Apparently, she wanted to turn it into a community centre.'

'A what?' Now Mrs Mardle looked thoroughly shocked.

'A community centre,' repeated Libby, wondering just what Mrs Mardle thought that was. 'For – I don't know, actually. For Arts and Crafts and...' she cast around for something else to say. 'Well, for people to get together.'

Mrs Mardle's wispy eyebrows drew together. 'Whatever for, dear? We've already got the pub – and your theatre; and of course Flo's Carpenter's Hall, and the church hall. Plenty of places for people to get together. And that Harry of yours – his cafe. Very popular, I hear.'

Libby suppressed a smile. 'Oh, yes, very. And I have to say, Mrs Mardle, that when Mrs Darling told me what she wanted to do, I said exactly what you've just said.'

'Well.' Mrs Mardle sat back in her chair and gave her thin bosom a quick hitch. 'Has she bought it, then? The Garden?'

'No, she was simply lent the keys.'

'Colin gave her the keys?' Now the eyebrows were lost under the thin fringe. 'Never! He'd never do that.'

'Is that Colin Hardcastle? You knew him?' Libby's interest quickened.

'Knew him? Bless you! I practically brought him up.'

Libby gaped.

'Oh, yes, dear.' Mrs Mardle nodded and leant forward.

49

'See, Lil and Bert, they were so taken up with the Garden –
making it work, you know, spending all hours turning it
into a proper hotel and learning the business, they had no
time. I started by going up there to help with the cleaning
and that, but soon I was looking after Colin as well. When
he came home from school, you know. And I'd have him
down here at weekends, although he didn't like that much.
Preferred being up there. He loved the bat and trap –
wanted to play himself, but they wouldn't let him till he
was eighteen. And it wasn't much after that he went off,
anyway. Headstrong, he was, even though he was delicate,
like.'

'Delicate?'

'Yes. Well, he looked it. Slim, and not over tall. Thin
face like his mum. Never liked football or anything like
that. That was why we were so surprised he liked bat and
trap.'

'Where did he go off to?' asked Libby.

'Oh, college somewhere. University, they said. He came
home holidays, but never for long.'

'And Flo and Het said he wouldn't come home to help
his mother after his dad died. Is that right?'

'Well, you couldn't expect it, really, could you, dear?
He'd never taken an interest, and he had his own job by
then. In a bank was it? Something like that. But Lil was
still living there, so although she closed the hotel after a bit,
she didn't sell it.'

'What I can't understand,' said Libby, 'is why Colin
hasn't sold it since she died. There seems no reason to keep
it.'

Mrs Mardle shrugged thin shoulders. 'I don't know, dear. But perhaps *that's* why he lent this Mrs Darling the keys. Perhaps she's going to buy it.'

'Not now she's found a body there!' said Libby.

'No, dear, perhaps you're right.' Mrs Mardle gave an odd little titter.

'Anyway, it wasn't Colin who lent her the keys but some builder or other. We'd never heard of him. Oh!' said Libby, as if the thought had just struck her. 'Perhaps your Gary knows him?'

Mrs Mardle leant forward again. 'Oh, yes! What was his name?'

'Ted Sachs. He comes from over near Felling, I think.'

'Sachs,' repeated Mrs Mardle, frowning. 'I've never heard Gary mention anyone of that name, but I'll ask him. Now why should he have the keys?'

'Well, if the police could find him, or Colin, they could ask,' said Libby, wondering why on earth Ian hadn't leapt at the chance when he saw Ted Sachs on Saturday.

'Oh, Colin's in Spain, dear. That's where he lives now.' Mrs Mardle nodded smugly. 'Asked me over, he has, but I don't fancy it. Not at my time of life.'

As if she was at least a hundred, thought Libby, instead of a well-preserved eighty-five-year-old.

'But he still has an office in this country?' she said aloud.

'Oh, an address – I expect so. I've got his one in Spain. Would you like it? Then you can find out why that builder had they keys.'

Libby left Mrs Mardle with a feeling of extreme

gratitude. Talk about falling into your lap!

She switched on the electric kettle in her own kitchen, and began scrolling through the numbers on her phone. Her finger hovered over Rachel Trent's, then over Rob Maiden's, before eventually settling for Ian Connell's private number.

'Yes?' came the curt response just as Libby lifted the kettle. She almost dropped it.

'Er – Ian? Is this a bad time?'

'Yes.' She heard him say something to someone else. Then, 'DS Trent is dealing with witness statements.'

'Um – yes. I'll call her.' She felt a prickle of embarrassed perspiration along her browline. Why had she thought -

'All right. I'll pass on the information.' His voice had softened, although he still hadn't mentioned her name.

'It's Colin Hardcastle's address in Spain,' she said hurriedly, and heard a smothered expletive.

'Are you at home?'

'Yes.'

'Someone'll be round.' The connection was cut.

Libby blew out a gusty breath of relief.

She was just finishing the tea and thinking about what, from her extensive repertoire of cheat's cooking, she could cook for tonight, when there was a sharp rap on the front door.

'That doesn't sound like Rachel,' she said out loud to Sidney, as she went to open the door.

'No, it sounds like an exasperated Ian,' said DCI Connell, stepping over the threshold.

'You could have sent Rachel,' said Libby meekly, following him into the sitting room.

'And you could have called her,' said Ian, sitting down. 'Why didn't you? What's the use of the superintendent telling me to stay in the office when members of the public insist on calling me out of it?'

'I...' began Libby, and stopped. 'Sorry.'

'Well? Where's this address? And what's the story?' His mouth twitched. 'And where's my tea?'

Relieved, Libby grinned and went to switch the kettle back on. When she had refreshed her own cup and given Ian his, she pulled out the piece of paper Mrs Mardle had given her, and repeated the story.

'So you see, there's more to the story of Colin Hardcastle than we thought,' she finished up.

'How do you make that out?' Ian frowned at her.

'Well, he was obviously a neglected child, for a start.'

'But didn't want for anything, by the sound of it.'

'No, except love.'

'But he got that from your Mrs Mardle.'

'It's no wonder he didn't want to come and run the hotel, though, is it?'

'No.' Ian shook his head. 'But when did he give Ted Sachs the keys? And how did he know about him? Have you found out anything about him yet?'

Libby hid a smirk. 'Not yet. But I've got my spies out.'

'What? Come on, Libby, now what?'

Libby laughed. 'Same source – Mrs Mardle next door. And do you know, I didn't have to ask a single question. I simply asked if her Gary knew of Ted Sachs. Because Mrs

Mardle wanted to know how Fiona Darling had got the keys to the Garden. Quite indignant, she was.'

Ian put his head on one side and surveyed her through narrowed eyes. 'You know, you're just like those old women amateur detectives. Put you in a room full of people, and suddenly you've got all this information the police would take weeks to get hold of.'

'Well, thank you for the compliment, but it's more that this is a close-knit village, and despite being a comparative newcomer, because of my association with Ben and Hetty and Peter, I'm a safe person to gossip with. Which, on the whole, is quite a good thing, isn't it?'

Chapter Seven

'One thing I was going to ask you,' said Libby, just as Ian was going out of the door. 'Hardcastle Holdings. Rachel – or Rob Maiden – said the police hadn't been able to raise anyone there. Even if Colin himself is away, someone should be there, shouldn't they?'

Ian turned reluctantly. 'You do ask the damndest questions.' He sighed. 'Well, yes. And there is. It's actually the registered offices of the company. And you know what that means?'

'Oh – a bank? Solicitors?'

'Exactly. In fact there are whole companies set up to act as Registered Offices these days. In Hardcastle's case it's his solicitors.'

'Didn't they tell you about him being in Spain?'

'No – because Ted Sachs only knew the name. We could find no trace because it was the weekend, and sadly, unlike other professions, both solicitors and Companies House close over the weekend. And now we've lost Sachs again, and Colin Hardcastle.'

Libby looked puzzled. 'But surely you've got hold of them by now?'

Ian's exasperated look had come back. 'Well, of course we have! Otherwise I wouldn't know where the registered office was, would I? And apparently, the only person the solicitors ever see is a woman. They don't think they've ever seen Hardcastle himself.'

'The amazing vanishing man,' murmured Libby. 'I suppose he is real?'

'Well, someone gave the keys to Sachs – and he says it was Hardcastle.' Ian looked at his watch. 'I must go. Thanks for the information, and…' He paused.

'Keep my ear to the ground?' suggested Libby with a grin. 'Sure!'

She sat on the stairs and called Fran on the landline. Sidney tried to get on her lap.

'Guess what!' she began, as soon as she heard Fran's voice.

'I can't be bothered to guess,' answered Fran wearily. 'And you're going to tell me anyway.'

So Libby told her.

'That's really interesting,' said Fran, who had perked up as the tale went on. 'Mrs Next-Door talked about him as a real person, and Ian talked about him as a cipher.'

'Well, I must say that's rather what I thought. No one's seen him, he lives in Spain, and doesn't come near either his old childhood home or his offices. Do you suppose someone's bumped him off and is milking the profits?'

'I should think that's a bit extreme,' said Fran. 'And why wouldn't they have sold The Garden? Is it listed?'

'I think so,' said Libby doubtfully. 'Quite old. Two hundred and fifty years, give or take?'

'What's next to it?'

'Next to it? Why?' Libby was surprised.

56

'I just wondered. Trying to get the layout in my head.'

'I should have taken you over there on Saturday – or Sunday morning.'

'There wasn't time,' said Fran. 'It stands just by the end of the high street, doesn't it? Almost into the Nethergate Road?'

'Yes – but what of it?'

'Oh – just a thought. You in tomorrow?'

'Yes – I'm trying to finish off those two commissions for Guy.'

Libby painted what she called "pretty peeps" after a favourite detective series character's paintings, mainly on commission for Guy's gallery.

'I might see if I can pop over. We're not too busy in the week, and the school holidays haven't started yet.'

'I don't see that has much to do with anything,' said Libby with a sniff. 'I thought British family holidays were always taken abroad these days. Not the good old English seaside holiday.'

'Oh, Libby!' Fran was laughing at her. 'Have you not heard of the staycation? Everyone staying at home instead of off to the Costas? The boom in caravan and camper van sales? We've even got a brand new site up on the cliffs!'

'Oh,' said Libby, deflated. 'Well, anyway, yes, I'm in. Perhaps we could go to Harry's for lunch?'

'Lunch out two days running? That's a bit excessive!'

'Oh, go on. That's the way things are done these days. You know, like staycations,' said Libby mischievously.

Later on that evening, as Ben was pouring out a nightcap for them both, Libby said, 'Fran's coming over tomorrow. She wants to look at The Garden.'

'Good Lord!' said Ben, handing her a glass. 'Whatever for? Or is it a moment?'

'She said she wants to get the layout in her head,' said Libby. 'What's the other side of it?'

Ben frowned. 'There's that little lane. Cuckoo Lane. Where you can cut off back to behind the church.'

'Not down the lane, though,' said Libby. 'That's got houses, hasn't it?'

'Yes – it's a footpath leading off it that goes behind the church.'

'So what's down the lane? I know there are houses – or some anyway. Old redbrick ones, like ours.'

'I know about the footpath, but that's almost at the beginning. Come to think of it, that runs right behind The Garden. Right behind the bat and trap pitch, in fact. That was where everyone used to come in.'

'Didn't you?' asked Libby.

'No, we always went via the bar. Do you think Rob Maiden would let me have a poke around the back there?'

'I shouldn't think so for a moment,' said Libby with a grin. 'But you could always join Fran and I on our nosymongering tomorrow. I expect if they see us pottering around they'll think it's entirely normal.'

Ben grinned back. 'I must just do that. See – I've been thinking. I've got a bit of an idea.'

Libby felt a sense of foreboding. 'Oh, yes?'

Ben's grin grew wider. 'Don't worry about it. I'm not going to be stupid.'

'I think,' said Libby, the following day when Fran

58

arrived, 'that he's going through the male menopause. First it was the micro brewery -'

'Well, you must admit he's making a success of that,' said Fran.

'Yes,' conceded Libby, 'but now he's revived our own – or his own – hop gardens, so by next year he'll have to buy in fewer hops. What's he up to now?'

'I wouldn't worry about it,' said Fran, amused. 'If it keeps him happy…'

'And out of my hair, you mean?' Libby laughed. 'There is that.'

'Come on, then, if we're going. Do you mean to call Ben to meet us there?'

Together they walked down Allhallow's Lane from number seventeen. The redbrick cottages led straight onto to the lane, all single-fronted, some two-storied, some three. On the other side of the lane there was a small green space almost opposite Libby's and Mrs Mardle's cottages, but otherwise nothing, until you came to the high brick wall which surrounded the vicarage, overhung by a huge lilac tree.

They turned right here, past the front of the vicarage and onto the high street, with its few shops interspersed with cottages. There was nothing in the high street younger than mid-eighteenth century, other than the replacement shop windows. Most of the buildings were brick under tile, but at the far end, beyond the Manor drive which turned off to the right past the Pink Geranium and the pub, and beyond Peter and Harry's home, were a few much older cottages, whitewashed under thatch with crooked windows set into

59

it. Libby did not find these as eerie as she found the 'eyebrows' of Steeple Farm, just up the lane on the right.

On the opposite side of the high street, just before it turned up the hill into the Nethergate Road, stood what had been The Garden Hotel. Libby and Fran stopped. It, too, was mainly brick under tile, and looked forgotten and dejected, until one noticed the blue and white police tape fluttering across the doorway and all the way round the sides of the building.

'That's the lane Ben was talking about,' said Libby. 'Cuckoo Lane.' At the side of the hotel, a rough track led off and out of sight behind a hedge and wall on the right-hand side.

'Those must be houses leading off the Nethergate Road,' said Fran. 'And that cottage on the left looks empty.'

'What's the building before it, though?' said Libby. 'Look – part clapboard. Looks almost like another pub.'

'That,' said Ben's voice behind her, 'is because it was.'

Both women swung round.

'How did you find that out?' asked Libby.

'I always knew.' Ben was grinning widely.

'Then why didn't you tell me? You didn't say last night you'd been down there.'

Ben's eyebrows rose. 'Why? And I haven't been down there recently. It's nothing to do with this murder – if it is a murder.'

Confounded, Libby looked at Fran for help.

'Why did you know about it?' asked Fran.

'I grew up here, remember? And I played bat and trap

for the Garden. Backed right on to that pub.'

'What was it called?' asked Libby, interested in spite of herself.

'The Hop – or Hop Pocket. It was always just known as the Hop. It had closed by the time I was old enough to drink in there.'

Libby turned back to peer at the dingy white building. 'What happened to it? It hasn't been standing empty all this time, has it?'

'A cafe was tried there at one time, but it's off the high street, there's no parking, and let's face it, Steeple Martin's never been much of a destination for tourists.'

'I wonder why it hasn't been turned into a house,' said Fran. 'That's what usually happens, isn't it?'

'No idea,' said Ben. 'Let's go and have a look.'

'A look?' repeated Libby. 'At that place?'

Ben held out a bunch of keys. 'Oh, yes.'

Libby and Fran exchanged glances. Libby's said 'What did I tell you?'

They crossed the road and stood in front of the Garden Hotel. Libby shivered.

'Well, this is it, Fran. Now, you wanted to know what was beside it, didn't you? Well, there's Cuckoo Lane and the Hop.'

'And this side,' said Fran, 'what appears to be a chapel?'

'It was,' said Ben. 'It's been a house for years. I think there was a dispute for a few years because the Hardcastles wanted to buy it as it shares a driveway with the hotel.'

'Doesn't look as though they did, though,' said Libby,

surveying the neatly kept driveway, which now led to a rather glaringly new garage.

Ben shook his head. 'I gather that was dropped when Colin refused to come back and help his mother run the place.' He cast a critical eye over the dilapidated hotel. 'Can't say I blame him, can you? He was a young man, living his own life in London. Why should he come down here to bury himself?'

'You did,' said Libby.

'But I didn't, did I? I came back to set up my practice in Canterbury. Dad was still alive then. I didn't have to do anything until I'd officially retired and was living with you.'

'Hmm,' said Libby. 'Anyway, Fran, why did you want to know what was next to the hotel?'

'Well, because you said it was obviously being used by kids. I wondered how they got in.'

'Round the back, I expect,' said Ben. 'There was a big garden – where the bat and trap pitch was – and a car park at the end of that drive there. And if they went round the back by the lane...' He led the way round the other end of the building into Cuckoo Lane. 'See? This is the pathway that leads past the garden and the backs of all the other houses right round the back of the church.'

He indicated a very overgrown footpath that ran down behind the hotel on one side and beside the equally deserted Hop pub on the other.

'So there you are. Now, as there is still a good deal of police tape around, we won't be able to go into the Garden or we'll spoil their harvest, or whatever it is, so shall we look at the Hop?'

Fran looked interested, so Libby shrugged and acquiesced. Ben struggled with a padlock and a rusty lock, but eventually, the door opened with an ominous squeak.

'Here we are,' he said, throwing out an arm and beaming at Fran and Libby. 'Welcome to the Brewery Tap!'

Chapter Eight

Libby stood still in the doorway and gaped, her eyes round with astonishment. The door they had come through was in the side of the building. The ceiling was low and nicotine brown. The bar, three sided, was high and solid. A few tables and chairs stood in dispirited looking attitudes and a couple of fly-blown advertising mirrors hung crookedly on the walls. On the front wall were four windows, partly boarded up, and a heavy front door.

'Well – what do you think?' Ben had gone past her and threw out an arm. 'Fran?'

Fran, too, had gone past her and now peered over the bar.

'It's a pub,' she said.

'What do you mean, Brewery Tap?' said Libby at last.

Ben sighed. 'Just that. You do know what a Brewery Tap is, don't you?'

Libby ventured into the bar. 'Yes. The bar that goes with a brewery. But this is nowhere near your brewery.' She was aware that her voice was accusing.

'No, it's not, but it's near enough. No one would ever find it if we attached it to the brewery.' He looked at her sideways. 'You don't like it, do you?'

'It's not that.' Libby felt awkward. 'It's just – well, how

would Tim feel about it? You'd be taking custom away from him.'

'I've talked to him,' said Ben.

'Before you talked to me?' Libby gasped. Fran walked pointedly past the two of them and outside.

'It was to be a surprise.' Ben sounded exasperated. 'You can turn anything into an argument, can't you?' He thrust his hands deep into his pockets and walked round to the front of the bar.

'Argument? I'm not arguing!' Libby pulled nervously at her jacket. 'I was just...'

'Just what?' Ben looked at her through narrowed eyes. 'The first comment you made was negative. They always are. I'm surprised you even allowed me to set up the brewery.'

'Ben!' Libby was horrified. For a long moment they just stared at each other, until finally, Ben dropped his taut shoulders and his eyes.

'I'm sorry, Lib. I shouldn't have said that.'

Libby moved hesitantly towards him. 'You really want to do this?'

He looked up. 'Yes, Lib. I do.'

'I won't have to work here, will I?'

He threw back his head and laughed. 'No, my darling, you won't!'

Fran put her head round the door. 'There's a policeman here,' she said.

Ben and Libby looked at each other, eyebrows raised, then went outside to join Fran, who was subjecting a young uniformed constable to an alarmingly superior stare.

'Sorry, sir,' he managed to stammer out, 'but this area -'

'Isn't a crime scene,' said Libby kindly.'

The officer looked uncomfortably over his shoulder. 'Well...'

Ben stepped forward. 'These are different premises, officer,' he said. 'Mine, in fact.'

'Oh,' said the officer, going rather red in the face. He swallowed hard and struggled to pull a notebook from his pocket. 'And could I have your name, sir?'

'Certainly,' said Ben, to the accompaniment of grins from Libby and Fran. 'Ben Wilde, the Manor and the Manor Brewery, Steeple Martin.'

The officer, looking agonised, stuffed the notebook back in his pocket.

'Sorry, sir,' he said. 'I'm just here -'

'We understand, officer,' said Libby. 'We're locals and you're not. But we aren't trying to get into the Garden.'

'The garden?' he repeated. 'But the hotel...'

'The hotel is called The Garden,' said Ben. 'Haven't they told you that?'

The officer looked confused, then took a step forward and said confidentially, 'They haven't told me much, actually. Just that I've got to keep an eye on the premises. They've got some forensic people coming down, apparently. Specialists.'

'Ah.' Libby nodded. 'And they don't want anything messed up before then. Do you happen to know if Colin Hardcastle has been located yet?'

Looking even more confused, the officer shook his head. 'Er – no. I mean – I don't know.'

'Well, tell DS Trent we were here,' said Libby. 'I'm sure she'll vouch for us.'

The officer nodded, stood irresolute for a moment, then turned away towards the front of the Garden.

'To be fair,' said Fran, watching his retreating back, 'no one knew anyone would be here.'

'And it isn't actually yours, yet, is it?' said Libby, eyeing Ben sideways.

'Believe it or not,' said Ben, looking guilty, 'it is.'

'What?' said Fran and Libby together.

'Well, the freehold is.' Ben turned to lead the way back inside.

'But you said,' protested Libby, 'you didn't know why it hadn't been sold when I said why hadn't it been turned into a house.'

'Well, I don't.' Ben led the way round the bar and opened a door into a what appeared to be a store room. 'The last tenant still owns the lease. He can't sell the freehold. But I don't know why he's hung on to it so long.'

'And what happens now?' asked Fran.

'The solicitors are getting on to the tenant. I expect we'll find he or she is dead and nobody's bothered to tell us. It's part of the original Manor Estate, you see. Even the Garden Hotel was at one time. Everything from the bottom of our drive to the Canterbury Road in one direction and Steeple Lane and the Nethergate Road in the other. We've got maps up at the house – I'll show you some time.'

'And most of it's sold off?' said Fran.

'Gradually, over the years.' Ben pulled a canvas cover from a tall bench and revealed barrels. 'No cellar, which

67

makes it ideal for us. The barrels could be changed whenever we wanted.'

'When was the Garden Hotel sold off?' asked Libby.

'Don't ask me.' Ben was poking around on the bench. 'Probably some time in the eighteen hundreds – long before our family bought it.'

'Why?' asked Fran.

'I just wondered. About the history of the building. How old would you say it was?'

'I would have said seventeen hundred and something,' said Fran. 'Perhaps it was just the land that was sold off?'

'And the buyer built the house. Not as a hotel, though,' said Libby.

'Whereas this was,' said Ben from behind a large cupboard. 'Originally an alehouse – you know, where they hung a sheaf of corn or something over the door for the ill-educated peasants who couldn't read.' He poked a dusty, grinning face round the cupboard door. 'In this case it was a hop pocket. Naturally.'

'What *is* a hop pocket?' Fran whispered to Libby.

'It's a jute sack which the dried hops would be put into for sale to the brewers,' explained Libby.

'So this would be going back to its original purpose,' said Fran.

'Well, yes.' Ben came back to them, dusting his hands. 'Now I'm restoring the hop gardens – the only thing that's new is the brewery.'

'Wouldn't they have brewed the beer themselves, then?' asked Fran.

'Probably, but it wouldn't have been a brewery as they

are today. Anyway, what do you think?'

'I like it,' said Fran. 'As long as it doesn't put Tim's nose out of joint, as Libby said.'

'I like the building,' temporised Libby. 'As long as you aren't going to end up spending every hour of the day and night working.'

'No, I'll put in a manager. And as for Tim – he's fine. He's expanding his restaurant and he carries a range of drinks. We'll be an alehouse – going back to the roots. Just selling our own beer.'

'Is there living accommodation?' Libby looked up at the low ceiling.

'Yes, stairs through that door.' Ben pointed. 'Now the thing I was thinking about...'

'Oh, here we go,' said Libby.

'No, listen. We were talking about it on Sunday – and I mentioned it earlier.' Ben grinned into both their faces. 'Bat and trap!'

'What?' said Fran. 'You've mentioned that a couple of times and I have no idea what you're talking about.'

Libby and Ben explained between them.

'And what I thought was,' continued Ben, 'we could get the pub going and if Hardcastle would let us use the pitch, we could set up a team here.'

Libby was looking interested. 'Now that's not a bad idea,' she said. 'I bet all the new "locals" would love that.'

'You mean the ones who've bought a little place in the country?' said Fran with a grin. 'What do they call them? DFLs?'

'Down From London, yes,' said Libby.

69

'Although,' said Ben, 'a lot of them don't mix. They're probably a bit disappointed that this village doesn't provide an alternative wine bar for them, rather than a village pub.'

'We've got the caff!' said Libby indignantly. 'That's Mexican, *and* vegetarian. Couldn't be trendier if it tried.' She looked thoughtful. 'And that's a word I hate.'

'And your Fiona Darling's trying to mix with the village,' said Fran.

'She's not *my* Fiona Darling,' said Libby with a sniff. 'And I bet she's doing that because she's disappointed, like Ben said.'

'Anyway,' said Ben, opening another door and revealing a steep staircase, 'I shall need someone to come in and do the renovations.' He grinned over his shoulder.

'Ted Sachs!' said the women together.

'Well, perhaps just to get a quote from – I don't fancy actually employing him. I shall use the Tindall brothers as usual. If they can fit me in. They did the brewery, after all.'

'Well, I think it's an excellent idea,' said Libby. 'How soon can you start?'

Ben and Fran burst out laughing.

'Whoa!' said Ben. 'Only five minutes ago you weren't happy about it!'

Libby felt herself going pink. 'I've changed my mind.'

Outside once more, Ben led them down the lane, which really was little more than a dirt track which petered out in front of a five-barred gate, behind which a large golden retriever greeted them with a violently wagging tail.

'Oh, you're beautiful!' said Libby going to stroke the head which was now resting on the top of the gate, tongue lolling.

'Careful!' said Fran. 'You don't know him.'

'No, but I do,' said Ben. 'This is Colley. No idea why they called him after another breed of dog, but there you are.' He went over and joined Libby and Colley, who was now in a positive frenzy of excitement. 'Where's your mum, old boy?'

'Dad's here, old son!' said a voice from behind them, and Libby turned to see a large figure emerging from the undergrowth carrying a shotgun.

'Dan!' said Ben, holding out a hand. 'You don't know Libby, do you?'

Dan stepped forward and shook the proffered hand. 'We've not actually met, but living in this village you can hardly help knowing *of* her!' He turned to Libby and held out a hand. 'Nice to meet you, Libby.'

'And this is Fran Wolfe,' said Ben. 'We just came to look over the old Hop.'

'Oh?' Dan looked interested. 'Want to come into the house? Moira's around somewhere.'

He led the way through the gate, where they were nearly knocked over by an enthusiastic Colley. The house looked to be roughly the same age as Edward and Ian's, but Georgian grey stone instead of white, and slightly bigger. Colley pranced ahead of them through the open front door.

'Why have I never met him before?' Libby whispered to Ben.

'You don't usually go into the back bar at the pub,' said Ben. 'He's often there. They both are, sometimes.'

At that, a woman emerged to meet them. Her long curly

71

hair was bound round with a trailing scarf, and her ankle length velvet skirt and waistcoat came straight out of the early seventies.

'Hello,' she said. 'I'm Moira.' She looked past Libby to Fran. 'And I know who you are. I've always wanted to meet you.'

'She's fascinated with the whole psychic stroke supernatural stuff,' explained Dan, his expression saying only too clearly what he thought. 'Now, coffee?'

Chapter Nine

Seated at a kitchen table which almost equalled Hetty's in size, Moira supplied them all with coffee.

'So, what were you looking at the old Hop for?' asked Dan, looking at Libby. 'It's nothing to do with the body that you found, is it?'

'I didn't find it!' said Libby, shocked. 'Is that what they're saying in the village?'

Dan shrugged. 'I expect it's people jumping to conclusions.'

'Natural, in a way,' said Moira. 'You've been involved with so many bodies over the years.'

'Oh.' Libby glanced at Fran, who sat serenely stirring coffee. 'Well, no, I just showed the woman who found it over the place. Come to think of it, I don't know why she wanted me with her.'

'Couldn't you just have let her have the keys?' asked Dan.

'*Me*?' said Libby.

'Libby didn't have the keys,' said Ben. 'It was a builder called Ted Sachs. Yes, Lib, why did she want you with her?'

'I don't know. I assumed she just wanted someone to hold her hand and she doesn't know many people here yet.'

'Ted Sachs?' Dan was frowning. 'I don't think I've heard of him.'

'No, none of us have,' said Ben. 'I'm going to get him to have a look at the Hop.'

'Thinking of buying it?' Dan looked even more interested.

'He already owns the freehold,' said Libby. 'Comes with being landed gentry.'

Ben scowled at her and the others laughed.

'Well, I'm all for it. A pub next door! My idea of heaven.' Dan beamed. Moira sighed theatrically.

'I've got to get hold of the people who last held the lease – they seemed to have slipped out of sight,' said Ben.

'Old Newman?' said Dan, looking surprised. 'He died years ago – didn't you know?'

'No, I certainly didn't!' Ben sat up straight. 'Do you know who were his executors? Or who he left things to?'

'His son, I expect,' said Moira. 'He went to live with them, and we only know because he left the key of the Hop with us so we could collect mail. They told us when he died and we returned the key.' She looked at her husband. 'I suppose we assumed the son was now the owner.'

Dan was on his feet turning out the contents of a dresser drawer. 'I've got his address here somewhere. Course, I don't know if he's still there… Ah – here we are!'

He held out an old envelope with a torn corner.

'Felling?' Ben looked round at Libby and Fran.

'Yes.' Dan looked puzzled. 'Why?'

'That's where that builder comes from – Ted Sachs. Probably just a coincidence.'

74

Moira was looking at Fran. 'Don't you feel anything about that?' she said. 'Coincidences aren't always what they seem, are they?'

Fran smiled gently. 'Usually just that,' she said, 'coincidences.'

'Oh.' Moira sat back in her chair and looked sulky.

Ben had unearthed a pencil from a pocket. 'Got anything to write on, Lib?'

'Oh, keep the envelope,' said Dan, waving a careless hand. 'We don't need it any more.'

Shortly afterwards, they were able to call a halt to the visit by Fran saying she had to get back to the gallery. Moira brightened up and said she must come and visit.

Dan and Colley came with them to the gate.

'You mustn't mind Moira,' he said. 'She gets very enthusiastic.'

'I've got one of those,' said Ben, with a hard look at Libby.

'And keep me informed about the Hop, won't you?' said Dan. 'Anything I can do to help.'

They walked back up the lane.

'Looks as though the new forensic experts have arrived,' said Ben. A large white van was parked with its back doors open at the side of the Garden, and an expensive-looking dark saloon with blacked out windows was parked in front. A uniformed policeman in a high-vis jacket gave them a hard look as they walked past, Libby's footsteps slowing noticeably. Fran and Ben took an arm each and hurried her past.

'Do you think Rachel would tell me what's going on?'

she asked wistfully, looking back over her shoulder.

'Not until they release something to the press,' said Ben.

'Are we going to lunch, then?' Libby asked as they crossed the high street.

'I really ought to get back,' said Fran. 'Lunch at Harry's tends to drag on.'

'Sandwich at the pub?' suggested Ben.

'Good idea,' said Libby.

'So you can ask Tim what he thinks about the Hop?' said Ben.

'We-ell...'

'I think I'll go home anyway,' said Fran. 'If you don't mind. You can let me know if there are any developments.'

Ben and Libby went in to the pub, waving Fran off as they did so.

'I think she was embarrassed about us arguing,' said Libby. 'Sorry, Ben.'

'She's known us long enough not to worry about it,' said Ben, giving her a squeeze. 'Come on and interrogate Tim.'

Settled at the bar with drinks and sandwiches ordered, Libby began the interrogation.

'What do you think about Ben's idea for a Brewery Tap, then, Tim?'

Tim grinned at them both. 'Ah! Told her, then?'

'We've just been to look at it,' said Ben. 'Lib was worried on your behalf.'

'That was nice of you, Libby, but honestly, I think it would probably be good for both of us. Ben doesn't plan to

76

be open as long as I am, and doesn't plan on doing food, do you, Ben?'

Ben shook his head.

'But how exactly will it benefit both of you?' asked Libby. 'I don't get it.'

'I told you, I will only be doing our own ales whereas Tim will do the full range of drinks.' Ben looked at Tim. 'That's right, isn't it?'

Tim nodded. 'And all the old lags who like real ales will be able to go to the Hop and moan about modern pubs.'

'If you say so,' said Libby doubtfully.

'And it will give me a chance to turn this place into a real destination pub,' said Tim. 'You know, step up the events and dining experiences – and even the hotel side. Even though we haven't got many rooms.'

'Yes, I see,' said Libby, still looking unconvinced.

Ben laughed. 'Never mind, Lib, it'll take ages to set up, anyway. I shall have to apply for a licence, although there shouldn't be any problem about change of use.'

Their sandwiches appeared. 'And now, fill me in on your latest murder.'

'It's not mine!' said Libby, startled. 'I wasn't there.'

'Do you know anything about this builder?' asked Ben.

'What builder?' Tim looked from one to another. 'Come on, tell me all.'

So Libby did.

'Who is this woman?' asked Tim, when she'd finished. 'Does she come in here?'

'Her name's Fiona Darling, and she and her husband have bought a converted barn out at Steeple Well. He works in the city, or something. And this builder did some work on it for them. Ted Sachs, his name is. Heard of him?'

'Haven't heard of either of them,' said Tim. 'And I thought I'd been here long enough now to know all the local builders and plumbers. Does he come from here?'

'Somewhere over Felling way, apparently,' said Ben. 'He's done some work for our friend Edward, too. Oh, and did you hear about Ian?'

'Your copper friend? No, what's he done?'

And they settled into a cosy conversation about Ian's surprise move to Shott.

'It is a bit odd, isn't it?' said Libby, as she and Ben walked back to Allhallow's Lane. 'No one knows anything about Fiona or Ted.'

'Except Edward,' said Ben.

'But he doesn't know much, and he's a newcomer himself.'

'Did you find out where he got Ted from?' asked Ben.

'Did I? Was it a leaflet? We'll have to check.'

'Mind you, the police will have done all this anyway,' said Ben. 'They'll have had teams of people beavering away in the background, the same as those expert forensics people over there now.'

'I don't know what they can hope to find, though,' said Libby. 'After all, it isn't a new body.'

'Oh, there'll be all sorts of tiny details to pick up. I wouldn't be surprised if they don't find out exactly who he is.'

The truth of this was soon borne out when later in the

78

afternoon a knock on the door announced DS Trent and a uniformed officer.

'What's up, Rachel?' said Libby, alarmed.

'Oh, nothing to worry about, Libby - er, Mrs Sarjeant,' Rachel corrected herself, with a look at the officer. 'We're just making some enquiries about the, um, deceased.'

'Do you know who it is, then?' asked Ben, coming up behind Libby.

'We think so.' Again, Rachel cast an anxious glance at the officer, who stood stolidly behind her and kept his gaze fixed in the middle distance.

'Well, come and sit down,' said Libby. 'We saw the forensics people up at the Garden earlier. Did they find something?'

'I'm afraid we can't tell you that,' said Rachel, 'but we do have a tentative identification.' She opened the tablet she was carrying and swiped at the screen. 'He was an Oscar Whitelaw, known as Ossie. Here.' She turned the screen to show them an obviously cropped shot of an apparently teenaged boy wearing the ubiquitous bomber jacket and beanie.

Libby and Ben peered at the screen.

'No,' said Libby. 'Never seen him as far as I know.'

'Was he part of a gang?' asked Ben. 'I've never seen him either.'

Rachel sighed. 'A couple of people who told us some teenagers had been using the hotel as a sort of den. We thought he was one of them. And forensics have confirmed the identity.'

Ben frowned. 'That's odd in itself, isn't it? After all, he

only looks about fourteen, so if he was with a gang of his peers none of them would be old enough to drive. How did they get out here?'

Rachel sighed again. 'We don't know.' She stood up from where she had been perching on the edge of a chair. 'Well, thank you both. Can you suggest anyone else we might ask?'

'Does Beth still run the youth club?' Ben turned to Libby.

'I think so, although it isn't as well patronised as it used to be,' said Libby. 'You could try her, Rachel.'

'Beth?'

'The vicar. You know, you've met her. She lives in the vicarage on the corner of this road.'

'Oh, yes!' Rachel was enlightened. 'She's lent us her church hall, hasn't she?'

When she and her shadow had departed in the direction of the vicarage, Libby went into the kitchen to put the kettle on.

'Do you think Beth will be able to help?' Ben wandered in after her.

Libby shook her head. 'I doubt it. Not many youngsters want to go to an old-fashioned youth club these days, do they? I don't know what Beth does with them, to be honest.'

'I wonder if it's just the latest example of this awful knife crime epidemic among youngsters?' said Ben.

'I wouldn't say that outside of this room,' warned Libby. 'It sounds a bit ageist to me.'

'Sorry.' Ben made a face. 'I never know what we're

allowed to say these days. But the truth is, we've not had any trouble with gangs of kids of whatever flavour, have we? And do we think that's the reason he was killed? Or was there another reason?'

Chapter Ten

'Tell you what you ought to do,' said Libby, 'get in touch with that whatsisname, Newman. You've got to find out about the lease of the Hop, anyway, and it sounds as though he might have known Colin Hardcastle – they might have been round about the same age.'

'I don't see that I could have any reason to ask that,' said Ben, fishing the crumpled envelope Dan had given him out of his pocket. 'And anyway, the police know where to find him, don't they? You passed on the Spanish address and they already had the registered address in London. And,' he went on, fixing Libby with a look, 'what would he have to do with a teenager's body in a derelict hotel he hasn't been near in years?'

Libby hitched a shoulder and turned away. Ben sighed and pulled his mobile out of his pocket and wandered back into the sitting room. Libby carried on making tea.

'Well?' she said, when she took in the two mugs. Ben was putting the mobile back in his pocket looking smug.

'John Newman's still at the address Dan gave us, and said he thought the solicitors would have been in touch when his dad died. Apparently on the paperwork, it says the lease dies with him, and can be renewed at the freeholder's discretion.' He beamed. 'That's me!'

'And does he want to renew it?'

'What do you think? Of course not. He's still got a lot of the paperwork and offered to send it to me. Again, he thought the solicitor would have taken care of all that. But,' he took his mug from Libby and sipped, 'I thought perhaps we could go over and collect it. He'll be in tomorrow morning.'

Libby gave him a kiss. 'Genius!' she said.

Wednesday morning was dull. Libby loaded the dishwasher and made the bed while Ben went up to the Manor to fetch the 4x4 which he preferred to travel in rather than using Libby's 'silver bullet'.

They drove across country, skirting Bishop's Bottom, and entered Felling through the Sand Gate, the enormous stone gatehouse that was the only way into the little town, passing on to the ring road, which enclosed it almost like a castle wall.

'Does he live in the town itself?' asked Libby.

'We're not meeting him there,' said Ben. 'He said it's a bit difficult to find and to park, so we're meeting him in a cafe in the town square.'

'Not the "Tea Square"?' said Libby. 'Fran and I had tea there during that business of Patti's at St Aldeberge.'

Ben gave her a swift grin. 'So you'll know where to park, then? I don't know the place at all.'

'Oh, yes,' said Libby confidently. 'In the car park by the Quay.'

'Odd place,' said Ben, when he'd parked. He strolled over to the stone wall above the moorings. 'That's the way to St Aldeberge, is it?' He pointed to the narrow stream

83

leading out of the yacht basin. 'And that's inland?' At the other end of the basin, a much broader river went under the bridge to the ring road. 'Only one way in by road, and only one by water, seemingly.'

'Like a medieval walled town,' said Libby. 'Which it once was. Come on, I'm dying for a cup of tea.'

They crossed the square to the self-consciously named "Tea Square", which Fran had commented probably got past most people, and went inside, to find a table already set out with tea and coffee pots, two plates of cakes, and a very thick buff folder. The man sitting at the table rose with a smile and an outstretched hand.

'You're Mr Wilde?' he said.

'Oh, call me Ben!' Ben shook the offered hand. 'And this is Libby Sarjeant. You must be John Newman? I'm sorry I never met you.'

'Oh, well, you'd gone to London,' said John, sitting down again. 'I didn't know if you'd prefer tea or coffee?'

When they had settled down with Ben's coffee and Libby's tea, Ben turned to the subject of the Hop Pocket.

'I'm really sorry no one ever contacted you,' said John. 'Dad's affairs weren't in the best state, and I just handed the whole lot to the solicitor. It never occurred to me that we were still holding on to the lease.' He glanced nervously at Libby and back to Ben. 'Do we owe you a huge amount of rent?'

That explains the lavish elevenses and the willingness to be helpful, thought Libby cynically.

'No, no!' said Ben, smiling. 'Don't give it another thought. I've been as lax as your solicitor – I should have sorted it out, but my father died, too, and the estate got a bit on top of me.'

'Oh!' John smiled in relief. 'Thank you.'

'As a matter of fact, it's rather fortunate,' Ben went on, and outlined his plans for the Hop and his brewery.

'Do you think you could make it pay?' asked John, doubt written all over his broad, ruddy face. 'Dad said it was a struggle, especially with the other pub and the Garden next door.'

'The new landlord at the pub says it will allow him to develop the dining and hotel side of his business,' said Libby, 'and the Garden's been closed now for years.'

'Colin didn't sell it, then?' John looked interested. 'I thought he would once he went to London. He didn't want to run it after his mum died, did he? No more'n I wanted to run the Hop.'

'Oh, you knew Colin, then?'

'Well, yes.' John grinned. 'We were next-door neighbours, weren't we, and almost of an age. I'm a bit older, o' course. How is he?'

Ben and Libby looked at each other.

'The problem is, we don't know,' said Ben. 'No one's seen him.'

John frowned. 'Not even Nanny Mardle?'

'No – not even her,' said Libby. 'She lives next door to me. and the police want to see him.'

'The police?' John's bushy eyebrows shot up. 'What for? He was never a one to get into trouble!'

'He's not now,' said Ben. 'Have you not seen the local news in the last week?'

John's face got even ruddier. 'Don't take much notice these days, especially as we don't get proper papers anymore.'

'No – even the *Mercury*'s online-only these days, isn't it?' Libby shook her head. 'So sad.'

'So you haven't heard about the murder?' said Ben.

'Murder?'

'A body was found in the old Garden. A young teenager, as far as the police can tell. Not been there long. So they have to speak to Colin. They've got his address in Spain from Mrs Mardle, and the company's registered address in Holborn somewhere, but the only person available has been a woman who goes to collect stuff.'

'Oh, yes.' John looked down into his coffee cup. 'What was her name? Carol? Caroline? I know!' He clicked his fingers. 'Carina! Not that I've met her, but Colin told me last time he was over.'

'Oh, you've seen him recently, have you?' Libby was surprised. John looked equally surprised.

'Oh, yes! That was why I wondered about no one in Steeple Martin being able to find him. He comes over regularly.'

'He comes to see you, does he?' asked Ben.

'Yes, sometimes, although I'll often go up to London to meet him.' He frowned again. 'I know he isn't keen on Felling, but I thought he was all right about his home village.'

'What do you mean?' asked Libby.

'Oh, he used to get the horrors about that girl that disappeared here – do you remember? About twenty years

86

ago? Maybe more. Yes, must be more than that. The singer.'

Ben and Libby shook their heads.

'Well,' John leant forward over the table, 'we were both at the party where she disappeared!'

'Goodness!' Libby said, round eyed.

'Luckily for us, we weren't involved. I'd been invited by my girlfriend, who's now my wife,' said John, looking coy, 'and I took Colin along with me. We came home together, too, in my car, but of course everyone was quizzed by the police. It really seemed to affect Colin. But then, he was always a bit soft.'

'Yes, Mrs Mardle said something similar,' said Libby. 'Said he was delicate, I think.'

'Yeah, well,' said John, looking at her sideways.

'Oh,' said Ben, with sudden understanding. 'He's gay!'

John looked relieved. 'Didn't think Nanny Mardle would understand. My dad didn't, not really, and Colin's mum never knew.'

'Things have changed quite a bit now,' said Ben. 'My cousin's gay, and married to his partner who owns our village restaurant. You'd be surprised.'

John was looking duly amazed. 'The little Mexican restaurant? The missus and I have been there loads of times!'

'Well, give us a shout next time you come over and we'll have a drink,' said Ben.

'So tell us about this singer. Was she famous?' asked Libby.

'Not really. She was local and been to one of these

87

special schools or something. And she'd been on the telly. And o'course we still had those local papers then and they made a fuss about her, saying she was the next big thing. So there was a hoo-ha when she went missing.'

'I bet there was!' said Libby. 'How old was she?'

'Eighteen? Nineteen? Young, anyway.' John shrugged. 'Col had always been a bit squeamish, and it put him right off. So off he went to London. Said he could be more himself up there. But we stayed mates.'

'Well, if he gets in touch soon, could you tell him the police would like to talk to him?' said Ben. 'If he hasn't already heard, of course.'

'Course,' said John, nodding firmly. 'And I'll let you know.'

'Well,' said Libby, as they drove back out of the Sand Gate. 'What do you make of that? Bit of a surprise, wasn't it?'

'Was a bit,' said Ben. 'Do you think we ought to pass it on to Maiden?'

'Or Rachel Trent.' Libby thought for a moment. 'And at least it seems as though he isn't actually in hiding. But what about that missing girl? Don't you remember anything about it?'

'No – I wasn't down here then, was I? But a missing teenager would have made the nationals, I would have thought.'

'Hm. Can't have anything to do with this case, though, can it?'

'I don't see how.' Ben sighed. 'Anyway, it looks as though I'm safe going ahead with plans for the Hop Pocket.

I'll get everything over to the solicitor this afternoon.'

And I'll get in touch with Rachel Trent, thought Libby.

As soon as Ben had dropped her off at Allhallow's Lane and gone on to the brewery, Libby called Fran and told her the results of the trip to see John Newman.

'And this helps how?' asked Fran, when she'd finished.

'Well, not sure, but at least we now know why Colin Hardcastle took against Kent. Although I don't see why he abandoned his mum and the hotel.'

'It sounds more as if he was one of those people who don't like the rural lifestyle. More of a big city boy.'

'But he's living in Spain!'

'Not all of Spain's rural,' said Fran, amused.

'No, all right. But we should tell the police, shouldn't we? Ben asked John Newman to tell him the police want to speak to him, but we should. Tell them, I mean.'

'I suppose so, but I expect they've found out by now, with all their resources.'

'Mmm. As it's Wednesday, Ian might come to the pub this evening, so -'

'Oh, Libby, don't! Poor chap needs to relax if he comes to the pub. After all, you're not really concerned in this murder, and anyway, he might not be able to get away.'

But, when Ben and Libby arrived at the pub later that evening to join their friends Patti and Anne, a weekly tradition, Ian was already there. And leaning on the bar speaking to him, a very slim man with dark hair and a thin, nervous-looking face, wearing a rather loose light grey suit.

Ian turned to greet them.

'Libby, Ben, meet Colin Hardcastle.'

Chapter Eleven

Luckily for Libby, who was uncharacteristically bereft of speech, Ben stepped forward with outstretched hand.

'Colin! Pleased to meet you. I don't think we've run across each other before.'

'I remember you, though.' Colin shook hands with a slight smile. 'You played bat and trap with your dad, didn't you?'

'Yes, I did!' Ben was delighted. 'Not for long, because I left the village. But actually - '

'Give him a chance, Ben!' Libby, recovered, smiled and held out her own hand. 'Hello, Colin. I'm new, so you won't remember me.'

'Not exactly new,' said Ian. 'Libby's been here several years and made herself – well, part of the village.'

'No, I know about you.' Colin's smile became a little broader. 'You live next door to Mrs Mardle, don't you? She's told me all about you.'

'Are you joining us?' asked Ben, as he spotted Patti and Anne coming into the bar. 'Or are you here to talk to Ian?' He looked at Ian. 'Sorry, DCI Connell.'

Colin looked from Ben to Ian and back. 'I don't know!' he said.

'We'll finish our chat first, Ben,' said Ian. 'If Colin wants to join us afterwards, he's welcome.'

By this time Libby had already joined Patti, who was pushing chairs aside to position Anne's wheelchair by their regular table. Ben called over to ask about drinks and the women sat down.

'So who's that?' asked Anne.

In a low voice, Libby briefly explained.

'How do you do it, Libby?' said Patti, shaking her head.

'Do what?' Libby looked offended. 'I didn't do anything! I merely went with the woman looking over the old Garden Hotel. I wasn't even there when she found the body.'

Ben arrived with a tray of drinks. 'I suppose she's told you all about our newcomer? He might be joining us, if you don't object.'

'Oh, no!' said Anne. 'Not at all. So he's the owner of this old hotel, is he?'

'Yes,' said Ben. 'Oh, and we were over at Felling this morning, Patti.'

'Yes, first time I've been back since your little bit of bother,' said Libby. 'It hasn't changed.'

'Why were you there?'

'Long story,' said Ben, 'but all to do with another pub.'

'Another pub?' echoed Patti.

'Yes,' said Libby. 'Here, next door to the old hotel that Colin owns.'

'I didn't know there was another pub here!' said Anne.

'I'd better explain,' said Ben, and was in the middle of doing so when Ian brought Colin to the table.

'Mind if we join you?'

'Of course,' said Libby, and they all shuffled round to make room for two more chairs. Colin was introduced to Anne and Patti.

'From St Aldeberge?' said Colin. 'Long way to come for a drink.'

'The Reverend Patti Pearson, actually,' amplified Libby. 'And they only allow her out once a week.'

'Don't take any notice,' said Patti to a rather startled Colin. 'I come over to visit Anne on my night off, and meet up with Libby. We have dinner in the Pink Geranium.'

'That's since my time, too, isn't it?' Colin turned to Ben.

Ben explained about the restaurant, Peter, and Harry to Colin. 'And we were over at Felling seeing your friend John Newman this morning.'

'Were you?' Colin looked even more startled.

'Yes,' said Ben. 'You see, it was my father who owned the land both your hotel and the old Hop Pocket stood on. Your parents bought the freehold from us, but John's parents hadn't, and now the lease reverts to me.' He looked round triumphantly at the company. 'And I plan to re-open it!'

There were gasps and exclamations of astonishment all round the table.

'But what about this place?' asked Anne. 'Won't Tim be upset? He's only just got this place going.'

'That's what I said,' said Libby, 'but apparently he's all for it.'

'And what I was wondering, Colin,' said Ben, 'was

92

about your bat and trap.'

'Here we go,' murmured Libby.

Now Colin was looking completely bewildered.

'Well,' continued Ben, 'the pitch will still be there, won't it?'

'Completely overgrown, I expect,' said Colin.

'We could see to that,' said Ben. 'And what about the equipment? Would that still be in the building?'

Colin shook his head. 'It was never kept in the hotel. Don't you remember, we had a proper shelter at the end of the pitch?'

'But that was open,' said Ben.

'With a locked chest. I don't know if that's still there.'

'What I was thinking was, if I could lease the pitch from you, I could start up a new team attached to the Hop Pocket. There's access from the footpath that runs behind the hotel and beside the pub, isn't there?'

Colin was beginning to look interested. 'Yes, there is. I might be tempted to come over more often if you did that.'

'Well,' began Ben, but Colin interrupted.

'Only I was planning on trying to sell the old place. How would that affect your plans?'

A somewhat loaded silence fell at this, and Ian stood up.

'Another drink, anyone?'

Only Libby and Ben answered and Ian went to the bar.

'Is that why you give Ted Sachs the keys to survey the building?' Libby turned back to Colin.

'Yes – I got his name from John.'

Ben and Libby looked at each other. Mystery solved.

'We couldn't work out why you hadn't used someone

93

from here,' said Libby.

'John said he was just starting up and could do with the work. He vouched for him, so I took a chance. I didn't want a lot done, just tidied up, really.'

'And do you know why he let Mrs Darling have the keys?' asked Ben.

Colin frowned. 'No, I don't. I wasn't pleased when I heard about that from the police. I don't think Mr Sachs will get the job after all.' His face turned gloomy. 'If they ever let me do anything with it, of course.'

'Who, the police?' said Patti. 'They will when they've finished their investigations.'

'Are you sure?' Colin made a face. 'And will anyone want to buy it?'

'It depends on what you were selling it for,' said Ben. 'Presumably not a hotel/restaurant?'

'Oh, no,' said Colin with a sigh. 'For development. Flats, or something.'

'So the purchaser would have to pay for complete re-modelling anyway,' said Libby.

'That's why I didn't want Ted to do much,' said Colin.

Ian, who had returned with the drinks during this conversation, said: 'There would have to be a change of use application.'

'Up to the purchaser, isn't it?' said Colin.

'You'd find it hard to sell without one,' said Ben. 'I don't have to apply for one for the Hop Pocket, as it always was a pub.'

Libby was looking thoughtful. 'I don't think Fiona Darling knew any of this.'

Ian's lips twitched. 'I'm pretty sure she didn't. And Ted Sachs hadn't told her anything.'

'I must see him,' said Colin. 'You've spoken to him, haven't you?'

'We have,' said Ian.

'Have you?' said Libby. 'When? Not on Saturday?'

'No, you know I didn't. And Inspector Maiden doesn't have to tell you what progress has been made.'

'Oh,' said Libby, chastened. 'But I thought…'

Ian sent her a warning glance. Anne, brightly inquisitive, looked from one to the other. 'Was he being a bit elusive, then, this Ted? And who was he, exactly? A builder?'

'Apparently,' said Ian. 'He's been working on Edward's summerhouse.'

Libby looked at him suspiciously. He returned the look with a bland smile, and she knew she would get nothing more from him – certainly not in company.

The conversation turned to more general subjects, including the St Aldeberge Summer Fete. Ben went into a huddle with Colin, presumably about bat and trap, until Colin pushed back his chair and stood up.

'Sorry, everyone, but I'm done! I was up at the crack of dawn this morning to get here.'

'Are you staying here?' asked Libby.

'Yes.' Colin nodded towards Ian. 'The police fixed it up for me. So I'll say goodnight.'

'So,' said Ben, when Colin had departed to his bedroom, 'not such a mystery after all. When did you get hold of him?'

'I didn't,' said Ian. 'Inspector Maiden did. And no – not such a mystery.'

'Didn't you find it a bit odd, though?' mused Libby. 'About the change of use - he was bit vague, wasn't he? I thought his business was property development. He should know all about that.'

'Hardcastle Holdings, isn't it?' said Ben. 'Oh, well, perhaps I can get him chatting about it tomorrow.'

'Tomorrow?' said Libby and Ian together.

'We're meeting at the back of the hotel to see if the bat and trap pitch will still be usable, and if the equipment is still there.' Ben grinned happily at Ian. 'That won't compromise the crime scene, will it?'

Ian sighed. 'I'd check with Inspector Maiden first, if I were you.' He stood up. 'Peter! Harry not with you? What will you have?'

'I'll get them, Ian. Not coffee this time?' Peter grinned across at Ian. 'Harry won't be a moment. He's just mopping up his tears because Donna's told him she's having another baby.'

All three women exclaimed with pleasure and Ben and Peter looked amused.

'So will he lose his right-hand woman permanently this time?' asked Ian.

'I doubt it. She'll still carry on doing the books and ordering and so on from home. He's been bloody lucky up till now. Anyone else?'

There was a chorus of 'No thanks' and Peter went to the bar just as Harry came in with a flourish and threw himself into a chair.

'We were just hearing about Donna,' said Libby. 'Is she feeling all right?'

'Oh, *she's* fine,' said Harry disconsolately. 'I'm the one with the problem.'

'You've got plenty of waiting help these days,' said Anne, 'and I gather young Adam's getting quite handy in the kitchen.'

'Well, maybe,' said Harry grudgingly.

'And,' said Peter, coming back to the table, 'she and her husband have just bought a house here, so she can wheel her babies round in the mornings to pick up or deliver orders and things.'

'The older one's school age now, though,' said Libby. 'Thank goodness we've still got a school. Where's the house?'

'Steeple Well, I think,' said Harry. 'All posh people out there.'

'That's where Fiona Darling lives,' said Libby. 'They'll be neighbours.'

'Don't start interfering, Libby,' warned Ian.

Libby looked back innocently.

'Come on, you old trout,' said Harry. 'What have you been up to now?'

'Nothing,' said Ben, 'for a change. Just speculation.'

'About Colin Hardcastle mainly, and how I'm going to manage the old Hop.'

'Definitely going ahead with it, then,' said Peter.

'I suppose he told you all about it, too,' said Libby, with a hard glare at Ben.

'Just mentioned it,' said Peter carelessly.

97

'So, Ian,' said Patti, tactfully changing the subject, 'have you actually moved in to your new home yet?'

'I'm camping out at the moment,' said Ian, 'but I'm moving in properly at the weekend.'

'You didn't tell me that!' Libby looked affronted.

'I've hardly had a chance,' said Ian, amused. 'But yes. Removals firm all booked.'

'You didn't walk here tonight, did you?' asked Ben, eyeing Ian's pint of bitter.

'Taxi,' said Ian, finally bursting out laughing. 'You're all so concerned!'

Harry leant over and patted his knee. 'Nosy and interfering, that's what,' he said. 'You ought to be used to it by now. I wonder that you wanted to move closer.'

'So do I,' said Ian. 'I must be a masochist.'

Chapter Twelve

'You know what we should be concentrating on,' Libby said to Fran on the phone on Thursday morning.

'Eh?'

'The poor boy who was killed. Everybody's been talking about Colin Hardcastle and Ted Sachs, and even Fiona Darling. We've hardly mentioned the body. What was his name? Ossie.'

'Ossie? Who told you that?' said Fran.

'Rachel. She came round with a photo. Oscar Whitelaw, apparently. She didn't tell us anything about him, just asked if we recognised him. She was going to ask Beth if he was a member of the youth club.'

'Do kids go to youth clubs these days?' asked Fran doubtfully.

'I don't know,' said Libby. 'I'll ask Beth. We don't know anyone with children that age, do we?'

'I don't, but Sophie might. And you could ask Adam. But why? The police are obviously on the case.'

'Don't they say that in a case of murder the answer is the victim? Who he or she was and why were they killed.'

'Yes – and that's what the police are doing,' said Fran. 'I expect they know where he came from, who his parents were, things like that. They aren't likely to tell you, are they?'

'They have in the past.' Libby sniffed.

'When it was necessary,' said Fran, 'and when Ian was SIO.'

'Well, he is now, except he's supposed to be deskbound.'

'And Inspector Maiden is the actual SIO on the ground. And you aren't anything to do with the case.' Fran sighed. 'Look, Lib. You've had this pointed out to you. Leave it alone.'

'Well, what about your chair?' countered Libby. 'Your room with a chair? You've been thinking about it, too.'

'It has been rather thrust under my nose,' said Fran, sounding amused. 'To be honest, I'm far more interested in the Hop Pocket and bat and trap.'

Now Libby sighed. 'That's where Ben is this morning. He and Colin Hardcastle were going over to inspect the old pitch, and to see if the equipment was still there. Frankly, I'd be surprised.'

'It can be any area of flat land, though, can't it? I've been looking it up.'

'I suppose so. I don't know anything about it, except that it exists,' said Libby. 'Colin seems quite enthusiastic about it.' She thought for a moment. 'I wish I knew more about that girl who disappeared, though. I didn't like to ask him yesterday.'

'Why?' Fran sounded exasperated. 'What's that got to do with the murdered teenager?'

'I don't know. Nothing. I just wanted to know. Neither

100

Ben nor I remember anything about it. She was a singer, apparently.'

'You could always ask Jane. She might know.'

'I don't like to interrupt her at work,' said Libby. Jane Baker was assistant editor on the *Nethergate Mercury*, and other local newspapers in the group.

'She works at home a lot,' said Fran. 'She's told us that in the past. You could always send her a tweet, or something. Or a text message. Then she doesn't have to answer you if she's busy. Like we do sometimes with Ian.'

'Yes, I could.' Libby was thoughtful. 'And I wouldn't be treading on anyone's toes, would I? Like the police, I mean.'

'No, Lib. And it'll give you something else to think about.'

For the rest of the morning Libby tried, fairly ineffectually, to catch up on neglected housework, before giving up at lunchtime and sending Jane a text. Ten minutes later, while she was stirring her soup, her phone rang.

'What do you want to know for?' asked Jane, without preamble.

'Hello, Jane! How lovely to hear from you,' said Libby, moving the soup pan off the hob.

'Hello, Libby, nice to hear from you, too. Now, why do you want to know about Shareen Wallis?'

'Who?'

'Shareen Wallis. The singer. Is she something to do with your body?'

'Oh! Was that her name? How ghastly. And no, she

101

isn't - wasn't. And it isn't *my* body.'

'Oh.' Jane obviously thought for a moment. 'Why are you asking, then?'

'Someone over in Felling mentioned her yesterday. One of Ben's former tenants, actually.'

'Who? Why did he mention her?'

'What's the matter, Jane? Why are you asking all these questions? Have we touched a nerve?'

Libby heard Jane sigh. 'It was one of the great local mysteries. Made all the nationals, too. I'm surprised you didn't remember it.'

'Yes, John said it hit the headlines. You can't have been here, then, though. Before your time.'

'Yes, but it's one of those things that keep cropping up. One of our old reporters had a real bee in his bonnet about it. She'd been on TV, you see.'

'So John said. Was it a talent show?'

'No, she'd been spotted singing in a local pub, I think, and put up for a spot on a Saturday morning children's show. Remember them? Before umpteen channels?'

'Oh, yes.' Libby remembered. 'So she got a spot on a kids TV show – how old was she?'

'As far as I know, she was about seventeen, then. And then she got a regular slot on someone else's show – just a song a week sort of thing – and she was starting to get really popular. I believe she was just signing her first record deal, something like that.'

'So she was obviously good. John said she was at a party where he was, and it was the party she disappeared from. Do you remember anything about that?'

'No. But I'll see if there's anything I can drag out of the archives, if you like. We've managed to get everything digitised, now. Pity old Barrett isn't still here, he'd have talked you to death about it.'

'Is he dead?' said Libby.

'I don't think so – I'd have heard. But he must be positively ancient. I'll ask if anyone knows.'

'Thank you,' said Libby. 'How's Imogen?'

'Oh, fine – thriving. Quite grown up, now.'

'I suppose she must be. And Terry – and your mum?'

'Fine, too. Mum's a lot slower, and is beginning to find the steps a bit of a bind, but she says they keep her fit. So, come on. What about this body?'

'Honestly, Jane, it isn't anything to do with me.'

'Why has your name cropped up, then?'

'Has it?' Libby squirmed uncomfortably. 'How? Who from?'

'Oh, just around.' Jane was evasive. 'What happened?'

'I'm not telling you if it's going into a news story.'

Jane sighed again. 'All right, I promise.'

So Libby once again told the tale of Fiona Darling, Ted Sachs, and the Garden Hotel.

'So you *nearly* found the body,' said Jane.

'Yes – a near miss. And I know nothing more about it. Except that it's brought the absentee landlord back from the continent.'

'Absentee landlord?' Libby could almost hear Jane's nose twitching.

'Well, not exactly, his parents ran the hotel – bought the leasehold from Ben's dad – but after they'd both died, he
103

didn't want to come back and run it. So that's why Ted Sachs had the keys. He was surveying the place to see how much renovation it would take to get it sale ready.' It sounded quite reasonable put like that, thought Libby, wondering why there'd been such mystery surrounding Colin Hardcastle's absence.

'So why was the body there?' Jane was persistent, as all good reporters should be.

'No idea. And I don't know what the police know, either. No inside track on this one. The only other bit of news is that Ben's going to re-open the other pub in the village.'

'Other pub? What other pub?'

'I know – I didn't know anything about it, either. It's called the Hop Pocket and it's in a little lane off the end of the high street, just behind the Garden Hotel actually. And Ben's planning to re-start the bat and trap team at the same time.'

'I didn't know there'd been a team in Steeple Martin!' said Jane. 'We used to print all the league results on the sports pages.'

'It was attached to the Garden Hotel, but the pitch is still there, and accessible from the Hop. People seem quite enthusiastic, but I've never seen it played.'

'Well, that's going to make a story,' said Jane. 'Re-opening of a village pub – will Ben be selling his own beer?'

'Yes, that's the whole point; it'll be an old-fashioned ale house. Tim at the other pub is quite happy. He says it'll leave him free to make more of his events and hotel business.'

'Excellent,' said Jane. 'And reviving bat and trap! There's a huge appetite for nostalgia these days. People seem anxious to return to what they see as happier, more uncomplicated times.'

'Even if they weren't really,' said Libby.

After finally consuming a bowl of soup, Libby decided to wander down the high street and see if Ben was still furtling in the undergrowth behind the old hotel. However she met him and Colin crossing the road just outside the Pink Geranium.

'Lunch?' suggested Ben.

'Come on, Libby,' said Colin, sounding a lot more cheerful than he had the day before. 'I'm buying.'

'I've just had soup, thank you,' said Libby, eyeing the open door wistfully.

'I'm sure you could manage a glass of wine, though,' said Colin, and successfully urged her inside.

Harry greeted them with raised eyebrows. 'To what do I owe the pleasure?' he asked, showing them to their usual table in the window, after being introduced to Colin.

'We've just been inspecting the old bat and trap pitch,' said Ben.

'Ah – bucolic frolics.'

'I know some books about bucolic frolics,' said Libby, 'but not the bat and trap sort. Is the pitch still there?'

'It is, although as we thought it's a jungle. But the old shelter is still there, and believe it or not, so was the equipment!' Ben grinned triumphantly.

'Dad kept it in a locked safe sort of thing,' said Colin.

'It was still there, and the key was on the hotel bunch. It'll need a bit of restoration, and the bat wasn't there.'

'But the ball and the posts were,' said Ben, 'so all we've got to do is get the ground cleared.' He and Colin shook hands and beamed at each other delightedly. Libby and Harry looked at each other and grinned.

'Big kids,' muttered Harry. 'Now, are you eating, or just drinking?'

When Harry had supplied them with wine and gone away to assemble Ben's and Colin's lunches, Libby asked how they were going to set about reviving the bat and trap team.

'I'll just ask for volunteers,' said Ben. 'There'll be a lot, I should think. Very popular, it was. There's only eight players in a team, but you can have as many teams as you want! We'll just advertise for friendly matches, first, before applying to join the league.'

'You're going to take it seriously, then?'

'Oh, yes! No point in doing it otherwise,' said Ben.

'And what about the pub? And the brewery?'

'They go hand in hand,' said Ben. 'And I've got a Master Brewer now, haven't I? So as long as I'm still around, the brewery's fine. And I shan't run the pub myself – I told you, I'll get a manager.'

'Very organised, isn't he?' Colin said to Libby. 'I must say, I'm impressed with the way the village seems to operate these days.'

'Why? Was it different when you lived here?' asked Libby. 'Most of the people I know who've been here a long time don't seem to think so.'

'It wasn't as friendly,' said Colin, looking uncomfortable, and Libby suddenly realised what he meant.

'I don't think all the oldest generation have quite got round to accepting the entire LGBT community,' she said, 'but everyone else is more or less happy with it. I think Harry here, and Ben's cousin Peter, helped a lot. I was their best woman when they got married,' she added proudly.

'Were you?' Colin gazed at her admiringly. 'So perhaps I should have stuck it out?'

'But that wasn't why you went away, was it?' said Libby. 'I thought it was because you were upset about Shareen Wallis.'

Chapter Thirteen

Colin's face froze, and Libby was instantly contrite. She leant forward and put a hand on his arm.

'I'm sorry,' she said. 'It's just what John Newman said.'

Colin shook his head and looked down at the table. After a moment he took a deep breath.

'I'm sorry, too,' he said, looking up into Libby's concerned face. 'I honestly didn't think it would still affect me. And you're right. It was why I went away.' He looked from Libby to Ben. 'And it's a nonsensical reason, really, isn't it? A girl I was at a party with disappeared – that was all.'

'John said you were all questioned by the police,' said Ben. 'That can be scary in itself.'

'It was.' Colin sat back in his chair. 'Not something I'm proud of, but it completely spooked me.'

Harry appeared carrying two plates. 'Here you go, gents,' he said. 'I'll just go and fetch the accoutrements and a glass for myself, if you don't mind.'

Libby looked round the restaurant and realised that since they had been seated, it had emptied. 'If Colin doesn't mind,' she said.

Colin smiled rather shyly at Harry. 'I don't mind.'

Harry grinned and went of to fetch bread, tapenade, and butter, as well as another glass.

'Well then,' he said, seating himself. 'What were you all looking so serious about?'

Colin took another deep breath. 'Actually about why I left the village.'

Harry's eyebrows went up. 'Really? When?'

'Nearly twenty years ago,' said Colin.

Harry looked at Libby. 'Before our time, ducky.'

'And not quite so tolerant,' said Ben. 'Although it's hard to believe, now.'

'Ah.' Harry nodded. 'Amazingly enough, there were quite a few people who were quite upset about Pete and me, and thought we should never have been allowed to open a restaurant here. Anyway, if you come back, you're among friends. Drink up!'

The atmosphere relaxed again, although Libby was convinced Colin still had something on his mind.

'There must be more to that story, you know,' she said to Ben on their way home, leaving Colin and Harry happily chatting over the last of the wine.

'What story?'

'About that girl disappearing. Why did it affect Colin so badly? It was nothing to do with him.'

'We don't know what went on.' Ben looked sideways at Libby. 'And don't go questioning him.'

'Is it to do with him being gay? You forget how much prejudice there was even recently.'

'I don't see the connection,' said Ben. 'Anyway, to my surprise, I like the guy. Shame he doesn't want to re-open the Garden, really.'

'That would be proper competition for Tim,' said Libby, 'so I hope he doesn't.'

'No, he doesn't want to. He's got no background in "hospitality" as he calls it, and was never any good with the customers when he used to help out when he was still at school. He said Mrs Mardle was better at it than he was.'

'Perhaps it wasn't actually to do with the girl – perhaps something horrible happened to him at the party.' Libby returned to the original subject. 'Abuse or threatening behaviour – something like that.'

'Could be. But unless he comes out with it of his own accord, we are NOT going to pry, Lib.'

'No, Ben,' said Libby meekly.

Ben went back to the Manor estate office, from where he also ran the brewery, intent on getting his plans for the Hop Pocket underway. Libby went into the conservatory and stared at the easel which held her latest painting. She painted originals of the area – mainly Nethergate – for Guy to sell in his shop-cum-gallery. He turned some of them into smaller prints, which had proved very popular over the years, and very occasionally she had been commissioned to paint something for a specific customer. However, as she was essentially undisciplined, progress on any particular painting tended to be erratic.

Today, the scene was from the top of the cliffs that rose up behind The Sloop and the jetty and included the redundant lighthouse on the headland, the little island in the middle of the bay, and a portion of the headland on the opposite side of the bay. She decided it was *not* inspiring.

110

The mobile ringing from the kitchen interrupted her thoughts.

'Listen, you old slapper,' said Harry. 'Colin has suggested dinner here for you and Ben and those mates of his from Felling. Apparently the bloke came from the pub Ben wants to do up.'

'Has he? When?'

'He thought tonight was a bit short notice, so he suggested tomorrow. I can just squeeze you in, I think. What d'you reckon?'

'Yes – great,' said Libby. 'As far as I'm concerned, anyway. Do you want me to ask Ben?'

'Save me a phone call, won't it? And if he says yes, can he let Colin know?'

Ben was duly informed and promised to let Colin know. 'And the solicitors don't think there'll be any problems about the Hop Pocket, although it's listed, so I shall have to submit plans to the relevant authorities. The Tindall brothers have said they'll take it on, bless 'em. Oh – and I asked them if they'd heard of Ted Sachs.'

'And had they?'

'Funnily enough, they had. Although they didn't know he'd set up on his own.'

'How did they know of him then?

'Apparently, he was apprenticed to a local carpenter when he left school.'

'Where?'

'They didn't say.'

'Oh, well, that's his credentials established, then,' said Libby. 'I wonder if Mrs Mardle's Gary turned out to have heard of him, too?'

'It doesn't matter, now, does it?' said Ben. 'We know why Colin used him, and there's no mystery about it.'

Libby called Fran to update her on the results of her enquiries about Shareen Wallis, Colin's invitation to dinner and the fact that Ted Sachs seemed to be genuine.

'No one to be suspicious of, then,' said Fran.

'Fiona Darling,' said Libby promptly.

'Oh, for goodness' sake, Lib!' Fran burst out laughing. 'Why?'

'She's the mystery at the centre of it all.'

'Not simply because she's the only one left?'

'Well, there is that…'

'She's a newcomer to the area, she's obviously younger than Colin Hardcastle -'

'How do you know that?' Libby interrupted.

'I'm assuming. He left years ago, so he's got to be in his forties, and I've seen her, don't forget. No more than early thirties, I would have thought.'

'But what difference does that make?'

'She's too young to have had any contact with Colin.'

'But what about young Ossie? Oscar Whitelaw?'

'Who? Oh, the body.'

'He is the actual victim in all this. I think Colin and even Ted Sachs are simply red herrings. Just because no one could work out why Sachs gave Fiona the keys and we couldn't locate Colin,' said Libby.

'And now all that's settled,' said Fran. 'And I'm sure the police are well ahead with their investigation.'

'Mmm,' said Libby. 'By the way, did I tell you Harry's

Donna is going to have another baby? And she and her husband are moving to Steeple Well?'

There was a short silence. 'Where the Darlings live,' said Fran eventually.

'Well, yes.'

'And you're suddenly going to become Donna's best friend?'

'Of course not!' said Libby, with an air of injured innocence.

Fran sighed. 'Look, Lib, just leave it. There's nothing to look into. Just get on with painting that picture for Guy and start thinking about next season's pantomime, or something.'

'I'm off panto,' grumbled Libby. 'And we've got enough outside hirers at the theatre to keep us going right through the season.'

'Lost interest?' asked Fran.

'A bit,' admitted Libby. 'It takes so much more effort than it used to, and there are so many more laws and regulations to comply with.'

'You've got dedicated staff to deal with that, now, though, haven't you?'

'Yes.' Libby sighed. 'It's taken all the fun out of it, somehow.'

'What about *Puss in Boots*, though? I thought our favourite Dame was keen to bring that production to the Oast.'

The previous winter, The Alexandria in Nethergate had staged its first ever pantomime, starring Dame Amanda Knight, an old friend of Libby's and Fran's, and her

113

daughter Clemency. It had not been an untroubled run, but Dame Amanda had thoroughly enjoyed returning to the stage in panto, and wanted to do it again.

'She does,' admitted Libby, 'and I suppose we ought to let her. She'll organise everything, including the director, so I can stay out of it.'

'There you are then,' said Fran. 'Get hold of her and start negotiations. That'll take your mind off the Garden Hotel.'

Libby consulted briefly with Peter and Ben, her co-directors of The Oast Theatre, than called Dame Amanda and, after a short chat with her husband, Coolidge, set up a meeting at the theatre for the following week.

'So that's that,' she said to herself. 'Now what do I do?'

'I think Fran was right,' she said to Ben later in the evening. 'I've just been trying to find things to look into.'

'That's a first!' said Ben. 'You admitting that.'

'I know.' Libby sighed and shrugged her shoulders. 'Perhaps I should just concentrate on helping you with the Hop project.'

'Oh, there's no need for that,' said Ben, looking nervous.

Libby looked undecided, then wandered back into the conservatory and stared at her painting again. She heard the knock on the front door, and Ben's voice as he opened it, but was not prepared for the voice that sounded suddenly behind her.

'Libby.'

Libby swung round. 'Beth!'

Bethany Cole stood in the doorway, tawny hair as usual

114

breaking free from its constraining plait. She smiled.

'Surprised?' she said. 'But you sent the police to me, didn't you?'

'Oh, sorry! But you were the only person I could think of in the village who might know something about teenagers. Because of the youth club – except I didn't even know if you still ran it.'

'As a matter of fact, it's still going, although I've only got about fifteen members. Mainly the children of the more – er – conservative with a small c parishioners. But yes, Ossie Whitelaw had been a member.'

Chapter Fourteen

On this bombshell, Libby let out a 'Whoosh!' of surprise.

'This needs a glass of something,' she said firmly. 'Come on – we'll sit in the kitchen if Ben's watching something in the sitting room.'

'I'm not,' said Ben, appearing behind Beth. 'You two go in there and I'll bring refreshments. Red? White? Something else?'

'Are you trying to nobble the clergy?' asked Beth with a grin. 'Red, please, if there's some open.'

'And for me, too, Ben, please,' said Libby. 'Actually, Beth, we haven't seen you and John in the pub recently. I wondered if you'd renounced the demon drink.'

'John's been working late recently, and I don't like to come on my own,' said Beth, following Libby into the sitting room.

'That's daft,' said Libby. 'You know we're always there on Wednesday evenings, and if we aren't for some reason, Patti and Anne are. I shall have to make a point of calling for you if you're not careful.'

'You're a bad influence,' said Beth, sitting opposite Libby and welcoming Sidney on to her lap.

'Now, about Ossie Whitelaw.' Libby fixed her visitor

with an enquiring eye. 'How did he come to be a member of the youth club? I didn't think he lived here.'

'No, he didn't, his parents lived at Steeple Well.'

'Not Steeple Well again,' groaned Libby.

'Eh?'

'Oh, it just keeps cropping up. You said lived – have they moved?'

Ben appeared with two glasses of red wine.

'Thanks, Ben,' said Beth. 'Yes, they moved – oh, about a year ago? Yes, it must be.'

'And they didn't report their son missing?' asked Ben, frowning.

'He wasn't missing when they moved.' Beth sipped her wine.

'Where did they move to?' asked Libby.

'Right out of the area, I think. Something to do with the father's job. He worked for a pharmaceutical company.'

'So the boy wasn't a – a – err…' Libby struggled for the right word.

Beth gave a crooked smile. 'No, he was a perfectly ordinary middle-class boy. But he got into bad company.'

'Here?'

'Well, yes. His father sent him to Foxgrove.' Beth paused and looked at each of them in turn. 'Foxgrove? You don't know it?'

Libby shook her head. Ben was frowning again.

'It's a very exclusive independent school,' he said. 'At least, it thinks it is.'

Beth sighed. 'Indeed. Ossie just didn't fit in. He was bullied and – and *taunted*.'

117

'But why?' Libby gasped. 'Wasn't he, oh, I don't know, the right sort? I thought that was illegal?'

'Oh, it is. And they have an "open" policy. Which means, in effect, that they'll take on the sons and daughters – mainly sons, but daughters at a pinch – of overseas millionaires who haven't quite made the grade for the more established public schools. So their students are, let's say, not tolerant of those they consider inferior.'

'How do you know all this?' asked Ben.

'Ossie told me.' Beth shifted in her seat, looking uncomfortable. 'Some of the others in the club said something about him carrying a knife, so I tackled him about it.'

'That was brave,' said Libby.

'No, sensible.' Beth smiled. 'He was really a very nice boy, and he was having a horrible time. His father didn't understand, he said, and in the end he deliberately got in with a gang. If they were going to treat him like that, he said, he might as well behave like it.'

'Is that why they moved?' asked Ben.

'I think so, partly. Ossie said his father would only enrol him in the same sort of school, wherever they went, and he felt, obviously mistakenly, that he'd found his niche here.'

'With the gang?' said Libby.

Beth nodded. 'That's one of the problems – they get a hold on these young people. Although I talked to Ossie, I knew I wouldn't do any good.' She shrugged. 'And then they moved.'

'What do the police think happened?' asked Libby.

'I've no idea. I thought you might know.'

Libby and Ben looked at each other. 'Not a thing,' said Libby. 'I'm afraid I – we – have been concentrating on the hotel itself. Who owned it, and that sort of thing.'

'Who did?' Beth looked interested.

Ben explained.

'And who found the body? It wasn't you, was it?' Beth looked at Libby.

'No.' Libby explained about Fiona Darling and Ted Sachs.

'The Darlings!' said Beth. 'Why – they're the people who bought the Whitelaws' house!'

Libby's mouth dropped open. Ben said 'Shit. Sorry, Beth.'

Beth laughed. 'I say it frequently myself, Ben! Well – I can see this has come as a bit of a shock.'

'It certainly has,' said Libby, recovering. 'Did you tell the police all this?'

'Only about Ossie. Should I tell them?'

'Is it relevant?' Ben looked at Libby.

'It sort of ties things together, doesn't it?' said Libby.

'Yes, but I don't see how.' Ben pulled at his lower lip.

'Fiona Darling found Ossie's body, and she lives in his old house. That's quite a connection. Beth?' Libby turned to her.

'It is quite a connection, I'll grant you that, but unless the Darlings knew the Whitelaws before...'

'And Fiona didn't recognise the boy,' said Ben.

'Well, the body was pretty much unrecognisable,' said Libby, 'to be fair. But what I can't understand is why he was here in Steeple Martin if he and his family had moved

119

away. If he'd disappeared before or just at the same time as the move, he would have been reported to the police here.'

'I expect wherever he was reported they looked here, too. It would have been natural, wouldn't it?' said Beth. 'His family knew he had friends here, even if they disapproved of them.'

'I wonder when it was, though? Nobody's said much about that. I've got a vague idea it was about six months, but that's going on the word of the pathologist.'

'I suppose,' said Ben reluctantly, 'we had better let the police know.' He looked at Beth. 'Shall I do it?'

Beth looked relieved. 'Would you? Oh, thank you, Ben.'

'The ubiquitous text message?' suggested Libby. 'Who to?'

'Have you got Rachel Trent's number?'

'Um – yes.' Libby picked up her mobile and scrolled through. 'Here.'

While Ben sent the message, Libby offered Beth more wine.

'I haven't finished this one yet,' said Beth with a sigh. 'And I really ought to be getting home. John'll be home soon, if he isn't already.'

'I'll watch you down the lane,' said Ben, putting his mobile away, and obviously remembering the occasion some years before when Libby had been attacked on the short walk home from the vicarage.

'I don't think there's a mad murderer lurking around at the moment,' said Beth.

'You never know,' said Ben darkly.

120

But just as he was opening the door, his mobile started a muffled warbling in his pocket.

'Rachel,' he mouthed at the two women. 'Yes, Rachel?'

He repeated the gist of Beth's information, nodded, and said, 'Hang on, I'll ask.'

He turned to Beth. 'Would you mind telling Rachel in person? She could be here in half an hour, or would the morning be better?'

Beth looked doubtful. 'I don't know – it's a bit late. But Friday mornings tend to be busy. There's the coffee morning – oh, I suppose it had better be tonight.'

'Did you hear that, Rachel? Yes, OK, I'll tell her.' He put the phone away

'She says that's really good of you, but it could be important.'

Beth smiled half-heartedly and stood up. 'Right. I'd better go home and warn John.'

'Tell him I'll buy him a pint if he wants to avoid Rachel.'

'Shall we all walk down together, then?' suggested Libby. 'I can be moral support for Beth – if you want me to, I mean.'

'Oh, yes, please. Honestly, I'm being a wimp, aren't I? I'm not usually like this.' Beth stared at the floor for a moment. 'I think it's because I feel so bad about poor Ossie. I should have been able to help, and I couldn't.'

John Cole, pleasant and understanding as ever, was only too pleased to be dragged off to the pub by Ben, while Libby and Beth went into the large vicarage kitchen.

'I'll see if I've got a bottle of red somewhere,' said

121

Beth. 'I need a drop of Dutch courage, now.'

'Don't worry on my account,' said Libby.

'I'm not,' said Beth, grinning over her shoulder. 'It's on mine!'

They were just about to start on the wine when there was a ring on the doorbell.

Rachel Trent came in with a uniformed officer, impossibly young and nervous-looking, behind her.

'Sorry about PC Robinson,' she said, 'but I need him to take notes.'

Beth indicated to the other chairs round the table and they all sat down.

'Now,' said Rachel. 'Tell me again.'

Beth obediently repeated all she knew about Ossie Whitelaw, including the fact that the Darlings had bought the Whitelaws' house.

'What do you think it means?' asked Libby, when she'd finished.

Rachel leant back in her chair and sighed. 'I honestly don't know. Have you got any ideas?'

PC Robinson looked startled. Rachel smiled. 'Don't worry. Mrs Sarjeant has helped us before.'

PC Robinson looked even more startled.

'No,' said Libby. 'It could just be a coincidence, but we thought you should know.'

'Oh, quite right. We'll have to look into it.' Rachel frowned. 'Do you think perhaps the Darlings knew the Whitelaws?'

'Maybe.' Libby looked doubtful. 'But I still don't get it.'

Rachel looked at Beth. 'What about you, Reverend?'

'Oh, don't call me that!' Beth laughed. 'I'm just Beth. And no, I don't get it, either.'

They all sat in silence for a moment.

'Should have offered you tea or coffee,' said Beth, standing up.

'No, thanks,' said Rachel, also getting to her feet. 'We'll be getting back. I'd better report to DI Maiden.'

'And I bet he won't know what to do about it, either,' Libby said to Beth, when they'd left.

'What about your friend Ian? Isn't he in charge?' asked Beth, finally pouring out the wine.

'Well, he's the senior officer in charge, but Rob Maiden is on the ground, so to speak. What's the betting Ian comes round any minute now?'

But it wasn't until Friday morning that Ian appeared at number seventeen Allhallow's Lane.

'Ian! What can I do for you?' asked a surprised Libby, as she opened the door.

'Coffee?' was all Ian said, as he came in.

Libby went into the kitchen and put the kettle on. 'Well?' she said, turning round to face Ian, who lounged in the doorway.

'I just wanted to ask you what you had to do with Mrs Cole's remarkable statement to DS Trent yesterday.'

'*Me*? It was nothing to do with me! Why?'

'DS Trent said you were with Mrs Cole when she interviewed her. And it was Ben who told her on the phone.'

'Well, yes. Beth came to ask me if the police had

followed up her information about Ossie Whitelaw, and it came out that the Darlings had bought the Whitelaws' house. We thought you ought to know.'

Ian sighed. 'So just happenstance?'

'Of course.' Libby poured water in to mugs. 'It honestly wasn't anything to do with me.'

'As it happens,' said Ian, taking his mug and going back in to the sitting room, 'it was useful. Exactly how, we don't know. But every – or any – link has to be followed up. Maiden's out there talking to the Darlings this morning.'

'The husband will be at work, surely?'

'Probably. But Mrs Darling should be there. We've been keeping an eye.'

'On *Fiona*? But why?'

'She found the body. You know perfectly well – or you should – that the person who finds the body is always of interest. The same as family.'

'But the family aren't here any more.'

'We know that.' Ian leant back in the armchair. 'We had already found out about young Ossie Whitelaw. His father accepted a transfer to Northumberland, but Ossie ran away. It was reported to the police, and to us, as his parents, quite rightly, assumed he might have returned here, where he had friends.'

'We thought that might be the case,' said Libby. 'Not very nice friends, either, Beth told us.'

'No. And they were questioned. Most of them were known to us.'

'Oh, you have been busy,' said Libby.

Ian gave her a knowing smile. 'You don't always know

124

everything we do, Libby.'

'No,' said Libby humbly. 'I realise that.' She paused. 'Is it done to ask where exactly you are in the investigation?'

'No, it's not, but you'll ask anyway.' Ian chuckled. 'And off the record, I'll tell you. Not all of it, of course.'

'Of course not.' Libby tried not to sound too eager.

'Well, you now know about Ossie's connection to the village and his background. It appears that he and some of his so-called friends had taken to using the old Garden as a sort of headquarters.'

'Here? But weren't they based in Canterbury? We haven't got anyone like that around here.'

'Several of the slightly older members of the gang had cars, and I believe there was a good deal of taking and driving away. I think the reason they came out here was precisely because it *wasn't* in Canterbury. According to a couple of them, after Ossie reappeared, hiding out at the Garden, they didn't want to come here because they thought he might be traced here.'

'And they'd be discovered.' Libby nodded. 'But what were they doing here?'

'Drugs, I would think,' said Ian. 'And some of the other disreputable goings on that you don't need to know about.'

'I've read a bit about that culture – if you can call it that,' said Libby, 'and seen it on television, but you don't always know how true it is.'

'Quite,' said Ian. 'But rest assured, as far as we can tell, unless we've missed something vital, none of his friends had anything to do with his death.'

Chapter Fifteen

'So,' said Libby, after a pause to digest this, 'what about his parents? His father? Did he follow him down here?'

'There's no evidence of that,' said Ian. 'He did come down, as you would expect, and went to the school Ossie had been attending.'

'Foxgrove,' said Libby. 'But not attending much, by all accounts.'

'No,' agreed Ian, 'but Mr Whitelaw didn't know anything about Ossie's "friends". He did go to Steeple Well, but didn't say anything about speaking to the Darlings. Inspector Maiden will be asking Mrs Darling about that.'

'It's amazing how much people don't know about their offspring,' said Libby, thinking of her own three. 'Does Ted Sachs feature anywhere?'

'Only in as far as Colin asked him to survey the building and he gave Mrs Darling the keys.'

'I still don't understand that.' Libby shook her head. 'If she wanted to look at it, why didn't he take her himself? They appear to be – um – close.'

'Maybe,' said Ian. 'We need to have a chat with Mr Sachs.'

'Haven't you seen him yet? I thought you would have spoken to him last week at Edward's party.'

'It wasn't the right time,' said Ian, 'and I wasn't on duty. They left before we came down from my flat. He hasn't been around since.'

'Isn't that suspicious?'

'Hardly. He wasn't connected with the Garden or Colin Hardcastle when we think the body was hidden, and he comes from Felling.'

'Mmm. And it was only John Newman recommending him to Colin that sent him over here.'

'Well, it appears that he was already working for the Darlings. .' Ian put down his mug. 'Anyway, nothing for you to investigate, is there? You can hardly go nosing around the street gangs in Canterbury. And if you're seen over there, I'll have you arrested.'

'As if I would!' said Libby. 'Can I tell Fran about this?'

'You will whatever I say,' said Ian with a grin.

'Colin's invited us to dinner at Harry's tonight, by the way. Ben and me, and the Newmans.'

'Well, don't start telling them what I've told you,' warned Ian, standing up. 'And now I'm off to sort out the flat.'

'Oh! Have you moved in at last? You said you had the removal men booked.'

'Yes. So don't get into trouble. I'll be virtually round the corner.'

As soon as Ian had left, Libby called Fran.

'Well,' said Fran when Libby had finished her saga. 'You have been busy.'

127

'That's what I said to Ian. He said he didn't have to tell me everything.'

'And what the rest of us have tried to tell you for years,' said Fran. 'So which bit are you going to investigate, apart from the street gangs?'

'Well,' said Libby slowly, 'I thought I might go and have a chat with Fiona.'

'On what pretext? She hasn't exactly shown any inclination to seek you out.'

'No.' Libby reflected for a moment. 'I thought she would have been in touch after she'd found the body, actually. After all, I was nearly with her.'

'She didn't seem keen to talk to you last Saturday,' said Fran.

'No... but she was with Ted Sachs, wasn't she. I think that was a mistake actually.'

'She can't have known you would be there, or that there would be a detective there, too.'

'True. So shall I go?'

'On the off-chance? If you warn her she'll make an excuse. Not that I think you should.'

'I know. But I think I will, all the same.'

Before she could lose her nerve, Libby grabbed the car keys and her basket and left the house. On the way to Steeple Well, past the Cattlegreen Nursery, she wondered what, exactly, she was going to say if, indeed, Fiona was in. It was all very well thinking there was more to Fiona's visit to the Garden Hotel, but putting it into words without giving offence was another matter.

Steeple Well was a collection of disparate houses of

different periods. An old well, long since dried up and now filled in, had presumably been the reason the first houses had been built there, but now they simply hung around with no particular purpose. There was no village shop, church, or pub, and not even a proper street layout. The Darlings' house, a converted barn which had once belonged to Taylor's Farm, a mile or so away, had just arrived, so to speak, sometime in the eighteenth century. It now stood apart, its front door, double height, facing away from the other houses. Taking a deep breath, Libby stepped out of the car.

The door was opened almost immediately.

'Oh!' Fiona Darling took a step back. 'L-Libby! I didn't expect you.'

'I was just passing,' lied Libby. 'Well, sort of. I was on my way to Cattlegreen and realised I was quite near you, so I thought I'd come and see how you were doing.'

'Oh, that was – kind of you.' Fiona hovered in the doorway, obviously unsure how to deal with her unexpected visitor.

'Well, it's only a week since...' Libby trailed off. 'Have you recovered? Have the police been back?'

Fiona frowned and stood back to allow Libby to come in. 'Actually, yes. I had that inspector here this morning. Honestly, the things they ask!' She shut the door. 'Come into the kitchen. I was just going to make coffee.'

Libby breathed a silent sigh of relief. Proper coffee, she noted, as she followed Fiona into the huge kitchen, fitted, predictably, with every gadget and labour-saving device known to man.

'What a lovely kitchen!' she said. 'Was it like this when you moved in?' She hoped this sounded suitably ingenuous.

'Oh – er – no, not exactly.' Fiona turned her back to perform esoteric rites with the coffee machine.

'Oh – part of the renovations Ted Sachs did?'

Fiona gave a rather forced laugh. 'Yes, I suppose so. Not exactly renovations, though. Just a bit of remodelling.'

'I suppose everyone wants to put their own stamp on a place when they move in, don't they?'

'Yes.' Fiona turned from the coffee machine. 'Do sit down.' She waved vaguely at the table. 'Americano suit you?'

'Yes, fine,' said Libby, who had no idea. 'So it wasn't to your taste, this house?'

'No.' Fiona's eyes moved sideways to Libby. She turned back to the machine, did something to it and then presented Libby with a cup of coffee. She sighed and sat down. 'I suppose the police have told you we bought this place from that boy's parents?'

'The police didn't, no,' said Libby, mentally crossing her fingers.

'Oh?'

'Ossie went to the youth club, apparently.'

'Ah, yes.' Fiona stared into her own coffee cup. 'Not that I knew him.'

'Of course not,' said Libby. 'They'd gone before you moved in, hadn't they?'

'Well, yes.' Fiona looked up. 'It's all a bit awkward, though.'

130

'Oh?' Libby stirred her cup, took a sip and discovered it was basically black coffee.

'Well, it turns out David already knew Ossie's father. That's how he heard about the house.'

Once again Libby was taken by surprise. 'Why is that awkward?' she asked.

Fiona sighed again. 'It makes a connection. I had that inspector – I told you, didn't I? – here this morning asking about it. They'd found out about it.' She scowled. 'I wish I'd never *heard* of the bloody place!'

'I don't see how it could have anything to do with you,' said Libby, and realised this was true.

'I know, but the police are obviously suspicious. But I found the body, didn't I? And apparently -'

'I know,' said Libby. 'The person who finds the body is automatically a suspect. But in this case, I really don't see it.'

Fiona smiled gratefully and impulsively reached over to squeeze Libby's hand. 'Oh, thank you! Honestly, I don't feel as though I've got a single friend here. That's why I went to that party last week. I thought I might meet people, but it – it wasn't like that.'

'No.' Libby hesitated. 'Was it Ted who suggested it?'

'In a way.' Fiona looked away. 'Ted felt sorry for me. That's why he suggested the Garden Hotel project.'

Libby felt as though she'd been hit by a truck. After a moment, she said, 'But I thought it was your idea?'

Fiona shook her head. 'He thought it would – I don't know – get me in with the community. But after talking to you, I realised it wouldn't. I'd tried already, joining the WI and that sort of thing. You know.'

'Yes.' Libby swirled the remaining coffee in her cup. 'But you tried to do it on your own. You could have come to me.'

'I didn't know you.' Fiona squeezed her hand again. 'But would you help me?'

Ah, thought Libby. This was difficult.

'Well, of course,' she said, 'but I'll tell you what. My friend Donna, who works for the Pink Geranium in the village, is moving to Steeple Well soon, and she won't know anyone here.'

'But she already knows people in the area,' Fiona looked sulky.

'That's just the point! And her husband's a surgeon at the hospital, so he works long hours just like your husband does.'

Fiona began to look interested. 'How would I meet her?'

'I'll introduce you,' said Libby, wondering how this would be managed. 'But tell me, how did Ted come up with the idea of the Garden project?'

'Oh, he'd seen something else like it somewhere else. You know, they let people come and work in a dedicated space, there's a café, and they run workshops. That sort of thing.'

'And he thought it would be just the thing for you? But didn't he tell you he was supposed to be sprucing up the building for sale?'

'Well, yes.'

'But as I said to you at the time, you wouldn't have got

132

enough interest to raise the purchase price. And I can't understand why he gave you the keys and didn't come with you.'

'The inspector asked that, too. I didn't even think about it.'

'How did you find him in the first place, by the way? He's not exactly local.'

'Oh, he was recommended by the Whitelaws. David saw to all that.' Fiona looked back at her coffee cup. 'And as I said, he was sorry for me.'

I'll bet he was, thought Libby. She decided she couldn't ask any more questions without Fiona becoming suspicious.

'I'm sorry things haven't turned out as well as you'd hoped. Do you think you'll stay here?'

'Oh, I suppose so.' Fiona shrugged. 'I'd prefer to go back to London, it would be much more convenient for David's work, and I could go back to my old job, too. But David says he likes the country life. Although he doesn't exactly see much of it.'

'What did you do?' asked Libby, filing this nugget away for future thought.

'I was in PR,' said Fiona proudly. 'But there's nothing down here.'

Libby nodded. 'Well, I'd better get back to Cattlegreen. We're out to dinner tonight, and I'm running late.'

She left Fiona standing in the doorway looking mournful, and drove straight to Cattlegreen to salve her conscience. She bought some unwanted vegetables and drove home.

'And what I was thinking,' she said, having called Fran to report on the visit, 'was that it sounds to me as though David Darling wants the lovely Fiona out of the way while he lives the life of Riley in town.'

'That's jumping to conclusions, isn't it?' said Fran. 'I'm more interested in why Ted suggested the Garden project to Fiona, and why he brought her to Edward's last week.'

'And whether there's any significance in the fact that it was Ossie Whitelaw's dad who recommended him to David Darling.'

Chapter Sixteen

Harry had managed to keep the round window table free for Colin's party, and when Libby and Ben arrived, they found Colin, John and his wife already seated.

'Libby! Ben!' said Colin, getting to his feet. 'You know John, don't you? And this is Emma, his wife.'

Harry appeared with a bottle of white wine. 'Red for you, Libby?'

'Yes, please.' Libby smiled at Colin. 'He does know me well.'

For a while, time was taken up by selecting from the menu.

'There was a time when Harry would cook me special Pollo con Verde in the kitchen upstairs,' said Libby.

'Haven't got time any more,' said Harry, placing a bottle of Libby's favourite Shiraz on the table. 'Or use of the kitchen.'

'That,' explained Libby, 'is partly because the rise in the popularity of Mexican street food has meant Harry's busier than ever, and partly because my son Adam lives upstairs.'

Adam, in his long Victorian style waiter's apron, grinned at the company and waved his notepad. 'Howdo!'

'What's Pollo con Verde?' asked Emma.

'Mexican green chicken,' said Harry. 'A sort of Mexican Thai green curry. Only much nicer.'

'And why can't you cook it here?'

'Because this is a vegetarian kitchen,' said Ben. 'No meat allowed.'

'Oh,' said Emma, still looking confused. Libby wondered how, in today's food aware culture, she could still be unaware of the upsurge in both vegan and vegetarian cooking, and its rules. She knew there were some people who considered it 'a load of nonsense', including Flo Carpenter, but that was a lot to do with their generation.

John, looking slightly embarrassed, changed the subject. 'I hear you're going to revive the old bat and trap pitch, Ben? Colin was telling us.'

'We hope so,' said Ben. 'I'm looking forward to getting a team together.'

'We've got a team in Felling,' said John. 'We'll come and play you!'

'Great!' Ben was enthusiastic. 'Friendlies only, of course, at first. Until we can join a league.'

Seeing all three men enter into the conversation, Libby turned to Emma. 'John was saying the other day that you've been here several times?'

'Yes.' Emma perked up. 'Of course it's different when you come with people like you. We've always enjoyed it, though. It's something a bit different, isn't it?'

'For rural Kent, yes, I suppose it is. Harry was ahead of the trend, really. What are the restaurants like in Felling?

136

I've only ever been to the café in the square.'

'The Tea Square? Yes that's quite good. And there's a couple of nice Indians and a Chinese takeaway. That's about it.' Emma looked vaguely dissatisfied.

'We've only got this one and the pub,' said Libby. 'Did John's family do food when they ran the Hop Pocket? Ben isn't going to.'

'I don't think so.' Now Emma simply looked vague. 'I lived in Felling when I met John. Didn't come over here much.' She looked closely at Libby. 'Have you always lived here?'

'Goodness, no! I'm originally a Londoner. When I married we moved to Kent – the other side of Canterbury - and when I divorced, Harry and Peter, his partner, who were already friends of mine, found me my cottage. I'd met Ben years ago, and we met up again, both divorced, and sort of stayed together. There!' she smiled brightly. 'Potted history.'

'I've only ever lived in Felling,' said Emma, her eyes wide. 'I don't know how I'd go on anywhere else.'

'Well, I expect your family are all there, aren't they?'

'Oh, yes.' Emma nodded, blonde curls bobbing. 'Mum and Dad, and my aunts and cousins, and my sister, of course...'

'Of course,' murmured Libby, the lines from *HMS Pinafore* running through her head: *And so do his sisters and his cousins and his aunts...*

Adam took their orders.

'Is there any more news about the murder?' asked John, when Adam had gone.

'No,' said Ben and Libby together.

'Not as far as we know,' added Libby. 'I expect the police will be working on it, though.'

'Shouldn't they tell you, as the owner of the property?' John said to Colin.

'I don't think so,' replied Colin, looking surprised. 'It's nothing to do with me, is it?'

'Will you still sell it?'

'Oh, yes. If anyone will buy it,' said Colin, looking gloomy. 'People don't like buildings where there's been a murder, do they?'

'A developer wouldn't care,' said Ben. 'That's what you were thinking of, weren't you?'

'Yes, that's why I told Ted Sachs just to give it a lick of paint. A developer would want to gut the place.'

'I wonder why he suggested the community project to Fiona Darling, then,' mused Libby.

'What do you mean?' asked Ben. Everyone was looking puzzled.

'I thought the community project was Fiona's idea,' said Libby, 'but apparently, Sachs suggested it.'

'He must have thought she was a possible buyer,' said Colin.

'But she thought she'd get funding,' said Libby. 'At least, that's what she told me.'

'Funding? From where?' asked Colin. By now, John and Emma were both looking confused.

'Goodness knows,' said Libby. 'I told her she'd be lucky.'

At this moment, Adam arrived with their orders, and

138

conversation revolved for a time around the food. But it wasn't long before Ted Sachs cropped up again.

'You recommended Sachs, didn't you, John?' said Ben. 'Do you know him well?'

'Not really. He's a Felling man, born and bred. Emma knows him better than I do.'

'I didn't know him that well,' protested Emma. 'He was just part of the crowd I used to go about with. He was at that party you came to, Colin.'

'Was he? I don't remember him.'

'I don't either, not from then,' said John. 'He worked for a builder we used to do some work for us, and when he retired, Ted set up on his own. We knew he was good because we'd seen his work.'

'Actually, he'd already done some work for the Darlings,' said Libby, 'and, apparently for the people they bought the house from.'

'Really?' Ben frowned. 'You mean Ossie Whitelaw's parents?'

'So Fiona said. I don't know how they knew Ted, though. They weren't originally local either, so I gather.'

'I don't understand,' said Emma. 'Is that important? Ted, I mean?'

Libby turned rather guiltily to John's wife.

'It's just puzzling,' she said. 'If it hadn't been for Ted, you see, Fiona wouldn't have been there and the body wouldn't have been discovered.'

Emma's brow wrinkled. 'But you could say that about anything, couldn't you? If it hadn't been for Colin's parents buying his hotel, he wouldn't be here buying us dinner. Or

139

if Ben hadn't been going to open John's parents' pub, we wouldn't have known anything about it.'

'She's right.' Harry leant over Libby's shoulder to top up her wine. 'Cause and effect. There's no organised story, just one thing happening and as a result something else is tripped into being.'

Everyone was regarding him with awe.

'What?' he said.

'I've never heard you so philosophical,' said Ben. 'Positively Grecian.'

'Very wise, Hal,' said Libby hastily, noting Emma's puzzled expression. 'And quite right, Emma. It doesn't matter, anyway, does it?'

For the rest of the evening, she managed to keep the conversation well away from Ted Sachs and the murder, but encouraged them all to concentrate on the re-opening of the Hop Pocket and the bat and trap pitch. However there was nothing she could do when over coffee Colin suddenly said 'You said Ted was at that party, John. Did you mean that one when the girl disappeared?'

John cast a quick look at his wife. 'Er – yes.'

'I don't remember him.'

'No reason why you should,' said John. 'You didn't know anyone there except me, did you?'

'No.' Colin looked round the table. 'It wasn't a very happy experience. Sorry, John, that sounds ungrateful.'

'That's all right, but why? You didn't say much at the time. I just thought you were upset about the girl.'

'It sounds as if you've never met Sachs,' said Libby. 'How did you get the keys to him?'

'I got the London office to send them.' Colin looked thoughtful. 'I wonder if I would have recognised him if I'd seen him.'

'And decided against it?' suggested Libby.

Colin smiled. 'Probably.'

Both John and Emma looked as if they wanted to ask why, so Libby jumped in with another change of subject.

'Did Ben show you inside the Hop yesterday, when you were looking at the bat and trap pitch?'

'Yes, he did. It's actually in a better condition than the Garden, so I'm told.' He turned to John. 'You should get Ben to show you, John.'

John smiled unenthusiastically. 'I'll come and see when it's open. Or when the bat and trap side's up and running.'

'And when will that be, do you think, Ben?' asked Libby brightly.

Ben looked at her suspiciously. 'We think we can get it cleared within a couple of weeks. Why?'

'I just wondered if Colin would still be here to see it.'

'I've already told Ben, if it's that soon, I will. I can attend to some things in London.'

'Have you got enough clothes?' asked Emma. Everyone looked surprised.

'Actually, Emma, no – but it's a great excuse to buy more, isn't it?' Colin gave her a cheerful grin.

Relieved that the conversation had moved away from what she felt was dangerous ground, Libby sat back and relaxed.

'But why did you think it was dangerous?' asked Ben on the way home.

'I don't know.' Libby stared into the distance. 'I just felt Colin was unhappy about both Ted Sachs and that party.'

'Well, yes, that was obvious. But it hasn't got anything to do with Ossie Whitelaw's body, has it?'

'No, I suppose not. I suppose I'm making mountains again, aren't I?' Libby sighed. 'I'll shut up, now.'

Saturday again. Libby decided it was time for another trip to the supermarket in Canterbury, and when she bumped into Donna in the bread aisle, was very glad she had. Having explained about Fiona Darling, Donna was only too pleased to offer to go round and introduce herself.

'Although as she hasn't got children, she might not find me quite – what? Congenial, I suppose.'

'Oh, I wouldn't worry about that,' said Libby. 'She's just lonely, and feels a bit of a fish out of water.'

Happy that she had solved a problem, or at least stuck a sticking plaster over it, Libby turned homewards, only to receive another surprise when she arrived.

'Look who's here,' said Ben, as she let herself in.

Edward stood up from the sofa and came to relieve her of one of her bags.

'Sorry to barge in,' he said. 'I just came over to drop someone off.'

'Oh?' Libby paused with the fridge door open.

'Yes.' He grinned and put the bag on the table.

'Go on, then. Who?'

'Don't tease her, Edward,' said Ben with a grin.

Edward leant towards her and whispered, 'Ted Sachs.'

Chapter Seventeen

Libby slammed the fridge door. '*Sachs*?'

'Yes. He turned up with my invoice and to collect some tools he'd left at the summerhouse,' said Edward. Ben went to put the kettle on.

'Didn't he know the police were looking for him?'

'Course he did. He's already seen them. Apparently, it wasn't such a mystery after all. He knew all about the body, but on the Sunday after my party he went away on holiday with his wife. Came back early yesterday and went straight to the police station.'

'So all sorted out, then?' Libby began putting things away, conscious of a slight feeling of anti-climax.

'Yes. He said he was a bit surprised at the fuss. He'd given his name to the police on the day the body was found, and no one had told him to keep himself available, so he'd gone off in his campervan and thought no more about it until he received a phone call from the Hardcastle Holdings office in London. Then they came back.'

'I wonder why the police didn't think of asking Colin's office to get hold of him earlier?' said Ben, putting mugs on the table.

'I don't think they were trying very hard to find him,'

said Libby, emerging from the freezer. 'Or they would have done so earlier. They're obviously working away in the background and not telling us everything.'

'Of course they are,' said Ben. 'So now you can settle down and find something else to worry about.

Libby sniffed and sat down at the table. 'So why did you have to bring him over here, Edward?'

'He said he was going to have to see Colin, so I said he was here and offered to bring him over. They're in the pub together.'

Libby slewed her eyes round to Ben. He sighed. Edward laughed.

'He said – Colin, that is – he thought you might want to come over for a drink? Ted's arranged for his wife to pick him up from here.'

'Do we?' asked Libby.

'I suppose so,' said Ben. 'The things you get us in to.'

'Nothing to do with me!' said Libby indignantly.

Colin was standing at the bar with the man Libby had last seen with Fiona when Edward ushered them into the pub.

Ted Sachs looked slightly embarrassed as Libby was introduced.

'Yes, we've met before!' she said brightly. 'At Edward's party last week. You were with Fiona, weren't you?'

Ben gave her a dig in the ribs on one side, while Edward did the same on the other.

'Can I get you a drink, Libby?' asked Colin, sounding amused.

Libby accepted graciously and allowed herself to be led to the round table in the centre of the room.

'Just shut up, Lib,' whispered Ben. 'Don't make things awkward.'

'As if I would.' Libby sat down and tried to look innocent.

'Colin was just telling me you intend to re-open the bat and trap pitch,' Ted said, as he joined them.

'That's the plan,' agreed Ben. 'Have you ever played?'

'Years ago,' said Ted vaguely. 'Don't remember much about it.'

'You'll have to come over and give it a try,' said Colin.

'Don't think it's my sort of thing. And I don't get over here often.'

'Well, now you've done work for me and the Darlings we'll have to get you some more work here,' said Edward. 'You've made a good job of the summerhouse, hasn't he, Ben?'

'Very good.' Ben nodded.

'Kind of you,' said Ted, unsmiling, 'but I've got a bit booked up now.'

Libby looked interested, and opened her mouth.

'Oh, never mind,' said Colin quickly, 'I don't suppose I'll be able to sell the Garden anyway.'

'You've said that before,' said Ben. 'I'm sure you'll have no trouble, once the police investigation is over.'

'How is it getting on?' asked Ted, not looking particularly interested.

'We don't really know,' said Colin. 'They haven't asked me to stick around, so I assume they have other lines of enquiry.'

'But you're going to stick around, aren't you?' said Edward.

'Yes.' Colin's thin, nervous face lit up with a grin. 'I want to help get the bat and trap pitch ready.'

'And it is his, after all,' said Ben.

Ted nodded and looked down at his beer. A strained little silence fell, until Edward cleared his throat and turned to Libby.

'We haven't heard anything about panto yet this year, Libby. Any news?'

'Libby's relinquishing the helm,' said Ben. 'You remember the panto at Nethergate last season? Well, Dame Amanda's bringing that over here.'

This subject tided them over until a small, thin woman with drawn back hair shot into the bar and came to a halt next to Ted.

'Ready?' she said.

Ted got to his feet. 'This is Kath,' he said to the company. 'My wife.'

Kath nodded curtly in the general direction of the table. 'Got to go,' she said, and turned for the door.

Ted shrugged. 'Nice to meet you all,' he said and followed.

'Well!' said Libby, as the door closed behind them.

Colin smiled ruefully. 'Not the charmers of the decade, were they? Quite pleased he won't be working for me.'

'Did he tell you why he gave the keys to Fiona?' asked Ben. 'That seems to be the main question.'

'He thought she was a "prospect", was how he put it,'

146

said Colin. 'Which, I assume, meant he thought she was a possible buyer.'

'I still think it's odd,' said Libby. 'According to Fiona she never gave him that idea.'

'Well, whatever was going on, if it was a scam of some sort, it's been knocked on the head now,' said Ben. 'He wasn't very happy was he?'

'Neither was she,' said Edward.

'It's probably all come out about his affair with Fiona now,' said Libby.

'You don't know for sure there was an affair,' said Ben.

'Course there was,' scoffed Libby.

'He wasn't interested in the bat and trap, either,' said Colin.

'Let's face it,' said Edward, 'he just doesn't fit in Steeple Martin.'

'Oh, do I then?' asked Colin.

'Oh, yes,' said Libby.

'You might even become one of Libby's Loonies!' said Edward.

'Eh?'

'Harry's idea,' said Ben. 'He says anyone who gets involved with Libby's – er – adventures becomes a member of the gang, and of course, they must be "loony".'

Colin grinned. 'I'd be flattered.'

'So was I,' said Edward. 'So flattered I've moved here. Well, nearby.'

'And it really isn't anything to do with me,' said Libby. 'These things just seem to happen.'

'Whatever it is,' said Colin, 'the village is a lot more

friendly than it used to be.'

'So you said.' Ben smiled at him. 'Tempted to come back?'

'Maybe to visit now and then,' agreed Colin. 'I'm going to see Nanny Mardle this afternoon.'

'She was the first one to tell us you were living in Spain,' said Libby. 'We had no idea she used to look after you.'

'Oh, yes. I'd have been lost without her.' Colin looked thoughtful. 'I've tried to persuade her to come and have a holiday with me, but she won't.'

'So she said. Too much for her at her age, she said.' Libby shook her head. 'Didn't think there was anyone who felt like that these days.'

'I'd better get back.' Ben got to his feet. 'I've got to go into the brewery.'

'I'd better, too,' said Libby with a sigh. 'I had a phone call this morning asking when the next painting will be delivered.'

'You paint?' Colin looked interested.

'Daub, really. I do stuff for our friend Guy's gallery in Nethergate.'

'If I walk with you to see Nanny Mardle, would you let me see some?'

'Of course.' Libby was surprised. 'Are you coming, Edward?'

'I've got to pick up the car, so yes,' said Edward. 'Then I'm going up to Cattlegreen for supplies.'

'Not coming to Hetty's for lunch tomorrow, then?' asked Ben.

'Don't want to push my luck,' said Edward, with a grin.

At Allhallow's Lane, Colin was ushered through to the conservatory, where he was shown the current masterpiece and some of Libby's previous work.

'Were you trained?' he asked, standing in front of the easel.

'Sort of,' said Libby. 'While I was at college doing drama I did a subsidiary course in set design. A bit of it must have rubbed off.'

'Your style reminds me a bit of Frank Sherwin – do you know him?'

Libby was surprised. 'Yes, I do! But I never expect anyone else to know him. And thanks – that's a real compliment.'

He smiled. 'Good. I'd like to buy something of yours before I go home, if that's all right.'

'Of course,' said Libby, now even more surprised.

'So would I,' said Edward from the doorway. 'It never occurred to me to ask.'

Gratified, Libby saw her guests off the premises, Edward to his car and Colin to knock quietly on Mrs Mardle's yellow front door. Inspired, she set about putting the finishing touches to the painting on the easel.

Saturday evening and Sunday passed in time-honoured fashion, and it wasn't until Monday morning that Libby was able to load the painting into her little car and drive it down to Nethergate. Once again, she had to park behind The Sloop. She called at Coastguard Cottage first, before going on to deliver the painting to Guy.

'Our new friend Colin said I had a look of Frank

149

Sherwin,' she told him. 'I was very flattered.'

Guy grinned at her. 'So you should be! He's becoming more and more fashionable – the rise of nostalgia! And Stanley Badmin, of course.'

'And all those jigsaw puzzles,' said Libby. 'Showing an England people would have liked to exist. Except it probably didn't.'

'Oh, the Derek Roberts ones! They are lovely, though. He did railway posters, too, like Sherwin and Badmin, and the whole idea was to present an idealised picture of Britain.'

'It did that all right,' said Libby. 'Anyway, is this one OK?'

'Perfect,' said Guy. 'Now I want you to paint a couple more from our window. That's always gone well.'

Libby went back to Coastguard Cottage to refresh her memory of the view from the front window and to beg a cup of tea.

'You hardly need to look at it again,' said Fran, retreating to the kitchen to make tea. 'You should be able to paint it with your eyes closed by now.'

'I know.' Libby grinned and perched on the window seat. 'It's an excuse.'

'Go on then,' said Fran, sounding resigned. 'What have you got to tell me?'

Libby recounted the events, or non-events, as she called them, of the weekend.

'So Ted Sachs is a no-go,' she said. 'Having thought about it, he must have thought Fiona Darling was a genuine prospect and decided the community project was a good excuse for not having to do too much work.'

'Very risky, if so,' said Fran. 'And he didn't do his research properly, did he?'

'About Fiona?'

'Well, yes.'

'Suppose not. Anyway, all our mysteries seem to have been cleared up.'

'Except who killed the Whitelaw boy.'

'Of course. Poor kid.' Libby chewed her lip. 'He seems to have had a raw deal all the way through. Being sent to a school where he didn't fit in, being bullied, a father who didn't understand him...'

'It would be easier if we knew he was a tearaway, wouldn't it?' said Fran.

'Yes, but Beth said he was a good lad, really.' Libby sighed. 'Oh, well, there isn't anything else we can do, is there?'

Fran laughed. 'No, Lib, there isn't!'

They drank their tea in silence for a few minutes.

'You didn't have any more moments, I suppose?' asked Libby tentatively.

'No, not a one. I think that one was a fluke.'

'Oh.' Libby looked despondent.

'Stop digging!' said Fran. 'The only involvement you've got now is with Colin Hardcastle.'

'What – you mean the bat and trap pitch?'

'Yes. He seems enthusiastic about that, doesn't he?'

'Yes, but he won't be around much.'

'Pessimistic as ever!'

Libby sighed. 'I just need something to get my teeth

151

into.'

'Well, it isn't me. Why don't you try writing a book?'

'A book? Me?'

'Well, I tried, didn't I? And you used to write for the stage.'

'No. It doesn't interest me.' Libby thought for a moment. 'Tell you what I would like to do – archaeology.'

'Well, why don't you join the local club?' Fran pulled her laptop towards her, 'Here, look.'

'Canterbury Archaeological Trust?'

'You could join as a Friend,' said Fran. 'Here, see?'

'Hmm.' said Libby. 'I'll think about it. Meanwhile, I've got some proper excavating to do.' She grinned at Fran. 'Going to come and help? Ben wants us to start on the Bat and Trap pitch tomorrow.'

Fran grinned back. 'If Guy gives me time off, yes. I think I might enjoy grubbing around in the undergrowth. You never know what we might find!'

Chapter Eighteen

'I'm not sure we'll be able to do anything in this,' said Ben, peering out at the torrential rain.

'It might stop,' said Libby doubtfully.

'Doesn't look like it,' said Fran.

They had been sitting in the front room at Allhallow's Lane for the last hour. Fran, having taken the day off from the art gallery and shop, was getting restive.

'It's nearly midday,' said Ben. 'Shall we go and get a sandwich from the pub and review the situation with Colin?'

Libby sighed. 'Might as well. Fran?'

Fran shrugged and stood up. 'Come on then.'

They trudged through the deserted village, splashing through puddles. In the small bar in the pub, Tim had actually lit the fire, and they sat at the round table steaming gently. Colin joined them, dressed, as they were, ready for some undergrowth action.

'Is it worth going over there?' he asked, when they had given Tim their sandwich order.

'Would the rain make clearing the site any more difficult?' asked Libby. 'Or would it just mean getting even wetter?'

'It would make clearing the rubbish more difficult,' said Ben. 'I've got to bring the flatbed over to take it all away.'

'I vote we go anyway,' said Fran. 'I've come over specially.'

'And I won't be here for much longer,' said Colin. 'I vote we go, too.'

'All right by me,' said Ben. 'If you're willing to risk it. Lib?'

'You said we wouldn't be able to do anything in this,' said Libby.

'I said I wasn't sure. But if everyone's willing to give it a go... It'll take longer than a few hours this afternoon, anyway, so we'll just do as much as we feel like.'

By the time they had eaten their sandwiches, the rain had eased off a little. A few hardy villagers had ventured out, and Nella had opened up the Cattlegreen shop. Cuckoo Lane had turned itself into a mudslide, and the footpath leading to the bat and trap pitch was almost impassable.

'Oh, we can get through,' said Ben. 'Come on – keep to the edge.'

Grumbling, Libby followed, holding on to the back of Ben's jacket. Fran and Colin floundered behind, and Libby was surprised and rather put out to hear them giggling.

'What's funny?' she managed, as soon as they'd reached the pitch.

'Us,' said Fran. 'I feel like a teenager.'

'And I haven't done anything like for years,' said Colin. 'Actually – ever, come to think of it.' He unlocked the shiny new padlock that hung round the gate. 'Put this on when Ben and I came to look,' he explained. 'Not that there's anything to steal.'

'There's the stuff in the cabinet,' said Ben. 'The trap and the ball and posts. That reminds me, we've got to order a new bat.'

To Libby, the area looked like an overgrown patch of wasteland. At one end there appeared to be a corrugated iron shelter, which looked in severe danger of collapse.

'Where do we start?' she asked. 'I don't see how we can do anything without some sort of machinery.'

'How do you normally clear undergrowth?' asked Colin.

'I've brought a couple of weed slashers,' said Ben, 'and as long as we've all got good thick gloves, we can pull a lot of it out.'

'I brought my gardening gloves,' said Fran.

'So did I,' said Libby.

'I haven't got any,' said Colin.

'Good job I brought two pairs, then,' said Ben, with a grin. He lifted his face. 'I do believe it's stopped raining.'

'I still think we'd do better with a mini digger,' said Libby to Fran. 'Do you want to slash or drag?'

'I don't mind. Shall I slash for a bit, and you drag it out, then we can swap over.'

Ben directed them to start at the hotel end of the pitch, where there seemed to be fewer brambles, while he and Colin began on the other end. For a while, they worked in silence, until Libby announced she was getting rather hot.

'Me, too.' Fran lay down the slasher and began peeling off her thick jacket.

This was the cue for all outer garments to be shed, and

Ben collected them to put under the shelter.

'Colin!'

They all turned towards him. He was staring at the ground.

'Was there a cellar door out here, do you remember?'

'A door?' Colin frowned. 'No, I don't think so.'

'Why?'

'There's something here,' said Ben. 'It looks as though the rain's caused some sort of subsidence and part of it's washed away. There wouldn't have been a cellar drop, would there?'

'Yes, there was, at the front,' said Colin. 'Nothing at the back, I'm certain.'

Fran and Libby struggled over to where he was standing.

'Looks like a sink hole,' said Libby.

'A small one, but yes, exactly.' Ben climbed through a tangle of brambles and bent to where a battered-looking plank door was hanging half open.

'Don't touch it, Ben!' called Libby. 'It'll be dangerous.'

'I'm only going to pull it open,' said Ben.

'Hang on,' said Colin. 'I'll come and act as ballast.'

Fran and Libby watched as Ben got down on his front, and with Colin hanging on to this legs, reached for what looked like a Victorian bow-shaped door handle. As soon as he touched it, there was a creak, and the door caved in and fell into the darkness below.

Colin inched his way up next to Ben, and together they peered over the edge of the hole.

'It is!' He called. 'It's a cellar! Or perhaps part of our

156

cellar. There are steps!' He levered himself to his feet. 'Do you think it's safe to go down there?'

'No!' said Libby and Fran together.

'I think we ought to tell the police,' said Ben.

'The police? Why?' asked Colin.

'Because the hotel is still a crime scene,' said Libby. 'And who knows? This might be the way the killer – or the victim – got in.'

'Oh, yes!' Colin stood with an arrested expression on his face. 'Obvious, really. But how did they know it was here? I didn't, and I used to live here.'

'Poking around the back, I expect,' said Fran. 'Safer than the front, where anyone could see. This part isn't overlooked at all.'

'If it was cleared, you could probably see it from the upstairs of the Hop Pocket,' said Libby, 'But there hasn't been anyone there for years according to John.'

Ben got to his feet and pulled his phone from his pocket. 'DS Trent?' he asked Libby.

'DI Maiden, I would think,' she said. 'Hold on – I've got the number.'

When Ben got through, he was in fact put through to Rachel Trent.

'She says not to touch anything, and please wait here. I did say what happened if it rained again and all she said was "we'll be as quick as we can".'

'I suppose we could carry on clearing the ground,' said Colin. 'That would only help them, wouldn't it?'

'I don't much feel like it now,' said Libby. 'Can we go under the…' she gestured towards the collapsing shelter.

'I don't think it's very safe,' said Ben. 'Shall we go into the Hop?'

'The Hop?' Colin looked puzzled.

'You know – the Hop.' Ben waved a hand back towards Cuckoo Lane.

'Oh – yes.' Colin picked up his discarded slasher. 'Good idea.'

Ben led the way carefully back the way they had come, but had barely got out of the gate when they heard a car stop in the lane. A moment later a uniformed officer wearing a high-vis jacket appeared, picking his way through the overgrown path.

'Mr Wilde?' he asked.

Ben admitted he was.

'DS Trent put out a call. She'll be along as soon as she can. Can you show me what you've found?'

'Can we go, then?' asked Libby, already knowing what the answer would be.

'If you'd just wait for DS Trent, ma'am.' He gave her a charmless smile, and with a sigh, she turned round to follow him and Ben.

Back on the pitch, standing amid the piles of cut back vegetation, they watched as, directed by Ben, the officer got down on his front and leant over the gaping cellar door.

'You the owner, sir?' The officer looked over his shoulder at Ben.

'No, I am,' said Colin. The officer looked confused, opened his mouth and closed it again, deciding instead to clamber to his feet. He then moved away from them, taking out what Libby assumed was either a radio or a phone. 'Do they have radios anymore?' she whispered to Fran.

'I think so,' said Fran. 'So they can talk to everyone at once – something like that. Taxi firms have them, too.'

'Oh.' Libby stared thoughtfully at the officer. 'Who's he calling, then? Rachel Trent, or head office?'

'I don't know!' said Fran, sounding irritated.

'All right, all right!' Libby looked surprised.

'Sorry.' Fran hunched her shoulders. 'I've got rain dripping down the back of my neck, my feet are wet, and I've been stung.'

'A bee? In this weather?'

'No – nettles!'

The officer was coming back to them.

'DS Trent will be here in a moment,' he said. 'And more officers.' He looked round the pitch. 'I'm sorry to keep you standing here in the rain. What were you doing out here, anyway?'

'Clearing the bat and trap pitch,' said Colin.

They all waited for a reaction. And got none.

'Ah,' said the officer and nodded.

They heard another car. Within seconds, Rachel Trent was ploughing through the weeds, followed by PC Robinson.

'Ow!' she said.

'Nettles?' asked Fran sympathetically.

Rachel sucked at her wrist and grinned. 'Feels like it!' She looked round at the dripping group. 'So what's going on?'

Libby started to tell her, but was silenced by a glare from their equally wet officer, who reported in suitably official language.

'Right,' said Rachel. 'We'll have to seal off the entrance, as it's part of our original crime scene, and get SOCOS down again.' She sighed. 'And when the other officers get here we'll take a look ourselves.' She turned to Colin. 'When did you last use this door, sir?'

'Me?' Colin looked startled. 'I didn't even know it was here!'

Rachel frowned. 'But I thought you lived here as a boy?'

'I did, but I never even saw this door. And I'm pretty sure my parents never used it.'

'It looks like a cellar drop,' said Ben.

'A what?'

'Cellar drop. You know, where beer barrels are delivered to pub cellars. Usually double doors set into the ground outside a pub.'

'Oh.' Rachel still looked puzzled. 'Didn't your parents use it?' she asked Colin.

'We had one at the front. Wouldn't have been much use round the back here,' said Colin. 'The delivery lorry couldn't have got here.'

'Right.' Rachel turned and looked at the uninviting hole in the ground without much enthusiasm. 'I suppose I'd better go in.'

'I'll go down first, Sarge,' said Robinson, almost visibly throwing his chest out.

Rachel nodded, and allowed him to go past her.

'Steps aren't too clever,' he said, half in and half out of the hole.

They all drew a little nearer.

'OK, Sarge.' His muffled voice echoed up to them. Rachel took a deep breath and turned to go down the steps backwards. Colin and Ben both stepped forward to give her a hand down.

For a while there was silence from the hole. Then:

'*Shit*!' bellowed PC Robinson.

Rachel's head appeared out of the hole, her face white.

'Another body,' she said.

Chapter Nineteen

The group watching her were struck dumb, including the officer now on guard by the entrance to the pitch.

'Call it in,' she said now, holding out hands to Colin and Ben to be hauled out of the hole. PC Robinson followed, looking even paler than the sergeant.

'Who -?' said Libby.

Rachel shook her head. 'Skeletal remains.'

'Not recent, then,' murmured Fran. Rachel shook her head and took the radio held out to her by the officer.

'Could we go into my pub?' Ben asked PC Robinson. 'It's that building there. Just to get out of the rain.'

'I'll have to ask the sarge,' said Robinson in a shaky voice.

'Go with them, Robinson.' Rachel had obviously heard the request.

They all followed Ben onto the footpath and out into the lane, where he unlocked the side door of the Hop Pocket and let them all in. PC Robinson looked round dubiously.

'Sit down, Colin,' said Libby. 'You look as though you might fall down.'

She pulled up a chair and gave it a wipe with her wet sleeve.

Colin, looking positively green, collapsed onto it. 'Thanks,' he said. 'It's just…'

'I know. A bit much, isn't it?' Libby patted his shoulder. 'And just as you were coming round to Steeple Martin, too.'

Fran had rubbed a clear patch in one of the windows. 'Reinforcements have arrived,' she said over her shoulder. 'Oh, Lord.'

'What?' said Ben and Libby together.

Fran shot a look at PC Robinson, who was endeavouring to watch them all closely at the same time. 'Ian,' she said. PC Robinson looked puzzled, and Colin, relieved.

'But that's good, isn't it?' he said.

'He'll accuse us of meddling,' said Libby.

'But we weren't!'

'*We* know we weren't, but to Ian it will just look as if we were poking our noses in,' said Ben.

Colin looked faintly aggrieved. 'It is *my* property.'

'That,' said Ben wryly, 'is the problem.'

'Eh?' Colin looked at them all in turn. 'Why?'

'Why do you think?' said Libby.

'But I haven't been anywhere near the place for years! And I can prove it. My passport will prove it.'

'Watch out!' muttered Fran, and moved away from the window.

The door opened. PC Robinson came smartly to attention.

'Well, well, well,' said Ian. 'Fancy seeing you here.'

Libby glared at him, Ben rolled his eyes, and Fran
163

looked resigned.

'Sir?' said Robinson.

'It's all right, Constable,' said Ian. 'I know these people. You needn't wait.'

PC Robinson hesitated. 'Erm,' he said. 'Sarge…'

'DS Trent is fine.' Ian smiled at the confused constable. 'Off you go. Right.' He turned to the other four. 'What exactly were you doing, and what happened?'

They all began to speak at once, then stopped.

'Fran,' said Ian. 'You tell me.'

'Well,' she began, 'you know Ben wants to start up the bat and trap team again?'

'Yes.'

'And Colin's going to let him use the pitch behind the Garden Hotel?'

'Yes.'

'If ever we get out of this mess, I'm going to sell it back to him,' said Colin.

'Back to him?'

'It was part of the Manor Estate at one time,' said Ben.

'Anyway,' continued Fran, 'while Colin's still over here, they decided to start clearing the pitch and Libby and I came along to help. We didn't think it was part of the original crime scene.'

'I'm afraid it is now – it's a crime scene all of its own,' said Ian. 'It didn't occur to you to ask if it would be all right?'

'It's my land, and nowhere near where the body was found,' said Colin, sounding surprised. 'The first body, that is.'

'And without us, you wouldn't know about the second body, would you?' said Libby, feeling that this was unanswerable.

Ian inclined his head. 'Tell me how you discovered the cellar.'

Ben described how he had spotted the subsidence and what had happened next.

'It was a bit like a sinkhole,' he said. 'With all this rain we've been having, I'm not surprised.'

'And you had no idea it was there, Mr Hardcastle?'

'None.' Colin shook his head. 'I'll ask Mrs Mardle. She might remember.'

'Mrs Mardle?'

'I told you. Our next door neighbour who gave us Colin's Spanish address,' said Libby.

'Did you ever come here to the bat and trap pitch?'

'Yes,' said Colin and Ben together.

'I used to come and watch,' said Colin. 'I was too young to play.'

'I used to play before I left the village to go to college,' said Ben.

'And neither of you remember the cellar door?'

Ben and Colin looked at each other and shook their heads.

'But bat and trap had stopped by the time I left the village,' said Colin. 'I wouldn't have come out the back at all after that.'

'John Newman might remember,' said Ben.

'He wouldn't have any reason to come here, either,' sais Colin. 'And he left for good not long after I did.'

165

'But he lived here,' said Ben, patting the scarred bar counter. 'It overlooks the footpath and it would have been clear in those days.'

'What can you see from upstairs?' asked Ian.

'Let's go up and see,' said Ben, opening a door beside the bar and disclosing an enclosed staircase.

'Are we going up?' asked Libby, as she and Fran watched the men disappear.

'I'd like to see what's up there,' said Fran.

'Come on, then,' said Libby with a sigh.

There were four rooms, a kitchen and a bathroom, all in need of renovation, but commanding a good view over Cuckoo Lane, right down to Dan and Moira Henderson's house, and the other way over the footpath and down to the back of the Garden Hotel, and even to the back of the chapel next door. They could also see where Cuckoo Lane joined the high street.

'You can't actually see the pitch from here, though,' said Ben, peering through the window over the side door.

'Hmm,' said Ian. 'Not much help, then.'

They all trooped back downstairs.

'And you're going to do this place up?' said Ian.

'Yes,' said Ben. 'When all the relevant permissions come through.'

'Can we go now?' asked Colin. 'You don't need to ask us anything else, do you?'

Ian regarded him thoughtfully. 'Not at the moment. But you will all have to make formal statements. I think you might have to come into the station.'

There was a collective groan.

166

'This is where an incident room would come in handy,' said Libby.

Ian smiled. 'Well, you never know. Now we've got two bodies...'

'But they aren't recent,' said Fran.

'Nevertheless, it's now a double crime scene, whether or not the two are connected. We'll have to see. Resources are stretched, so...' He ushered them back out to Cuckoo Lane and Ben locked up.

'Will you be able to tell us about the new body?' asked Libby.

'Maybe. We'll have to see,' said Ian again. 'Go on, get off home. I know where to find you.'

In silence the walked back to the high street.

'I could do with a drink,' said Colin. 'Anyone else?'

'Not for me,' said Fran. 'I've got to drive home.'

'Come and have a coffee or something,' said Libby. 'We all need something.'

'All right,' said Fran, 'but I mustn't be long.'

They crossed the road, and as they did so, Harry appeared outside the Pink Geranium.

'What's happened now?' he asked, waving towards the police cars now parked outside the Garden Hotel.

'Another body - a skeleton,' said Ben. 'We're just going to have a drink.'

'Come on, then,' said Harry. 'More private in here.'

They followed him into the restaurant and sat down in the left hand window.

'Wine? Beer? Coffee?' asked Harry. 'Colin, you look as though you could do with a brandy.'

167

'Oh, I could!' said Colin gratefully, and pulled out his wallet.

'On the house,' said Harry. 'What about the rest of you?'

Ben and Libby opted for whisky and Fran for coffee. Harry disappeared towards the bar area.

'What do we think then?' asked Libby.

'What about?' asked Ben.

'This other body.'

'It has to have something to do with the first one,' said Fran.

'But why were they in different places?' said Colin.

'Do you think the two areas of the cellar link up?' said Ben. 'They must do, surely?'

'But the first body wasn't actually in a cellar, was it?' said Libby.

'I thought you were told Fiona fell through a cellar door,' said Ben.

'So,' said Harry, returning with the drinks. 'Did you actually find this one?'

Between them, they explained.

'Got to be linked, surely?' said Harry.

'It's a bit odd if they aren't,' said Ben.

'Ian said he might be able to tell us,' said Libby.

'What's he doing there? I thought he was supposed to be directing operations from afar?'

'He is, but we all knew he wouldn't,' said Fran. 'I bet he's resisting further promotion right now. I don't think he wanted the last one.'

'Why not?' Colin was frowning.

'The further up the ladder they go, the less front-line policing they do,' explained Ben. 'I didn't realise it, but most investigations are led by detective sergeants. Rachel's doing most of the leading on this one.'

'That's the girl we just met?' asked Colin.

'That's her,' said Libby. 'And Inspector Maiden's deputy SIO.'

Colin shook his head. 'I can't make sense of it all. I'm beginning to wish I hadn't come back after all.'

There was a chorus of protest, and he smiled. 'Well, if we get through this, we'll see.'

'You sound like Ian,' said Libby morosely.

'So what are you going to do now?' asked Harry.

'Us? Nothing,' said Ben. 'We can't clear the pitch now.'

'I meant about the case,' said Harry, looking pointedly at Libby.

'Nothing,' she said, flushing. 'There's nothing we can do. We don't know anything about the background and we don't have any connections to the case.'

'Except me,' said Colin.

'Yes, but you're merely the absentee owner of the property,' said Fran. 'Nothing to do with you.'

'You'll have to take up something else, then,' said Harry. 'How about tatting?'

Libby slapped his arm.

'She's already got paintings to do,' said Fran.

'I did say I'd quite like to get into archaeology,' said Libby. 'Perhaps get involved with a local dig. You know, be a scrubber or something.'

This provoked an explosion of laughter, into which a

169

puzzled looking Ian walked.

'Will someone tell me?' he asked, as they all struggled to control themselves.

'I think it's aftermath of shock,' said Fran, wiping her eyes.

'Well, now you're going to get another one,' said Ian. 'Your skeleton was much older than the first body.'

'There you are, Libby,' said Harry. 'An archaeological find!'

'Not quite,' said Ian. 'But certainly more than ten years.'

'Ten years!' said Colin. 'But I don't understand. The place was already empty by then.'

'If someone could get in six months ago, there's no reason why they shouldn't have been able to ten years ago,' said Ian. 'But it isn't a definite date, just a first impression. They'll know better after they do some tests.'

'Radio carbon dating,' said Libby knowledgeably.

'I don't think it'll go that far,' said Ian, 'but insect activity and fibres that have been found. That sort of thing. But you've already answered what I came to ask you, Mr Hardcastle. The hotel was empty ten years ago?'

'Yes. My mother closed it after my father died, and that was nearly twenty years ago. It's been empty since she died, in fact, before she died. She went to live with her sister.'

'And that was?'

Colin frowned. 'Fifteen years ago? They came to stay with me in London for a holiday about then, but Mum wasn't well.'

170

Ian sighed. 'So anyone could have got in there?'

'I suppose so,' said Colin, 'but I didn't even know about that cellar door – or even the cellar. But there wouldn't have been anything in there to steal. Did you find anything in there?'

'Not really.' Ian sighed again. 'So far, nothing in the main cellar room except a little gilt chair.'

Chapter Twenty

'A chair?' repeated Ben, Colin and Harry. Libby and Fran just looked at one another.

'Libby?' said Ian.

Fran sighed. 'It was me, Ian.'

'Ah,' said Ben and Harry. Colin looked puzzled.

'And why didn't you tell me?' asked Ian.

'Tell you what?' Colin almost yelped. 'Did you put it there, Fran?'

'Nothing like that,' said Ian. 'Do you want to tell him, Fran?'

'No. You tell him.'

Ian was silent for a moment. Then he turned to Colin. 'It's like this.'

'For goodness' sake sit down,' said Harry, and pulled forward another chair. 'Do you want coffee or something?'

'No, I can't stay,' said Ian, sitting down. 'You see, Colin, Fran's helped us out before. By us, I mean the police. She has a – well, I suppose you'd call it a gift.'

'Or a curse,' mumbled Fran.

'A gift?'

'Yes. You see, Fran can sometimes see things other people can't.'

'What? You mean...' Colin's eyes fairly bulged, 'like, *psychic*?'

'Yes,' said everyone else.

Colin sat back in his chair. 'I don't believe it.'

'That's what most people say,' said Ian, 'but it's true. When you've seen it proved, you can't help believing it.'

'Proved?'

'She's saved people's lives,' said Harry simply. 'I know, I didn't believe it, either. Just take us on trust, mate.' He turned to Fran. 'Tell us, Fran.'

'I didn't tell you,' said Fran, addressing Ian, 'because I didn't think it amounted to much. And I thought I should really have to report to Rachel – DS Trent – and she wouldn't understand. I just saw this room, empty except for a little chair, and a rather confused image of a boy.'

'When was this?'

'A few days ago. I was out for dinner with Guy when it happened.'

'So it wasn't something happening right at that time?'

'Couldn't have been, could it?'

'But we could have gone looking for a room with a chair,' said Ian. 'We might have found it sooner.'

'I'm sorry,' said Fran, 'but it wouldn't have made any difference, would it? The – er, events - had already happened.'

Ian sighed. 'I suppose so. But if it happens again -'

'Yes, I'll tell you.' She turned to Colin. 'I'm sorry, Colin.'

Colin looked confused. 'What for? Oh, I don't understand it, but that's hardly your fault, is it?'

'Well, there's one thing,' said Libby.

'What?' asked Ian.

'It proves that the two bodies are linked. Fran saw the room with the chair, which you didn't find until the second one was found, but she also saw the first body. Or the boy who it had been, if you know what I mean.'

'That's true, Ian,' said Harry.

Ian nodded. 'It gives me something to work on. Even if I can't tell DS Trent why!'

'What about Inspector Maiden?' asked Ben. 'He knows about the moments.'

'That's what we call, them, Colin,' said Libby. 'Fran's Moments.'

Ian nodded. 'Maybe. I can see I'm going to be getting more involved again.' He stood up. 'Even though I shouldn't. And now I'd better get back to the station. I'll see what I can do about an incident room.'

'Well,' said Harry, when Ian had gone, 'you see what an influence Libby's Loonies have on the local police force, Colin.'

'It doesn't work anywhere else, though,' said Libby. 'We went to the Isle of Wight once…'

'And not all of the force in Kent, either,' said Fran.

'Big Bertha,' agreed Ben.

'Who?'

'Pet name for Superintendent Bertram,' said Libby. 'She doesn't like me.'

'She doesn't like anybody, pet,' said Harry. 'Now, come on, you've been admitted to the charmed circle now, so what are you going to do?'

'Charmed circle?' asked Colin, who looked as though his head might be spinning.

'I think he means that we've got Ian on side,' said Fran, 'although I'm not sure about that. And I really don't see that there's anything we can do.'

'Until we have a bit more information,' said Libby. 'Preferably about this new body.'

'Which is at least ten years old,' said Ben. 'That means we might know who it is. We were all here then.'

'Oh, golly, yes!' said Libby. 'I never thought of that. Come to think of it, we were here when poor Ossie was killed, too. It's not long ago, after all.'

'But when did you ever see a gang of teenage boys prowling the streets of Steeple Martin?' asked Harry. 'That's the only way you would have known about Ossie.'

'They didn't prowl the streets, by all accounts,' said Libby, 'they came out from Canterbury in someone's car.'

'Which they would have parked round the back,' said Ben. 'Which, as we know, isn't overlooked.'

'What about Dan and Moira?' asked Fran. 'Could they have seen anything from their house?'

'It's down a dip, isn't it?' said Libby, 'so I doubt it.'

'Is that the couple who live down Cuckoo Lane?' asked Harry. 'They come in here sometimes.'

'We could go and have a look,' said Libby. 'Wouldn't hurt, would it?'

'But not now,' said Fran. 'I must get home.'

'Get hubby's tea on the table?' said Harry with a grin, and ducked. 'Go on then, petal. We know where to find you.'

After Fran's departure the other four sat on round the coffee table. Colin's thin face was troubled.

'Don't let it worry you, Colin,' said Ben. 'I'm sure it will all be cleared up soon enough. And Ian's very good. He'll get to the truth.'

'And it might be unpleasant,' said Colin.

Libby, Ben, and Harry looked at each other and nodded.

The following morning, Libby was sitting at the kitchen table with her second mug of tea when the landline rang.

'Sorry to disturb you so early, Mrs Sarjeant,' said DS Trent, 'but I believe DCI Connell did say he would have to ask you to come in to make a formal statement?'

'He did,' said Libby, stifling a groan.

'Well, I'm sure you'll be relieved to know we've managed to set up an incident room here in the village again.' DS Trent gave a little giggle. 'I think we might as well open a permanent station here, don't you?'

Libby heaved a sigh of relief. 'We do seem to get our fair share of bad luck,' she said. 'Church hall again?'

'Yes, and that's really convenient,' said Rachel chattily. 'You know that path along the back? Well, it goes all the way from the back of the Garden Hotel right past the back of the Church Hall!'

'It does indeed,' said Libby, amused. 'And right out to Lendle Lane the other way. But you can't get a vehicle along it, can you?'

'Not a full-size one,' said Rachel, 'but they brought in a mini digger to clear the path and the area behind the hotel where the cellar door is.'

'The pitch!' gasped Libby. 'Wonderful!'

176

'The pitch?'

'We told you – that's why we there yesterday! To clear the bat and trap pitch.'

'Oh, yes.' Rachel had lost interest. 'Anyway, could you come over this morning some time? We got most of the stuff in last night, and we've got a skeleton staff – oh.'

Libby swallowed a laugh. 'Right, I'll be there. What about the others. Do you really want Fran – Mrs Wolfe – to come in from Nethergate?'

'No, you and Mr Wilde will be fine. We've already been in touch with Mr Hardcastle.'

'OK. I'll get hold of Ben and we'll see you later.'

Ending the call, she thought for a moment, then rang the Manor estate office, where Ben would be at this time in the morning.

'And do you think we ought to ring Colin?' she said, after she'd relayed the message. 'He might prefer to go with us.'

'OK,' said Ben, 'I'll do it. But we can't keep babysitting him. I'll ring you back.'

But when he did, he sounded surprised.

'We're not needed,' he said. 'He's going with his other babysitter.'

'Eh?' said Libby.

'Mrs Mardle! They asked her in to answer some questions about the Garden, which I suppose they would, given that she's the only one left in the village who worked there and might know something about it, and she called Colin. As he'd already been asked in, he's coming round to collect her in about half an hour. I said we might as well all

177

walk round together, so I'm coming home now.'

Half an hour later, Colin knocked on the door of number seventeen.

'She's nervous,' he said, nodding towards the open door of number sixteen.

'Well, dear,' said Jinny Mardle, appearing in the doorway in a turquoise cardigan and floral skirt, 'I've never had anything to do with the police before.' She pulled her yellow front door closed behind her and dropped the key into a large white handbag. Libby guessed it was her summer handbag, to be replaced by a sensible black or brown for the winter.

'Nothing to worry about, Mrs Mardle,' said Ben. 'They're very nice.'

'If you say so dear,' said Mrs Mardle, looking unconvinced. 'Only you hear such things.'

The other three exchanged glances over her head.

They walked slowly down Allhallow's Lane, Mrs Mardle clinging on to Colin's arm. Yesterday's rain had disappeared, and the sun shone brightly on lush green foliage, having already dried up the puddles.

'I don't know why they wanted to talk to me,' Mrs Mardle went on. 'You could have told them anything they wanted to know about the old Garden, dear, couldn't you?'

'I've told them all I could, Nanny,' said Colin, 'but you were there after I went away, so you probably know more than I do.'

'Well, I don't know anything about any bodies,' she said querulously. 'The idea.'

Ben and Libby grinned at each other.

The high street was busier than it had been yesterday, and Mrs Mardle was greeted by several people as they made their way along towards Maltby Close. As they turned into it, Flo appeared at her door.

'Jinny!' she said, removing the cigarette from her mouth. 'Where are you off to, then?' She gave Libby a suspicious look.

'The police dear,' said Mrs Mardle, a little proudly.

'Blimey! What you done?' Flo came forward and stood in their way.

Libby sighed. 'We've all got to give statements, Flo.'

'Oh, about the new body, then, is it?' she said, nodding knowingly. 'Knew you'd be mixed up in it.'

'Everyone knows about it, do they?' said Ben. 'Can't keep anything quiet round here.'

'Course not,' Flo scoffed. 'Anyway, it was on the local news last night. That mate of yourn – what's 'is name?'

'Campbell McLean,' said Libby resignedly. 'And he's not a mate.'

The TV journalist had become acquainted with Libby and Fran some years before, and had, in fact, given them some help.

Flo sniffed. 'Yeah, 'im. All right, then, s'pose you'd better get on.' She stepped back and allowed them to carry on towards the church. They skirted it and waved at Beth, hovering outside.

'See you when we've finished,' called Libby.

The church hall had been converted into an incident room before, so was familiar to Libby and Ben, but Mrs Mardle looked terrified. Rachel Trent came forward, assessed the situation and, with a friendly smile, held out her hand.

'Mrs Mardle? How kind of you to come and help us.'

Mrs Mardle gingerly took the proffered hand, looking surprised.

'Mrs Sarjeant and Mr Wilde, the officer over there will take your statements.' She nodded towards a desk on the other side of the room. 'And Mr Hardcastle, DCI Connell will be along in a minute.'

She led Mrs Mardle away towards her own desk and left Ben, Libby and Colin looking at one another.

'Why -?' began Colin.

'I'm afraid the situation has become rather more serious, sir,' said Inspector Maiden, appearing on one side of Colin.

'The body,' said Ian, coming up on the other side, 'now appears to be over twenty years old. Dating from the time that you still lived here.'

Chapter Twenty One

Libby opened her mouth, but Ben's hand on her arm kept her silent.

'Sir?' said Ian, gesturing Colin in front of him.

DI Maiden turned away from his senior officer and gave Ben and Libby a friendly smile. 'Perhaps you'll come with me?'

'I thought Rachel said that officer over there,' said Libby.

'Yes, he's coming, too.' Maiden ushered them towards a corner of the room partially screened off by movable notice boards. Ian had by this time piloted Colin into the kitchen area and closed the door.

Libby and Ben took seats one side of a table, while Maiden and the other officer sat on the other. Maiden placed what looked like a fat mobile phone between them. Libby looked at it as though it might bite.

'New interview recording equipment,' said Maiden. 'Quite a bit better than the old tape decks. And easier to set up in incident rooms.'

'Er – yes.' Libby cleared her throat.

The interview began as most did, with the introduction of persons present, time and date. Then Maiden began.

'Can you tell me exactly what happened yesterday at the Garden Hotel site? Mr Wilde?'

Ben described their visit the previous day until the arrival of the first officer on the scene.

'Do you agree with that, Mrs Sarjeant?'

'Yes.'

'Nothing to add?'

'No.'

'And what about Mr Hardcastle. How did he seem?'

'Seem?' Libby looked bewildered.

'Yes. Was he behaving normally?'

'He was exactly as we've come to know him,' said Libby.

'He was looking forward to getting the bat and trap pitch up and running again,' said Ben. 'Why?'

'Ah, yes. The bat and trap pitch. Why was he so interested?'

Ben frowned. 'The same reason we all are. If it was restored, we could bring the game back here, as it's being brought back all over Kent.'

'Really?' Maiden looked unconvinced.

'You've heard of it, surely?" said Libby.

Maiden shrugged.

'Oh, yes,' said the other officer, earning himself a severe look from his superior. 'I've joined my pub team.'

'So Hardcastle had no other reason for wanting to join your expedition yesterday?' persisted Maiden.

'Why on earth should he?' said Ben. 'In fact, we decided together. He's only here for a short time, so we wanted to see if we could get the pitch clear enough to have

182

a scratch game before he headed back to Spain.' Ben sighed. 'Of course, we realise we won't be able to do that now.'

Maiden looked down at the desk. 'Very well,' he said after a moment. 'That'll be all. Interview terminated at...' he glanced at the clock, '11.18.'

'What do we do now?' Libby asked Ben.

Maiden and the other officer stood up.

'Sorry about that,' said Maiden, 'but it had to be a formal interview.'

'But I don't understand,' said Libby, although she was terribly sure that actually, she did, 'why were you so interested in Colin?'

The other officer excused himself and Maiden sighed. 'It's what DCI Connell said. Forensics have confirmed that the body is female and over twenty years old - I mean it's been hidden for over twenty years.'

Libby nodded.

'And do we know how old the female was?' asked Ben/

'The nearest that the pathologist would commit to was between eighteen and thirty.'

Libby looked at Ben, who nodded.

'What?' Maiden said sharply.

Libby tried to look innocent.

'Just that it probably didn't have anything to do with Colin Hardcastle,' said Ben, who had obviously thought quickly, 'because he's gay.'

'*What*?' said Maiden again.

'Oh, didn't you know?' said Libby, still innocent.

'No.' Maiden frowned. 'Right. Can you see yourselves
183

out?'

'We should probably wait for Mrs Mardle,' said Ben. 'Can we do that, do you think?'

'Er – yes.' Maiden looked round and failed to see a waiting area. 'By the door.'

Ben and Libby watched him go quickly to the kitchen area, knock and go in. A few seconds later he re-emerged followed by Ian, who glanced towards them and frowned. They began moving over to DS Trent's desk, where Mrs Mardle sat with a cup of tea.

'Finished?' said Rachel. 'Would you like to see Mrs Mardle home?'

'We thought we would,' said Libby.

'What about Colin, dear?' asked Mrs Mardle.

'I think he's still busy,' said Rachel, just as Ian arrived at her desk.

'Just a moment, please, Mrs Sarjeant, Mr Wilde,' he said formally. 'A word?'

Libby sighed.

Ushering them politely but firmly away from the desk, Ian said 'Now.'

'Now?' echoed Ben.

'You knew I knew Hardcastle was gay.'

'Well, I thought you did,' said Libby.

'So what was it you thought you knew?'

'What?'

'Inspector Maiden says you looked at each other and nodded. Then came up with this statement that he was gay. What was it you really meant?'

'Just that,' said Ben. 'What else?'

'Look, Ben,' said Ian, 'I'm used to Libby being a nuisance, but not you. You're usually the sensible one.'

'Oh, all right,' said Libby. 'We just didn't want to put something into your minds if you hadn't thought of it yourselves.'

Ian sighed. 'Like the fact that the body could be that of Shareen Wallis?'

They both looked shamefaced.

'So what do you know about that?'

'John Newman told us about the party he took Colin to,' said Ben.

'And it was after that party that the girl disappeared,' said Libby. 'But John brought Colin back here. Unless he brought the girl back, too, how could Colin have had anything to do with her being here?'

'Well, if it is her, and it isn't confirmed yet, she got here somehow, didn't she?' said Ian. 'Is that all you know?'

'I thought that was all there is to know,' said Libby. 'Jane said -'

'Oh, so you've been digging, then?' Ian frowned at her.

'I only asked Jane! And she wasn't around then, but she said one of the old reporters often spoke about it.'

'And no trace was ever found,' said Ben.

'If she was stashed away underground here, that isn't surprising.' Ian scowled at the floor. 'All right, go and take Mrs Mardle home. I know how to find you if I need any more.'

'Will we see you tonight?' asked Libby.

'Under the circumstances, I don't think so,' said Ian with a grim smile.

'Oh, dear,' whispered Libby, as they watched him walk away. 'I don't think we're popular.'

They took Mrs Mardle home, agreeing when she said how nice the young lady had been, and it wasn't a bit like the telly.

'When will Colin come back?' she asked as she let herself into number sixteen. 'Will he phone me?'

'We'll ask him when we see him,' said Libby. 'I'll let you know.'

'Phew!' she said to Ben as he closed their front door behind him. 'I didn't know what to say.'

'No.' Ben came into the front room, frowning. 'I don't know what to think, either.'

'About Colin?'

'Well, of course about Colin. Have we been wrong about him?'

Libby stopped on her way to the kitchen and turned round, aghast.

'You mean could he have done it?'

'We have rather taken him on trust, haven't we? From having been so suspicious before we met him.'

'But he couldn't have done it!' said Libby. 'How could he?'

'He could have gone back to that party after John brought him home,' said Ben.

'But why? What for? He's gay, for heaven's sake! What would he want with that girl?'

Ben shook his head and sighed. 'Oh, I don't know. But the body's in his house.'

'And what about young Ossie Whitelaw?' Libby went

186

on. 'He couldn't have done that. He wasn't even in the country.'

'How do we know that?' asked Ben. 'No one knows exactly when Ossie was murdered. Anyway, they might not be connected.'

'I bet they are,' said Libby darkly.

After a lunch of whatever Libby could find in the kitchen, Ben went back to the Manor and Libby called Fran.

'So I've got to do something,' she concluded. 'I can't just sit back and do nothing.'

'I notice you don't say "we",' said Fran.

'Well, you don't want to get involved, do you? You more or less said you didn't.'

'Did I?' said Fran slowly. 'I'm not sure...'

Libby let the silence go on for a heartbeat. 'What do you mean?'

'I said, I'm not sure. Anyway, Ben could be right.'

'Oh, I know,' said Libby impatiently. 'It looks so incriminating on the surface. But it can't be!'

'Libby, you're letting sentiment get in the way. How well do you know Colin? And what about the reservations you had before you met him?'

Libby was silent.

'All right,' she said at last. 'But that means I've got to find out for myself what happened. And you still haven't said. What did you mean, you're not sure?'

'Well, I'm not.' Fran paused. 'I like Colin, too, and as far as I could tell, he was nothing to do with the chair I saw, or the boy. But that isn't fact, as we know.'

'Ian took notice of it, though.'

'Ye-es, but it didn't actually tell him anything. No, for once, I think you're right. We need to have a look.'

Libby was so stupefied she was lost for words.

'So where should we start?' Fran went on. 'Felling? That seems to be the beginning of it all, with that party. How can we find out about that?'

Libby found her voice. 'John Newman, or possibly his wife, Emma. It was Emma who invited John to the party.'

'Right. Shall we go and see them?'

Libby's mouth opened and closed like a fish.

'Come on, Lib! Say something!'

'I can't believe you're being so – so – so *proactive*!'

Fran laughed. 'Just because I actually think there's something to look into,' she said. 'Come on, where do the Newmans live?'

'In Felling, you know that – Ben has the address and phone number, but we can't just turn up. And I somehow doubt Emma would welcome us. She was fairly ill at ease when we all had dinner together.'

'We have to do it by stealth, then.' Fran was quiet for a moment. 'Didn't you say they'd had some work done by Ted Sachs?'

'Yes, by him and the bloke he worked for at the time.'

'So you could ask for a recommendation?'

'But they know he did work for Fiona. And they know I know her. That would sound odd.'

'Hmm. OK, where does she work? I assume she does work? She's not one of the idle rich like you, is she?'

'I'm not! I work – I paint pictures!'

'Hmm,' said Fran. 'So, Emma?'

'I don't know. Under the circumstances, I can't ask Colin.'

'Why not? They haven't clapped him in irons, have they?'

'I don't know. I don't see how they can without any proper evidence.'

'Then, as it's Wednesday, you'll be going to the pub and he's staying there. Even if he doesn't come down for a drink, you can go up and see him. And get any information you can out of him. Ian won't go under the circumstances.'

'No, that's what he said himself,' said Libby. 'All right, I'll try. But I wish you were going to be with me. Ben'll get mad.'

'OK. Let me work on Guy – I might be able to get him to come over on the promise of a drink. Then he can keep Ben company.'

So it was that, later that evening, Ben, Libby, Fran, and Guy all entered the pub. And found Patti and Anne already there, with Colin and Edward.

Colin sprang to his feet.

'Oh, I'm so glad to see you!' he said. 'I wasn't sure you'd come.' He dropped his voice. 'The police think I'm the murderer!'

189

Chapter Twenty Two

Libby took a deep breath and eased Colin back into his seat. Ben gave her a speaking look before he and Guy went to the bar for drinks.

'Now,' she said, 'I take it you've filled everyone in on what the police said to you?'

There were murmurs of assent from the others round the table.

'So now tell us,' said Fran.

'They think the body is that – that girl.' Colin swallowed. Libby thought he looked frightened.

'The singer?' asked Fran.

Colin nodded. 'And they know all about me being at that party.'

'The one where she disappeared?' said Libby.

'Yes. They think I must have gone back after John brought me home.'

'I don't see it myself,' said Edward. 'Why would you? And why would she have come with you?'

'Honestly – I've no idea.' Colin shook his head. 'But after all this time, how do I prove it?'

'I don't know,' said Libby. 'But Fran and I will try and help.'

'Help? How?'

'You don't know them,' said Edward with a grin.

'They've got Miss Marple beat,' agreed Anne.

'You're *detectives*?' Colin gasped.

'No, just nosy,' said Patti, smiling at Libby. 'But they get results.'

'I don't understand,' said Colin.

At this point, Ben and Guy returned and between them the assembled company explained about Libby and Fran's various adventures.

'And that's where your – er – moments come in?' Colin asked Fran.

'Sometimes.' She nodded. 'But mostly, as Patti says, it's just us being nosy.'

'We look at things the police don't,' said Libby. 'For instance, what we'd like to do is go and talk to Emma Newman.'

'Emma? Why?'

'She was the one who asked John to the party. She knew a lot of the guests, didn't she?'

'I suppose so.'

'So she would have noticed who the girl was talking to that evening?'

'Yes. The trouble is, she was talking to me.' Colin coloured. 'She'll tell the police.'

'Was she?' Fran frowned. 'Why?'

'She didn't know me. She didn't know…' Colin trailed off.

'Don't worry about us,' said Patti. 'I may be a vicar, but you must have noticed that Anne and I are a couple.'

Colin stared at her with his mouth open.

'So she was making a move on you?' said Guy, who rarely contributed to this kind of conversation. Libby looked at him in surprise. Colin nodded.

'Will she remember that?' asked Ben. 'As you said, it's a long time ago.'

'I should think everyone would remember that evening,' said Libby. 'They will have been questioned by the police at the time. That sort of thing rather fixes things in the memory.'

'So we thought we might go and talk to her,' said Fran. 'If she'll talk to us.'

'Couldn't you talk to John?' asked Colin.

'We will, but he didn't know anyone at the party at the time, did he? He told us that. What would he know?'

'I don't know.' Colin looked down into his drink.

Libby raised her eyebrows at Fran.

Ben leant towards Colin.

'If you don't want to talk about it, just say so, Colin. But honestly, they are only trying to help.'

Colin looked up. 'Thank you,' he said. 'And I need all the help I can get. But I don't know what you can do.'

'Shall we leave it tonight, then?' asked Libby. 'I can come and talk to you tomorrow if you prefer.' She looked round at the rest of the table. 'On our own.'

Colin sat up a little straighter. 'No. They all know about it, now.' He shook his head. 'I really don't know what's come over me. I've never talked about – well, me – in front of anyone before. Especially people I've only just met. And you'd think, under the circumstances, I'd be even more

192

likely to keep myself to myself.' He shook his head again. 'I don't get it.'

'It's circumstances that have done it,' said Edward. 'Unusual circumstances – and, of course, the effect of the Loonies.'

Patti and Anne went on to explain that Harry had dubbed their band of friends Libby's Loonies.

'But of course you've heard that before,' said Libby.

'Yes.' Colin grinned. 'I said I'd be flattered.'

'There you are then,' said Edward. 'We will all bend our minds to the problem.'

Colin looked a little happier.

Now,' said Fran, 'have you been in touch with your solicitor?'

'Yes, but they're the Hardcastle Holdings solicitors – our registered offices in London. I don't know if they'd be able to help.'

'What did they say?' asked Libby.

'I had to leave a message,' said Colin. 'They haven't come back to me.'

'Then you need someone local,' said Ben. He looked round the table. 'Who do we know?'

'The only one I can think of is that one in Nethergate, Robert Grimshaw,' said Libby doubtfully.

'Well, there's the estate solicitor,' said Ben. 'I can ask him. They do criminal law.'

'Criminal law!' Colin lost his recent colour.

'Well, that's what it is,' said Ben kindly. 'Don't take it personally.'

'And tomorrow Fran and I will go to Felling and see if

Emma will talk to us,' said Libby. 'Do you know where she works?'

Colin frowned. 'I'm not sure. Part-time, I think. Maybe a shop?'

'The thing is,' said Libby, 'we don't want to ask John, because he might not want us to.'

'Why not?' asked Anne. 'If it's to help his friend.'

'They know what they're doing,' said Patti, patting her friend's arm. 'It's called tact.'

'Not something my beloved is normally known for,' said Ben, with a chuckle.

Libby sniffed.

'Anyway,' said Fran, 'we find out what we can about the party and the girl – Shareen, was it? – and then we'll think again. One thing we're certain of is that you couldn't have had anything to do with the death of the boy.'

'Well, no.' Colin looked surprised. 'They didn't ask me anything about that. Are they connected?'

'They must be!' said several voices together.

'Or are you just going for the obvious?' said Guy.

Everyone looked at him.

'They might not be,' he said reasonably. 'There are – what? Twenty years between them?'

'That's true,' said Libby. 'And whether they are or they aren't, we just concentrate on the death of the girl. Shame we can't find out more about her background.'

'What about the old reporter you said Jane mentioned?' suggested Ben.

'I'll ask her tomorrow. She said she'd try and find out if he was still around.' Libby smiled round. 'Now let's try and cheer Colin up.'

Not at all sure that they had cheered Colin up, the following morning, Libby called Jane.

'Hello! Got me in the office for a change,' said Jane. 'You still on the search about that girl singer? Guess you are, as her body's turned up.'

'Oh, have they confirmed it, then?' asked Libby. 'They hadn't yesterday.'

'Apparently. It came through on the wire earlier,' said Jane. 'No details, just the plain fact.'

'Oh, well, in that case Fran and I had better get on with it then.'

'Get on with what?'

'Looking into it,' said Libby. 'Did you find that old reporter?'

'Barrett? Yes, I did. And if you want to speak to him I'd do it fast. He'll be getting on to the police any minute I would think. It was his pet subject.'

'Yes, you said he was very interested. Where is he?'

'You'll never guess! Felling!'

When Libby had duly expressed surprise and taken down his address and phone number, she called Fran.

'So what do we do? Emma first, or this Barrett?'

'Barrett, before the police descend on him,' said Fran. 'I'll meet you at that tea shop in the square. We can phone him from there.'

Libby phoned Colin, but his phone went straight to voicemail. She then phoned Ben, who said he'd been in touch with the solicitors, who had arranged to see Colin that morning.

'I expect that's why his phone is off,' said Libby. 'OK, we're heading off to Felling, now. I'll keep you posted.'

Libby drove to Felling, pleased to see that the verges along the roadside had been left to develop into mini-meadows. The sun was shining, and if it wasn't for Colin's predicament, she would have felt that all was right with the world. But try as she might, she couldn't get rid of the feeling that the odds were stacked against him, and to wonder, treacherously, if they had all been taken in by him.

'But,' she reasoned to herself, 'why do we all feel the same way? Only Guy was doubtful. The rest of us all took him at face value.'

By the time she reached the car park in Felling, the sun had gone in and she felt even more unsure.

Fran was already waiting in the Tea Square, a pot of tea in front of her.

'You don't look very happy,' she said. 'I thought you'd be all fired up and raring to go.'

'I was,' said Libby, sitting down and pulling the pot towards her. 'I was just wondering why we're all so sure Colin's innocent.'

Fran's eyes widened. 'Where did that come from?'

'Well.' Libby carefully poured tea. 'After being so suspicious of him before we met him, when we couldn't find him, we all just accepted the fact that he wasn't guilty of anything. Why?'

'He wasn't guilty of the boy's death,' said Fran.

'No, but does it follow that he isn't guilty of this one?'

Fran put her head on one side. 'You've changed your tune.'

Libby sighed. 'I know, but I realised I was just barging ahead assuming that I was right.'

'But everyone feels the same,' said Fran.

'I know, that's what set me thinking. Did I do that? Set everyone on the wrong track?'

'No,' said Fran. 'Colin has been introduced to everyone, who accepted him without bias. You haven't said anything. He comes across as a little bit nervy, not sure that he'll be accepted, and appears to be delighted that he has been. Something obviously happened to him to put him off Kent – Steeple Martin and Felling in particular – but I don't see how he could have killed that girl without John Newman helping him with the body. So it isn't that.'

Libby heaved a sigh. 'I agree. I'm just doubting myself more than Colin. And I like him. I didn't think I would, but I do.'

'In that case, let's get on with it.' Fran took out her phone. 'Have you got the reporter's name and number?'

Libby fetched out the piece of paper on which she had scribbled the details. 'Are you going to ring him?'

'Unless you want to?'

Libby shook her head. Fran keyed in the number.

'Hello, is that Mr Barrett? Yes, I'm sorry to bother you – no I'm not selling anything. No – listen – Jane, the editor of the *Mercury* – yes, I'm a friend of hers. She gave me your name. No, perhaps she shouldn't have done, but – no, please listen. It's about that girl Shareen – yes.' Fran mimed relief. 'Well, did you know her body had been found?'

There was a longer pause, while Fran listened and Libby

seethed with impatience.

'Could we come and talk to you about it? Yes, I'm sure the police will want to talk to you, too, but it concerns a friend of ours. Yes, I have another friend with me. Oh, of course. You can call Jane and ask her. I'm Fran Wolfe and my friend is Libby Sarjeant. So can we come? Yes, I have your address. Can you tell me how to get there.'

Fran finally ended the call.

'I gather he was a bit – what? Annoyed?'

'Obstreperous,' said Fran. 'Anyway, we can go. I've got directions.'

'Whose car, then?'

'Neither.' Fran grinned. 'It's just round the corner.'

In fact, Fred Barrett's house was in a short terrace of Victorian cottages leading to the river. There didn't seem to be any access for cars, and Libby wondered what the residents did with theirs. The Barrett cottage was unadorned with hanging baskets or potted shrubs, unlike most of the rest.

'Bachelor,' whispered Libby, after Fran had knocked.

The door swung open almost immediately.

'Wolfe and Sarjeant?' barked the little old man standing before them, white hair standing up in a fringe round a shiny pate. A huge moustache concealed his mouth, and wire rimmed glasses perched on the end of his nose.

'Yes,' said Fran. 'I'm Fran Wolfe -'

'And I'm Libby Sarjeant.'

'Come in, then, come in. Haven't got all day.'

Chapter Twenty Three

Fred Barrett led them into a crowded sitting room and gestured towards the small dining table. They sat on uncomfortable upright chairs squeezed in between the table and an ancient sofa.

'Now,' said Barrett. 'What do you want to know?'

'What do you know about Shareen Wallis?' Libby plunged straight in.

Barrett narrowed his eyes at her. 'What do *you* know?'

Libby recounted all the information they had so far accrued.

'And now someone we know is under suspicion of her murder, we thought we'd try and find out a bit more. To help,' she concluded.

'And how do you know this person didn't do it?' asked Barrett.

'We don't, for sure,' said Fran, 'but we don't see how he could have done it.'

'Who is it?'

Fran and Libby looked at each other.

'Come on,' said Barrett. 'I can't work without all the information.'

'Colin Hardcastle,' said Libby reluctantly.

199

'Hardcastle,' mused Barrett. 'Hardcastle... No, I don't think I came across that name. Who is he?'

'He was taken to the party by someone else, who was invited by a local.'

'Names, woman! Names!'

Libby sighed. 'Emma Something invited a John Newman - they're now married - and he brought Colin with him. They both lived in Steeple Martin.'

'Ah – that's better.' Barrett thought for a moment. 'Now, when I looked into it, I did come across those two names.' He settled back in his chair. 'I'll tell you what I know. And what I thought.' He looked up at the ceiling and folded his hands across his stomach. 'The police tried to find out when exactly the Wallis girl had left the party – you know where it was, do you?'

Libby and Fran shook their heads.

'An old barn – outside the Sand Gate, it was. Think it's been pulled down now. Used to use it for those raves, the kids did. Well, that was where it was. And the police tried to get hold of everybody who'd been there. But no one knew when she'd gone. They all thought she must have been picked up by someone in a car, until someone said she'd insisted on walking and was seen on the road to Bishop's Bottom. You know where that is?'

'That's the way I came,' said Libby.

Barrett nodded. 'Well, the police got nowhere, as you obviously know.' He brooded for a long moment. 'And I thought they hadn't done their job. So I began to track everyone down.'

'And did you find all the guests?' asked Fran.

200

'Not all. But I found most of the people who had anything to do with the girl while she was there. Apparently, she was popular.'

'Because she'd been on TV?' asked Libby.

Barrett shrugged. 'Seemed so. Anyway, she had people clustering around her all night – men, of course. And I followed 'em all up.' He thought again. 'And I used to put little pieces in the paper – oh, not naming names, of course – just to jog memories. But they came to nothing. In fact, nothing made any sense. The closest I got was talking to the couple who'd seen her walking down the road afterwards. They stopped and offered her a lift, but she refused, and they got the impression she was going to meet someone.'

'It couldn't have been a guest at the party, then,' said Libby, 'or she'd have left with them.'

'Oh, no!' said Fran and Barrett together.

'Why?'

'It could have been someone she shouldn't have been with,' said Fran. 'Someone who was at the party with his wife or girlfriend.'

'Exactly, girl!' Barrett beamed at her approvingly. 'So I tried to find out if there was someone in particular who had singled her out. Or that she had singled out. And there was only one.'

'Who?' said Fran and Libby together.

Barrett scowled. 'I couldn't find out. No one knew him, apparently. And the strange thing was, he didn't seem happy about it. He tried to get away from her and she followed. They disappeared for a bit, as far as anyone could tell, and when she came back, he didn't.' He looked up at Libby. 'That could be your friend.'

'It could,' said Fran. 'He wouldn't be happy about being targeted by a girl.'

'Why?'

'He's gay,' said Libby.

Barrett kept on staring at her, a look of surprise developing on his face. 'Ah!' he said at last. 'Gay baiting.'

'Could it be? Was there much of that round here?' asked Fran.

'Come on, Fran,' said Libby. 'Remember all that stuff with Harry's friends? It was going on everywhere.'

'Worse in little places like this,' said Barrett. 'And youngsters were the worst of the lot.' He nodded wisely. 'And that girl would have seen him as a challenge.'

'Did any of the other guests disappear?' asked Fran.

'Any number of 'em. In and out all the time. Well, they would, wouldn't they?'

'So apart from that, did you find out anything else?' asked Libby.

'No. Oh, I followed up; if ever any of 'em made the paper I'd check 'em out, but there was nothing. I remember your John Newman and his Emma getting married. We still did weddings, then. You know, standard form sent out, colour of bridesmaids dresses, flowers in the bouquet, but that one we actually covered because Emma was a bit of a local celebrity.'

'She was?' Libby was surprised. 'Nobody said!'

'Met her?' asked Barrett.

'Yes, I have. What was she a celebrity for? I mean, had
202

she done something special?'

'She was a bit of a singer,' said Barrett..

'O-oh!' said Libby.

'*Was* she now!' said Fran.

Barrett smiled smugly.

'Was there bad blood between her and Shareen?' asked Libby, leaning forward over the table.

'Don't know personally,' Barrett looked disappointed, 'but it was reckoned there must have been. They both sang in local pubs, and the Wallis girl got the break.'

'We need to talk to John,' said Libby. 'Not Emma.'

'Don't reckon he'll have much to say,' said Barrett. 'Married the girl, didn't he.'

'Right.' Libby sat back. 'Is there anyone else we ought to speak to?'

'Can't think of anyone. Local yobs are all either inside or moved away. And to my mind it didn't look like that sort of crime.'

'How do you mean?' asked Fran.

'Mugging or gang rape gone wrong,' said Barrett. 'More deliberate.'

'Planned?' said Libby. 'Arranging to meet after the party?'

'Yup.' Barrett stood up. 'I reckon that's it. Let me know if you find anything out? Always bugged me, that case has.'

Libby and Fran stood up and squeezed out from behind the table.

'Who actually held the party?' asked Fran. 'It wasn't a – um – rave, was it?'

'No. Some rich kid, it was. Trying to get in with the locals, I reckoned. Now, what was his name?' He stared at his feet for a moment. 'No, can't get it. I'll give you a call if I remember. Got a number?'

Fran handed over a card with the number of the Wolfe Gallery.

'Nice little place,' said Barrett. 'Yours?'

'My husband's actually,' said Fran. 'He's an artist. Guy Wolfe.'

'Yes, I know, I covered the opening. Don't remember you, though.'

'We weren't married then.'

'Ah. Live there?'

'Just along Harbour Street.'

Barrett raised his eyebrows. 'Very nice. I liked living in Nethergate.'

'Oh, you haven't always lived here, then?' said Libby.

'No.' Barrett avoided her eyes.

'Came here to follow up his pet case,' said Libby, as they walked away from Barrett's house.

'Sounds like it,' said Fran. 'So what do we think?'

'Despite the fact that Emma was obviously jealous, she can't have had anything to do with it,' said Libby.

'Unless she killed Shareen and got John to take the body back with him.' Fran shook her head. 'No, that won't work. Shareen was seen well after John had left – on the Bishop's Bottom road.'

'But he had a car. He could have dropped Colin and gone back,' said Libby.

'And what? Killed her? Met Emma and they both killed
204

her?'

'Oh, I don't know. And John certainly didn't come across as guilty – or even knowing much about it.'

They were silent as they made their way back to the town square, where they wandered away to look out over the little river.

'I could bear to find out about the rich kid,' said Libby.

Fran nodded. 'And why Shareen was so set on making a move on Colin, if it was Colin.'

'Do we agree with Barrett that it was gay-baiting?'

'Possible. Do you think you could ask him?'

'I don't know. It's a bit delicate, isn't it?' said Libby. 'Funny – that's what Mrs Mardle called him. Delicate.' She sighed. 'I suppose I could get him in conversation and tell him what we know about the party.'

'I wonder where this barn was,' said Fran, turning round to stare back at the Sand Gate. 'Must be somewhere near the Bishop's Bottom road.'

'Shall we go and have a look?'

'Barrett said it was pulled down.'

'Yes, but we might get an idea. Come on.'

They crossed the square and walked up to the Sand Gate, and through the little pedestrian tunnel.

'This way,' said Libby, leading the way to the access road across the ring road. 'And here we are. That way to Nethergate -'

'I know.'

'And that way inland. And that's the Bishop's Bottom road. Let's try there.'

They began to walk along the narrow road, little more

than a lane.

'What's this?' said Fran, as they came to a locked gate in a high wall.

'Can't see anything through it,' said Libby. 'Perhaps it's the back gate of something.'

'Something on the Nethergate Road?' suggested Fran. 'Although I've never noticed anything.'

'Yes, but you're always driving. You might not.' Libby turned back.

They walked back down to the ring road and took the Nethergate road.

'Don't think there's anything along here,' said Fran.

'Well, there's a little lane,' said Libby, pointing to her right. 'Look.'

'Do you think it's private?' said Fran.

'It doesn't say so. Let's see.' Libby turned right.

'All this for a pulled-down barn,' muttered Fran.

Libby grinned over her shoulder. 'But we're actually *doing* something!'

The lane was very overgrown.

'You could only just get a car down here,' said Fran.

'And that's probably the idea,' said Libby. 'Look.'

To their right the lane opened out to another gate, obviously well used, set between magnificent gateposts.

'There,' said Libby. 'Local manor.'

The gates led to a broad drive, which in turn led up to a stately Victorian manor house, much turreted and towered.

'Buildings behind,' said Fran. 'See?'

'Coach house and stables?' suggested Libby.

'And what's the betting there was a barn,' said Fran.

'Possibly with access from the Bishop's Bottom entrance,' agreed Libby. 'Or are we making bricks without straw?'

'It makes sense,' said Fran. 'Right location, and handy for Shareen's walk home – or wherever she was going.'

'What's this place called?' Libby stepped back and peered up at the gateposts. 'Can't see a name.'

'I expect we could find out,' said Fran. 'And maybe who it used to belong to.'

'This sort of place, it's probably still in the same hands,' said Libby. 'And I bet I know whose.'

They looked at each other and spoke together.

'The rich kid!'

Chapter Twenty Four

'If this does belong to the rich kid and his family, I'm surprised Barrett doesn't remember his name,' said Fran. 'This would be a local landmark.'

'He did remember,' said Libby. 'Just didn't want to tell us.'

'And that makes you wonder what else he didn't tell us,' said Fran.

'Exactly. After all, if he was researching it for that long, he told us surprisingly little, don't you think?'

'Except for the nugget about John and Emma. Perhaps that was simply because we'd already mentioned their names.'

'Now why?' Libby scowled up at the gateposts. 'Does he not want us to find out any more?'

'Maybe.'

'Do you think he's been got at?'

Fran looked amused. 'By whom? The rich kid?'

'Well, that's the obvious answer,' said Libby, 'but if so, why did he mention him at all? He could have just said he didn't remember who hosted the party.'

They turned away and began to walk back towards the Sand Gate.

'I wish we could talk to John Newman,' said Libby, when they got back to the car park. 'Seems a waste of a journey as we're already here.'

'Two things,' said Fran. 'One, you don't know his address and two, you don't know where he works.'

'Or where Emma works, come to that,' said Libby.

'What about Ted Sachs?' said Fran. 'Isn't he based here? And he was at the party, wasn't he?'

'Oh, bother,' said Libby. 'We should have asked Barrett.'

'Oh, well, might as well call it a day, then. Will you try and talk to Colin?'

'I'll try.' Libby looked doubtful. 'He might not want to talk to me. Or maybe the solicitor will have warned him not to talk about it.'

'Let me know either way,' said Fran.

'I've just thought!' said Libby, as Fran turned away to get into her car. 'Patti! She'll know who the house belongs to!'

Fran looked at her watch. 'Do you want to go over there now? She might not be home.'

'Shall I phone?'

Fran sighed. 'Go on, then.'

Patti answered her phone, sounding somewhat out of breath.

'Did I interrupt something?' asked Libby.

Patti laughed. 'I'm up a ladder in the vestry.'

'There's a sentence you don't hear every day,' said Libby. 'Look, if you're not too busy, could Fran and I pop over to have a word?'

'Of course,' said Patti, sounding surprised. 'Have you had lunch? We've got the Pensioners' Lunch here and it's very good.'

'Gee, thanks,' said Libby.

Patti laughed again. 'No, it's actually open to everyone, it just used to be called the Pensioners' Lunch and the name stuck.'

'OK. We'll be over in about ten minutes.'

'Why? Where are you?'

'Felling!' said Libby and ended the call.

The village of St Aldeberge was on the coast where the little creek that flowed out of Felling spilled out into a rocky cove. Patti's church, of the same name, stood in the centre of the village, with the vicarage to one side. Libby parked on the vicarage drive and Fran pulled in behind her.

'I wonder what Patti was doing up a ladder,' said Libby, as they made their way into the church.

'Hello!' A woman Libby recognised from previous association with Patti's congregation waved to them. 'Patti's in the vestry.'

Patti had obviously got down from her ladder and was brushing down her jeans, which sported a liberal coating of dust and cobwebs.

'A leak,' she explained. 'Up there, see?'

Sure enough, an ominous crack showed just above the old wooden bookcase, with even more ominous evidence of damp around the edges.

'What were you doing, trying to mend it yourself?' asked Fran.

'Just investigating.' Patti quirked an eyebrow. 'Which is

210

what you two are doing, I take it?'

Libby moved a pile of sheet music off a chair and sat down.

'You remember last night?'

'It was only about twelve hours ago,' said Patti, grinning.

'You know what I mean. Well, Fran and I have just been to see an old reporter in Felling who looked into the disappearance of that girl.'

'Was it useful?'

'Up to a point,' said Fran. 'And that point is, do you happen to know who owns the big Victorian manor house just outside the town? On the Nethergate road? We couldn't see a name on the gateposts.'

'It doesn't need a name,' said Patti. 'Everyone knows it.'

'We thought they might,' said Libby, 'but we don't.'

'Hawley House,' said Patti. 'It's Sir Nigel's place.'

'Sir Nigel?' repeated Fran and Libby.

'Preece. Come on!'

'Nigel Preece!' gasped Libby.

'Sir Nigel now. Hereditary baronet,' said Patti.

'And disgruntled former MP,' said Fran. 'Goodness.'

'Why did you want to know?' asked Patti.

'Well, we think the party that Colin went to where the girl disappeared was held in a barn on that property, and there's a fair chance that it was a young Nigel who hosted it. All our reporter said was a rich kid.'

'He wouldn't like that being brought up,' said Patti.

'It's only supposition on our part,' said Fran. 'And we

211

can hardly ask him.'

'That's a shame,' said Patti. 'That might give you lots of clues.'

'It might,' agreed Libby, 'but we got the impression he was hosting in order to get in with the locals. But if he was already local himself, why would he want to?'

'He'd never mixed with the locals, as far as I can tell,' said Patti. 'He did the classic thing of prep school, public school, and Oxbridge. Oxford, I think.'

'Ah,' said Fran. 'So the locals wouldn't have had much time for him.'

'Probably not. He isn't very popular now, at any rate.'

'Well, that clears that up, then,' said Libby. 'A dead end, as far as we're concerned.'

'Unless you can find someone else who was at that party,' said Patti. 'Now, lunch?'

The lunch, served and cooked by the ladies of the parish, was, as predicted, an excellent shepherd's pie.

'Almost seems an anachronism, doesn't it?' said Patti, smiling round at her parishioners. 'Scenes like this have been familiar for at least the last hundred years or so. You wouldn't think they would have survived.'

'In these days of poverty and food banks, I expect they're vital,' said Fran.

Patti nodded sadly

As Libby and Fran were leaving, she said 'Would you like me to ask around? See if anyone here remembers anything about that party or the girl? Or even Sir Nigel?'

'If you can do it without raising suspicions,' said Libby, 'it would be helpful.'

They parted on the vicarage drive, and Libby was thoughtful as she drove back to Steeple Martin. The trip had done little to convince her or otherwise of Colin's guilt, but had added a few strands to the enquiry.

Once back at home, she tried calling Colin again, but again, it went straight to voicemail. She called Ben.

'He's still with the police,' Ben told her. 'It doesn't sound good, does it?'

'No. But we learnt quite a bit down in Felling.' Libby went on to relate their findings of the morning, including Patti's information on Nigel Preece.

'He always struck me as a nasty piece of work,' said Ben. 'I wasn't surprised when he was dropped as an MP.'

'No. There was a bit of a scandal, wasn't there? A woman?'

'Yes. Can't remember the details, though. Do you think you ought to let the police know what you've found out?'

'I would have thought they would have found it out themselves,' said Libby dubiously. 'They'll say I'm interfering.'

'Mmm.' Ben was obviously thinking. 'There's always the back door.'

'Eh? What back door?'

'Edward. He might be able to see Ian at home and tell him off the record.'

'He can hardly lie in wait for him to come home,' said Libby, 'but I suppose it's worth a try.'

Edward's phone also went to voicemail, which meant he was probably working. Libby wasn't exactly sure what his duties at the university were, but left a message. After

213

which, she didn't know what to do. Recalling Fran's rather unflattering attitude to her as a working woman, she reluctantly went into the conservatory and started preparing paper for another sanitised view of Nethergate. To her surprise, she became absorbed and her phone burbling in her pocket made her jump.

'Hi, Libby,' said Edward. 'What can I do for you?'

'I'm sorry, did I disturb you at work?'

'We're officially into the long vac now, so I haven't got lectures or tutorials. I was catching up on paperwork. Just about to go home.'

'Ah. Well, this is a bit difficult.' Libby chewed her lip and stared cross-eyed at her paper.

'Are you at home?'

'Yes.'

'Shall I pop in on my way? You can give me a cup of proper tea.'

'Oh, yes!' Libby was relieved. It would be much easier to explain face-to-face.

'About forty minutes then,' said Edward. 'See you then.'

In fact it was almost an hour before Edward arrived.

'What's the problem, then?' he asked, as she poured boiling water into the brown teapot. 'Is it to do with this business of Colin's?'

'Yes. You see, Fran and I went down to Felling today, and we learnt a few things. Ben and I didn't know whether we should tell the police, but I thought they probably knew it all already, and would say I was interfering.'

'So you thought if I passed it on to Ian at home, off the

214

record, so to speak, it would help?' Edward was smiling.

Libby felt the colour rising up her neck. 'Well, yes...'

Edward laughed. 'Go on, then. Tell me all.'

Once more, Libby recounted everything she and Fran had learnt that morning. Edward, smartly dressed as usual, stretched his legs out in front of him and contrived to make the very English sitting room look exotic.

'As far as I can see, nothing you found is anything but circumstantial, but the inference that it was Nigel Preece who hosted the party is worth looking into, surely?' he said, when she'd finished.

'But the police must know that!' said Libby. 'It would have been one of the first things they looked into at the time of the girl's disappearance.'

'You would have thought so. But you said your reporter friend said he couldn't remember who it was.'

'I'm sure that was a lie,' said Libby. 'And it's only supposition, anyway. Also, I feel that telling the police about Emma being jealous of the girl would be dropping her in it.'

'If it's off the record, Ian doesn't have to do anything about it,' said Edward. 'I think it's worth me passing it all on, anyway. We often have a drink together if he comes in late, so it'll be easy enough. He says it stops him feeling guilty for having a lonely nightcap.' He took out his phone, looked at it, then put it away again. 'I was going to send him a text asking him to drop in, but then it would look too contrived. I'll just loiter.' He grinned. 'I shall feel like a proper Loony.'

Libby laughed. 'Heaven help us! But thank you,

Edward, seriously. I don't know why, but I feel sort of responsible for Colin.'

'I don't know why, either. It isn't your fault he's here, after all.'

'It's just that he didn't have any friends here, unless you could call Mrs Mardle next door a friend. And we all suspected him before he arrived. I feel a bit guilty because of that.'

'Well, he's certainly got friends now,' said Edward. 'Let's just hope the friendship isn't misplaced.'

Ben arrived not long after Edward had left, and also seemed relieved that he was going to pass on the information. 'I feel guilty about him, too,' he said. 'And I like him.'

'So do I,' said Libby. 'As Edward said, let's just hope it isn't misplaced.'

Chapter Twenty Five

There was no word from Colin. Libby and Ben contrived a scratch meal from the remnants in the fridge and settled down to watch television, finally resorting to an old DVD as nothing appealed.

'We're getting old,' Ben said with a sigh.

It was nearly half past nine when there was a knock at the door.

'Colin?' said Libby, as Ben went to answer it.

But it wasn't Colin. It was Ian, followed by an anxious-looking Edward.

'Sorry, Libby,' said Edward. 'I didn't think he'd take it like this.'

'Like what?' asked Ben, looking at Ian's furious face.

'I said he'd say I was interfering,' said Libby with a sigh. 'Come on, Ian, spit it out.'

Taken aback, Ian stopped dead in the middle of the room.

'Well?' said Ben, putting hands on hips and looking mulish. 'What have we done now?'

The look of fury faded.

'*You've* done nothing,' said Ian. 'As usual, it's the interfering Mrs Sarjeant.'

'See? I told you,' said Libby. She turned to Ian. 'I won't ask you to sit down, DCI Connell, because you're just leaving. I shall be happy to come to the incident room in the morning and report to DS Trent. Good evening.' She turned her back and went into the kitchen, leaving dead silence behind her. Desperately trying to control her breathing, she found the whisky bottle and poured herself a double. A throat was cleared behind her.

'I'm sorry, Libby.'

She didn't turn round. 'Hmph.'

'I shouldn't have said that.'

Now she did turn round. 'No, you shouldn't. As I said, you thought I was interfering. Why do you think I didn't want to tell you myself? Edward agreed to tell you off the record to deflect your – er – *reaction*, but neither of us – *none* of us – thought it would be so extreme.'

Ian sighed and looked at his feet. 'If you'll come back and sit down, I'll explain.'

Head high, Libby pushed past him into the sitting room, where she took up her normal position in the corner of the sofa.

'I'm driving,' said Ian, 'but coffee…?'

'Can I have a whisky?' asked Edward.

'You deserve it,' said Ben, and went into the kitchen. They heard him put the kettle on, and a moment later he came back with Edward's whisky. 'Coffee in a moment,' he said.

'Right,' said Ian. 'Actually, Libby, we did, as you thought, know some of what you found out, but not all.'

'Then what made you so mad? All Fran and I did was

218

go and ask some questions of a couple of other civilians. We weren't treading on anyone's toes.'

'Which civilians?' Ian said sharply.

Libby raised her eyebrows at him. 'An ex-reporter called Fred Barrett and Patti.'

'Patti?'

'Yes. Fred Barrett said the party was hosted by a rich kid whom he couldn't remember. Fran and I found the house -'

'Found the *house*?'

'We went looking for the site of the barn and found a house. We didn't know who it belonged to, so we went and asked Patti if she knew. And she did.'

'And you put two and two together.'

'That's what we usually do.'

Ian sighed again and accepted the cup of coffee Ben held out.

'We knew Nigel Preece hosted that party. That came out in the first investigation, and Preece was under suspicion for a while. His family were outraged.'

'I can imagine,' said Edward.

'And,' Ian looked Libby in the eye, 'Sir Nigel, naturally, found out that the case was under investigation again and, via various channels, warned us off.'

'Ah!' came the collective response.

'Chief Constable intervention?' said Ben.

'And the Crime Commissioner.' Ian nodded. 'Not to mention the family themselves.'

'Above the common herd, of course,' said Libby. 'And you assumed Fran and I would go and put our size fives straight in the middle of it?'

'We-ell…'

'Unlikely,' said Libby. 'What were we going to do? March up to his front door and start asking questions?'

'No. You didn't did you? But he could have got wind of you asking questions.'

'From whom? Barrett? Who, presumably, has also been warned off. He was definitely lying when he said he couldn't remember who the "rich kid" was.'

'Yes.' Ian took a thoughtful sip of coffee. 'What was his other information?'

Libby repeated it.

'And we assumed that the man the singer was making a play for was Colin. No proof, of course.'

'It was. He told us all about it today.'

'Why was he with you for such a long time?' asked Libby. 'I couldn't get hold of him all day.'

'I'm afraid we had his phone,' said Ian. 'We saw your calls coming in.'

'Oh!' Libby looked indignant.

'Look, we had reasonable grounds for suspicion, you must admit that. So we had to question him. Luckily, Ben had provided a solicitor -' Ian gave Ben a wry look, 'and he quite understood. He's told us quite a lot more about the evening, and his reasons for leaving the area.'

'What were they?'

'I can't tell you that. He'll tell you if he wants to. But we've now let him go – with a warning not to leave the area.'

'So he's not under suspicion anymore?' said Edward.

'Not immediate suspicion, no.'

'Has he got his phone back?' asked Ben, taking his own out of his pocket.

'Yes, and he's back at the pub. But leave it until I've gone, will you?'

Ben nodded and put the phone away.

'Now what other information did you say you had?' Ian asked Libby.

Reluctantly, Libby told him about Emma and the possible jealousy between her and Shareen Wallis.

'I don't think it amounts to a row of beans, though. Shareen would hardly have agreed to meet her on the way home, would she?'

'And you think that's what happened? She arranged to meet someone?'

'That's what it looked like from the original investigation,' said Libby. 'Someone who had been at the party with a girlfriend, so couldn't openly leave with her.'

Edward was frowning. 'Admittedly, I don't know all the ins and outs,' he said, 'but if this girl was becoming well known as a TV personality, why would she be bothered meeting some local nonentity on the quiet?'

The answer struck them all at the same time. *Preece*. Ian sighed.

'Exactly. So you see why we need to keep this quiet.'

'But if it seems obvious to us now, and we're not even in the thick of it,' said Ben, 'why didn't it originally?'

'I told you – it did. He was investigated, and his alibi checked out.'

'What was the alibi?' asked Libby, frowning.

'Various partygoers who swore they were with him all the time.'

'Dubious,' said Edward.

'Quite. But after twenty years, how are we going to break them?'

'Do you know who they are?' asked Libby.

'A few. But I think we might ask your friend John Newman if he knows any of them.'

'He didn't live there, then, though, did he?' said Libby.

'His wife did.'

'Oh, hell!' said Libby miserably.

'We won't say where the information came from,' said Ian, 'we never do. Anyway, it came from the reporter Barrett, didn't it?'

'So, to sum up,' said Ben, 'the reason you were so mad was because you thought Libby and Fran might have stirred up Sir Nigel Preece.'

Ian had the grace to look slightly ashamed. 'I've said I was wrong. But, Libby, do you think you could bear to go in and give a formal statement tomorrow?'

'Won't DS Trent think it's all unsubstantiated and irrelevant?' said Libby with a grin.

'No, she won't.' Ian grinned back.

'And does this mean you think he's the man you want?' asked Edward.

'Not necessarily,' said Ian. 'Just worth looking at.'

'I know who else you could ask!' said Libby suddenly. 'Ted Sachs, the builder. He was there.'

'Good idea.' Ian nodded. 'If we can pin him down – he's rather elusive.'

222

'He was,' said Ben, 'but that was because you were suspicious of him giving Fiona Darling the keys. You're not looking into that, now, are you?'

'Who says we aren't?' said Ian, with another grin, and stood up. 'Time I left you in peace, once again, with apologies. Come on, Edward, let's go and have a drink at home.'

Libby got up and gave Edward a kiss. 'Thank you,' she said.

Ian put a tentative arm round her shoulders. 'Sorry,' he said.

'Is it too late to report to Fran?' asked Libby, when they'd gone.

'Yes,' said Ben firmly. 'You can have another whisky and then we're going to bed.' He took her glass into the kitchen and reappeared with a refill. 'You quite scared me, you know.'

'Scared you?'

'When you told Ian where to get off.'

'I scared myself,' said Libby. 'I was thinking we might never see him again.'

The following morning, before going to the incident room, Libby called Fran and reported.

'I wish I'd been a fly on the wall,' said Fran, laughing. 'To see the great DCI Connell humbled.'

'He wasn't very humble. Anyway, I've to go and make a formal report.'

'Do you think I should come, too?'

'Ian didn't say so.'

'Can't hurt, though, can it?' said Fran. 'I'll come.'

'Is Guy all right with you taking this much time off?'

'He's quite interested, and we aren't very busy at the moment. It'll be different when the schools break up.'

It was late morning when Fran and Libby entered the incident room, which seemed a lot busier than the last time Libby had been there. Rachel Trent saw them and came over, smiling broadly.

'We've been expecting you,' she said, 'but I didn't realise you were both coming.'

'We thought it best,' said Fran, neutrally.

It didn't take very long. When they'd both finished, Rachel sat back and looked them both curiously.

'You do seem to have a way with you,' she said. 'How do you do it?'

'Do what?'

'Find things out?'

'A mixture of nosiness and contacts,' said Fran.

'Nothing to do with your – er – abilities?'

Nothing at all,' said Fran firmly. 'We know Jane Baker at the *Nethergate Mercury*, and a lot of friends in the area.'

'Like the local vicars,' said Rachel.

'Vicars hear a lot of what goes on,' said Libby.

Rachel nodded. 'The one here knew Ossie Whitelaw.'

'The Reverend Cole,' said Fran. 'Yes.'

'So what are you going to do next?' asked Rachel.

They both looked surprised.

'Next?' said Libby.

'I just wondered if you were going to find anything else out for us.'

'We wouldn't dare,' said Libby. 'Your DCI would be

most unhappy.'

'Oh, I don't know,' said Rachel, with a sly smile.

'But,' said Libby, as they left the church hall, 'what *are* we going to do next?'

Fran looked at her watch. 'Lunch time. Let's go and see Hal.'

There were already lunchtime customers in the Pink Geranium, and Libby was surprised to see Donna standing behind the counter.

'What have you done with the baby?' she asked.

'Not exactly a baby any more,' said Donna, 'but she's at playgroup, here in the village.'

'Oh!' said Fran in surprise. 'Have you moved already?'

'No, but I had to take the place while it was available. We're acclimatising.' She beamed. 'I love it here. Are you eating?'

'Yes, please,' said Libby. 'Just soup and bread for me.'

'And me,' said Fran. 'Where can we sit?'

'Window table,' said Donna. 'I expect Harry will join you when he can.'

'Actually,' said Libby, when they were seated, 'That reminds me. I said to Ian last night they weren't investigating Ossie's death anymore, but he said they were. Which of course, they would be, it's just got a bit sidelined, I suppose.'

'They'll be trying to tie the two murders together,' said Fran. 'I'm glad it's not me.'

Donna arrived with two bowls of soup and a basket of fresh bread on a tray.

'Oh, I meant to tell you,' she said. 'Yesterday I popped

in to introduce myself to that friend of yours.'

'Oh, yes?' said Libby. 'She's not exactly a friend – just an acquaintance.'

'Well we've met. Actually, it was a bit awkward, so I said I'd come back another time.'

'Awkward? How?' asked Fran.

'She had someone with her. Looked a bit like that black detective on the TV.'

'Not our friend Edward?'

'Oh, no. Not as nice-looking. No, apparently he used to live in her house.'

'Whitelaw!' gasped Libby.

Chapter Twenty Six

'But I thought she told you she didn't know him?' said Fran.

'She did.' Libby frowned. 'I suppose he could have come down to see her because she found the body. Would make sense, wouldn't it?'

Donna looked from one to the other. 'Is this to do with your murders?'

'Um, sort of,' said Libby. 'If it is Mr Whitelaw, he's the father of the first body, the one Fiona Darling found at the Garden Hotel.'

'Oh, well, there's no mystery, is there?' said Donna. 'He'd naturally want to find out all he could.'

'About what?' Harry came up to the table.

Donna told him, and took herself off.

'And naturally, you two think there is a mystery.' Harry sat down.

'Well, no. It's like Donna said,' said Libby.

'Exactly. No need to rush off to the police with it.'

'No.' Fran took a mouthful of soup. 'Nice. What is it?'

Harry shook his head at her. 'Fancy not recognising vegetable soup.'

'It's just different,' said Fran.

'OK – fill me in with all the goss.' Harry sat back in his chair. 'I hear you've been up to your tricks again.'

'We were only trying to look into things,' said Libby.

'Surprise, surprise. So what did you find out?'

Once more, they repeated the events of yesterday between them.

'And the police know all this?'

'We've done an official report,' said Libby. 'And been warned off Sir Nigel Preece.'

'I'm not surprised,' said Harry. 'A nasty piece of work, so I've heard.'

'Yes.' Fran nodded. 'All the same, I don't see how he could have killed the singer and got her body here.'

'Got someone else to do it?' suggested Harry.

'Maybe. It's all very confused,' said Libby. 'We've no way of knowing who he knew well enough. We don't know anyone who was at that party except Colin, John, and Emma.'

'We're just going over old ground,' said Fran. 'Much as I hate to say it, I think we ought to give it a rest.'

'I think you're right,' said Harry. 'It's a complicated case and the police have many more resources than you have.'

They finished their lunch, said goodbye to Donna, and walked slowly back to Allhallow's Lane, where Fran had left her car. As they passed the vicarage, Beth appeared at the door.

'Hey! Guess who came to see me yesterday?'

Fran and Libby stopped.

'Ossie's dad?' said Libby.

'Yes! How did you know?'

'Lucky guess!' said Fran.

'Got a minute? I'll tell you all about it.'

They followed Beth into her kitchen and sat down at the table.

'We guessed because he also went to see Fiona Darling,' said Libby. 'What did he say?'

'He wanted to know what I'd told the police.' Beth frowned. 'I thought he would want to know how well I knew Ossie and what I thought of him, but he only asked what Ossie had told me, and if I'd told everything to the police.'

'You couldn't very well tell him Ossie felt his dad didn't understand him,' said Fran.

'No, I rather glossed over it. I told him I liked Ossie. I also told him the school hadn't been right for him.'

'Oh, I bet he didn't like that!' Libby said.

'No, he did poker up a bit at that. But I couldn't tell him anything else. He just said he wanted to find out as much as he could and would talk to someone else.'

'That would be Fiona,' said Fran. 'I wonder why he didn't go to her first?'

'Perhaps she was out. But he did go and see her. Not that she could tell him any more – even less, probably.' Libby was puzzled. 'Unless there was some other connection.'

'Ted Sachs,' said Fran. 'He did work for the Whitelaws, didn't he? They recommended him to the Darlings.'

'I do wish he wouldn't keep cropping up,' said Libby testily. 'He's too tempting.'

229

'Tempting? What do you mean?' asked Beth.

'As a villain,' explained Libby. 'See – he gave Fiona the keys. He'd been asked by Colin to do the renovations to the Garden. He turns out to have been at the party where the girl singer disappeared – who turned out to be the other body.'

'But it's all quite logical,' said Fran. 'He lived in Felling, where Emma lived, and was one of the crowd at the party. It looks as though half the young people in the town were there. Then, he worked for a builder in the town who did some work for John and Emma, so when Colin asked John if he could recommend someone to do the work, John recommended Ted, who had recently set up on his own. He'd already done work for the Whitelaws, who recommended him to the Darlings. Then he got a bit too close to Fiona and there you are!'

'It does seem logical,' said Beth. 'And you know what it's like in a village – or a small area – you could probably trace connections with dozens of people one way or another.'

Libby sighed. 'I guess you're right. I'm making bricks without straw, as usual.'

'Did you know the origin of that saying?' said Beth. 'Apropos of nothing.'

'Go on, then,' said Libby. 'The bible, I suppose.'

'Actually, yes! Exodus 5 – Pharaoh telling the Israelites off. Tells them to go and gather the straw themselves.'

'Perhaps that's we should do,' said Fran. 'Tell the police to gather their own straw.'

'I think they already do,' said Libby. 'With no help

230

from us.'

They left Beth and carried on down the lane. As they reached the door of number seventeen, Mrs Mardle put her head round her door.

'Have you heard from Colin today, dear?' she said. 'I don't like to bother him.'

Libby smiled. 'I'll try him now. I'd like to make sure he's all right, too.'

This time, she got through.

'I'm sorry I didn't get your calls yesterday,' he said in a subdued voice.

'It's all right, Ian explained. But Mrs Mardle and I both wanted to know if you were all right.'

'Yes.' Colin didn't sound sure.

'Do you want to talk?'

'Are you at home?'

'Yes. Fran's here, too. Come round. I'll make tea.'

She switched off the phone. 'He's fine,' she told Mrs Mardle. 'He's coming round for a cup of tea. Would you -?'

'No, that's all right, dear. Just ask him to give me a knock on the way past. Thank you.' She withdrew and closed the door.

'You will stay?' Libby said to Fran as she opened the door.

'Yes, of course.' Fran sighed. 'Seems we can't give it a rest after all.'

Colin arrived just as Libby was filling the brown teapot.

'Do you know what's happened?' he asked, slumping in to the armchair. Fran sat beside Libby on the sofa.

'We know the police had you in for questioning and took your phone from you,' said Libby. 'Ian told me last night and said you were back at the pub. Fran and I had to go to incident room this morning to make a report.'

'What about? Me?'

'No. About what we were doing in Felling yesterday.'

'Really?'

'Yes.' Fran smiled. 'And it turned out you'd given the police almost the same information we had.'

'Oh?' Colin accepted a large mug of tea. 'Do you mind telling me...'

So they did.

'That was me,' said Colin miserably, when they reached the part about the singer making a play for an unnamed guest.

'We thought it must be,' said Fran. 'Was she – unpleasant?'

Colin winced. 'Very.'

'Just her?' asked Libby gently.

'How did you guess?' Colin tried a shaky smile.

'Something Fed Barrett said. About gay baiting.'

Yes.' Colin sighed. 'Her, and a group of the boys – men. Trying to force me to – to – well -'

'No need to explain,' said Fran. 'But they left you alone in the end?'

'Only because one of them told the others to clear off, and then tried it on me himself.' He shuddered.

'Did you tell the police all this?'

'Yes. I think they thought it gave me even more of a motive.'

'Did you have any names?' asked Fran.

Colin shook his head. 'I only knew John. I didn't even really know Emma, then.'

'John said Ted Sachs was there. Didn't you recognise him the other day when you met him?' said Libby.

'No, but I don't suppose I would. It was twenty years ago and we were all much younger. We're middle-aged now.'

'Golly, what does that make us?' muttered Libby.

'What about Sir Nigel?' asked Fran.

'Sir Nigel?' Colin frowned. 'Sir Nigel Preece? What's he got to do with it?'

They didn't tell him, thought Libby. To try and trip him up?

'We think he might have been at the party,' she said non-committally.

'Wasn't he a local MP at one time?' said Colin.

'Until he got the sack,' said Fran.

'I wouldn't have known who he was, anyway.' Colin finished his tea. 'What else did you find out?'

Libby told him about the couple who had met Shareen on the Bishop's Bottom Road.

'And that Emma was jealous of Shareen,' said Fran. Libby scowled at her, but Colin gave a short laugh.

'Yes, that was very obvious! Whenever she was in our vicinity, you should have seen Emma's face! I don't know why she was worried, John was obviously besotted with her. Emma, I mean.'

'Because Emma was a singer too,' said Libby.

'Was she? I didn't know that!'

'They both sang in pubs, and Shareen was picked up for the TV and Emma wasn't.'

'Oh, I see.'

So that was it, was it?' asked Fran. 'You kept out of the way after... after...'

'Yes. I went outside, and eventually got hold of John and asked if we could go. He didn't want to, because of Emma, but I said he could always go back – oh!'

The three of them looked at each other in shock.

'But I'm sure he didn't,' said Colin. 'Anyway, if he had, he would have gone straight to Emma, wouldn't he?'

'And,' said Libby slowly, 'I don't think the timing fits. What time did he drop you home?'

'Early, as far as parties go. Somewhere between eleven and half past, I think.'

'So if he'd gone back he wouldn't have got there until just before twelve?'

'I suppose so.'

'Oh.' Libby thought for a moment. 'I suppose he would have had time, if she didn't leave until then...'

'John wouldn't have killed anyone!'

Libby and Fran didn't say they'd heard that before, but they both thought it.

'I'm sure he didn't,' said Libby in a robust voice, 'and I'm sure you didn't either. But was the – let's say attack – on you the reason you left the area?'

Colin looked uncomfortable, but nodded. 'It was vicious. The things they said. And did. I decided that if that was what people were like in the sticks, I was going. Oh, I'm sorry, I didn't mean...'

234

'It's all right,' said Fran, amused. 'We are a bit out in the sticks. Certainly Felling is. And things are a bit better these days.'

'Oh, yes.' Colin smiled. 'I never gave Steeple Martin a real chance, did I?'

'Well, you can now,' said Libby. 'Was that all you told them?'

'There wasn't any more to tell.' He sighed. 'They just said not to leave the area.'

'Oh, that's standard,' said Libby blithely. 'Don't worry about it. Oh, and Mrs Mardle said would you give her a knock on your way past, just to let her know you're all right.'

'OK.' Colin stood up. 'I won't take up any more of your time. Will you let me know if you hear anything else?'

Libby let him out and came back to the sofa.

'You know, I'm sure he didn't do it,' she said.

Fran nodded. 'But who on earth did?'

Chapter Twenty Seven

After Fran had gone, Libby decided to do some research on Sir Nigel Preece. She was very vague about the details of his life and career, and thought it might bear looking into. Although, she acknowledged to herself, the police would know all about it, and what bearing it had on the case she had no idea.

The internet threw up many pages of information, through which she dutifully ploughed, but apart from some would-be sensational headlines in the news from several years ago, learnt very little. He was unmarried, had stood for parliament and been selected, and following a much publicised affair with a married celebrity, had resigned, not, as rumour would have it, been sacked. After all, thought Libby, MPs had survived that sort of thing many times before. Some of his public comments were in very dubious taste, and revealed a distinctly elitist, arrogant, and patronising turn of mind. Libby suspected him of being both homophobic and racist, and decided he typified the public perception of the privileged upper classes.

She found few mentions of Felling, mostly concerning his father, Sir Reginald Preece, the heir to the family fortune, which stemmed from an engineering Preece in the nineteenth century, who had built Hawley House, named, apparently for his wife's family, the influential Hawleys, who appeared to have a finger in every local pie imaginable.

Fascinating though all this was, she resisted falling down the rabbit hole of internet research, and turned instead to Ted Sachs, who appeared to have nothing more than a very basic web page advertising his building services. Hardcastle Holdings, however, had a professional and bland website which gave very little away. Libby wondered about Colin's assistant – what had John said her name was? Carina? Colin had never mentioned her, which was odd, come to think of it.

She checked her watch to see if Fran would have had time to get back to Nethergate, decided she had, and called.

'I've only just left you! What's the matter?'

'I was just doing some internet research,' said Libby. 'Mainly on Nigel Preece.' She gave Fran the details. 'Then I looked up Ted Sachs – nothing – and finally Hardcastle Holdings. And it struck me – why hasn't Colin been in touch with them since he's been here? And he's never mentioned his assistant. I told you about her, didn't I? John Newman said she was called Carina.'

'No reason he should mention her,' said Fran. 'And we don't know he hasn't been in touch. He doesn't have to tell us who he's called when he isn't with us. He could be giving them hourly updates for all we know.'

'The police would know,' said Libby. 'They had his phone for the best part of Thursday.'

'Don't you go asking them!' warned Fran.

'Can I ask Colin?'

Fran sighed. 'If you like. Oh, and Guy wanted to know if you'd like to come down here for dinner tomorrow? And stay, obviously.'

'We'd love to. Any special reason?'

'Don't think so. Except, as I told you, he does seem very interested in this business.' Libby could almost hear the frown in her voice. 'I might ask him.'

Libby and Ben spent Friday night quietly at home, undisturbed by either phone calls or visits from anyone. On Saturday, Libby made another trip into Canterbury for her weekly shop, feeling slightly guilty as she did so for not patronising the village shops. But, she argued with herself, they don't stock everything I need.

To assuage her conscience, when she got home she went immediately to Nella's nursery shop for fresh vegetables and to Bob the butcher for pork chops.

'How's the investigation going?' asked Bob, as he wrapped her purchase in brown paper.

'Investigation?' said Libby innocently. 'Oh, the bodies at the Garden. I don't know.'

'Come off it, Libby. We know you've been over to the incident room, and you've taken that Colin Hardcastle under your wing.'

'Well, yes, but that's all. We – I – aren't involved.'

'Pull the other one!' said Bob. 'But we were wondering about the panto. That Dame Amanda's bringing hers over, isn't she?'

'Yes.' Libby looked nervous. 'Are you – I mean – don't you approve?'

238

Bob laughed. 'Oh, yes! We get a year off, don't we? Except for the techies, of course.'

'She'll obviously need those – you can't do panto without lighting and sound, or backstage crew. She's been in touch about that. You volunteering?'

'No fear! We all need a year off to refresh ourselves.'

'Have we been getting stale, then, do you think?'

'There's always a danger, isn't there?' said Bob. 'There you go. Enjoy.'

Another thing to worry about, thought Libby as she walked home. Had she taken her position as panto writer and director for granted? Was the Oast Theatre Company glad to see the back of her?

The weather was fine enough for the dining table in Fran and Guy's back yard to be put to use that evening. Balzac the cat eyed them balefully from a perch on the wall, obviously annoyed at having his retreat invaded.

'What's up, Libby?' asked Guy, as he poured wine. 'You don't seem your usual cheerful self.'

'She's decided that the theatre hates her,' said Ben.

'What?' Fran emerged from the kitchen with plates.

'Oh, it isn't as bad as that,' said Libby, squirming a little. 'I just think they might all be fed up with me throwing my weight around. They're all glad to be having a rest this season, so Bob tells me. They feel they might be stale. I think he meant me.'

'I doubt if they'd all come back each year, if that were the case,' said Guy.

'Exactly,' said Ben. 'I tried to tell her, but she won't listen to me.'

239

Fran looked at her friend with amusement. 'She can't get any further with the Garden Hotel case, so she's had to find something else to worry about.'

Everyone but Libby laughed.

'I know you all think I'm being silly,' she said, 'but I think I'm right.'

'Speaking of the case,' said Fran, indicating that they should help themselves to her version of paella, 'Guy has something to tell you.'

'Guy?' said Libby and Ben together.

'I don't know that it's any help, though,' said Guy, not looking at them.

'Why didn't you say anything before?' asked Libby.

'You'll see when I tell you.' Guy looked up. 'I think Fran said that Fred Barrett told you he came to cover our opening at the gallery?'

'Yes.'

'Well, we got chatting, as you do, and he asked me if I remembered the Shareen Wallis case. It was fairly recent back then. He was obviously – well, I suppose obsessed wouldn't be too strong a word. And he said he was sure Nigel Preece had something to do with it.'

'Really?' Libby asked with her fork half way to her mouth.

'That's why I hadn't said anything before, because his name hadn't come up in the current investigation, as far as I knew.'

'It hadn't, until we saw Barrett, who didn't mention it as such. We got it from Patti,' said Fran.

'Yes.' Guy looked uncomfortable. 'But I remembered it

because I'd had a run-in with Preece myself.'

There were various expressions of astonishment all round the table.

'How come?' asked Ben.

'He approached me to do a portrait of him. I refused.'

'On moral grounds?' asked Libby.

Guy smiled. 'I suppose you could call it that. And he took it rather badly. Threatened to blacken my reputation, in fact.'

'Just for refusing the portrait? But how could he do that?' said Ben.

'Well...' Guy took a deep breath, 'he also propositioned me.'

This time there was an astonished silence.

'And then he came up with some theory that I was a copyist. Claimed to have proof that I'd been painting fakes.'

'What?' Libby was aghast.

'Oh, it all blew over – he was all bluster, and if he had any proof it would have been manufactured, and to be honest, I didn't think he had the sort of criminal friends capable of that. But it left a nasty taste in my mouth. So when Barrett mentioned his name, I was quite ready to believe it. But, as I said, his name hadn't come up this time, so I didn't mention it.'

'And now it has.' Libby glowered at her plate. 'What a piece of shit.'

'Preece, not the paella, I hope,' said Fran.

That broke the tension and they all laughed.

'So he propositioned you?' said Ben. 'He's gay?'

241

'Certainly got leanings. I got the impression that he'd take it where he could find it,' said Guy.

'So he could be the one who was meeting Shareen,' said Libby.

'But how would he have got her to Steeple Martin? Or have known about the cellar at the Garden?' asked Fran.

'Oh, heavens, I don't know,' said Libby. 'I think I just want him to be guilty.'

Later, as she and Fran sat alone at the table while the men cleared up in the kitchen, she said, 'The trouble is, even if Preece had some involvement in Shareen's death, he couldn't have had anything to do with Ossie.'

'It's difficult to see how anyone could have had something to do with both of them,' said Fran. 'Unless it's someone we haven't heard about.'

'And that's always a possibility,' said Libby gloomily. 'I mean, there's all the people at the party we don't know. And what about someone connected with Shareen at the time? You know, in her career or something.'

'Or jealousy,' suggested Fran. 'Not Emma, she wouldn't have been able to do it, as we said. But there could have been others who were jealous, or whose career Shareen had wrecked.'

'She wasn't influential enough, surely?' said Libby. 'But I suppose she could be – oh, I don't know – using underhand methods to climb the ladder. Blackmail, even. We just don't know.'

'So that's the next research project, is it?' asked Fran.

'Can't hurt,' said Libby. 'Shall I fetch the laptop?'

'Not now,' said Fran. 'We'll have a quick look in the
242

morning.'

After breakfast on Sunday morning, Guy left them to open the gallery/shop, Ben went for a stroll along the sea wall and Libby and Fran sat down with the laptop.

'There isn't a lot,' said Fran, 'and most of it's to do with her disappearance.'

'Look, though – it says here she'd been signed up by some management company.'

'Yes, they've got some famous clients. Well, they were famous then.'

'Nothing much else, though, is there?' Libby scrolled through the information. 'Except some news reports about her body being found.'

'Speculation that it was a kidnapping for money, here,' said Fran, clicking on a link. 'Unsubstantiated, though.'

'Right,' said Libby. 'Who else can we look up?'

'The Darlings?' suggested Fran.

'Oh, yes, what's his name? Fiona's husband?'

'Can't remember. But what about the Whitelaws? Whitelaw Senior went to see Beth and Fiona the other day, didn't he?'

'Oh, good idea.' Libby hunched over the laptop again. After a moment she sat back, disappointed. 'Nothing. Except odd bits where the name comes up in some other context.

'Wait a minute, though,' said Fran, taking over the screen. 'Look. Nicholas Whitelaw, member of the campaigning team.' She looked up at Libby, shock on her face. 'For Nigel Preece.'

Chapter Twenty Eight

'What?' Libby grabbed the laptop. 'He supported Nigel Preece! When?'

'When he campaigned to be an MP, of course.'

'Blimey!' Libby sat back. 'He's got branches everywhere!'

'Tentacles, rather,' corrected Fran.

'But Whitelaw's got nothing to with anything!'

'Except as a victim's father.'

'Oh, yes.' Libby subsided.

'Come on, then,' said Fran. 'Nothing more we can do now, and I'd better get to the shop to help Guy.'

'And we'd better get home to get ready for Hetty's lunch,' said Libby.

'So what did you find out?' asked Ben, once they were in the car on the way home.

Libby told him. 'And do you know,' she said, 'I was thinking.'

'Oh, dear,' said Ben.

'No, listen. There was one link when we looked for Shareen that suggested she had been kidnapped for ransom.'

'No note, though,' said Ben.

'Yes, but just suppose she was taken, rather than killed, and then killed later. Her body could have been put in the cellar at any time. It didn't have to be that same night.'

'You've got a point there,' said Ben, much struck. 'Surely the police must have thought of that!'

'But she'd have to have been kept somewhere.' Libby stared out of the window. 'But where? Felling or Steeple Martin? Or somewhere in between?'

'As I said, the police must have thought of that, and they would have looked into that. In fact,' said Ben, 'they would have searched all over the place for her – not knowing she'd been brought back to Steeple Martin.'

'Oh, yes.' Libby sighed. 'Oh, well. As Fran said, nothing more we can do now.'

Ben dropped Libby in Allhallow's Lane before taking his car back to the brewery. She contemplated ringing Fran with her new theory, but decided against it, telling herself that it would look like obsessing over the subject.

Before they went up to the Manor for lunch, she wondered aloud if Ian would be there.

'Shouldn't think so. It'll be all hands on deck now, what with two bodies to investigate. And try and stay off the subject, eh?'

Sure enough, when they arrived in the Manor kitchen, Hetty was there alone.

'No Flo and Lenny?' said Ben, kissing his mother.

'They'll be along. And Edward,' said Hetty gruffly.

'I think you've got an adopted brother, Ben,' said Libby, with a grin.

'I like him,' said Hetty, turning away to her Aga.

245

'So do we, Mum,' said Ben. 'Oh – and here he is!'

The kitchen door opened to reveal Ian. Three people stared at him in surprise.

'It's all right, Hetty,' he said, 'I haven't come to gatecrash.'

'Welcome to stay,' said Hetty, who always cooked enough to feed the whole village.

'No, I've got to get back to the incident room, thanks all the same. I just wanted to catch up with Libby and Ben.'

Libby squinted at him. 'Oh, yes?'

'Yes.' Ian's dark brows quirked upwards. 'May I sit down?'

'Yes – and a glass of wine while you're here?' asked Ben. 'Might as well be comfortable.'

'We-ell,' said Ian, and sat down.

Ben went to fetch wine and Libby sat down opposite Ian.

'Go on, then,' she said.

'I wanted to know if you'd found out anything else since we last spoke.'

Libby gasped, and Ben stopped dead in the doorway.

'All right, don't look at me as if I'd grown two heads,' said Ian. 'It was simply that while we were having a conference down there,' he jerked his head in the direction of the village, 'both DS Trent and DI Maiden gave their opinion that you and Fran often thought of things that we – the police – didn't. Often irrelevant,' he added, frowning, 'but sometimes useful.'

Libby was smiling. 'I never thought I'd hear that'

'I never thought I'd say it,' said Ian, raising his glass.

'Cheers.'

Libby put her head on one side and thought.

'Well, there were a couple of things. One of them isn't mine to tell, so I suggest you ask Guy.'

'*Guy*?'

'Yes. He hadn't mentioned it before because – oh, well, he'll tell you. But don't bully him!'

'Bully - ?' Ian's eyes positively bulged.

'Anyway, the other thing was that Ossie Whitelaw's dad was part of Nigel Preece's campaign team when he wanted to be an MP.'

'I don't see what that has to do with anything,' said Ian.

'No, neither do I. But Mr Whitelaw called in to see both Beth Cole and Fiona Darling the other day.'

'What?'

'Yes. Donna saw him at Fiona's – you know, Donna at the caff – and Beth told Fran and me. He wanted to know what she'd told the police, which seemed odd. And she told him the school had been very bad for Ossie. He didn't like that.'

'You see?' Ian sat back in his chair. 'You do come up with little nuggets. We probably wouldn't have found that out.'

'In that case, can you tell me something?' asked Libby.

'What?' said Ian cautiously.

'Was kidnap considered when Shareen disappeared? And did the police search reveal anywhere she might have been kept – or killed?'

'So you've got on to that,' said Ian. 'How?'

'Just thinking about it. Her body didn't have to have been taken to the cellar the night she died, did it?'

Ian sighed. 'No. It was considered, of course, at the time, because there was a possibility she was still alive, but the search revealed nothing. They went over all the suspects' homes, including Nigel Preece, whose father was extremely annoyed about it, and every likely and unlikely place anywhere in the area. And there was never any ransom note, of course.'

'No.' Libby looked down into her glass. 'And her management? Her career? That would have been looked into, wouldn't it?'

'Yes, Libby.' Ian smiled and patted he hand. 'The police do think of some things by themselves.'

Edward arrived as Ian was leaving, and after being supplied with wine and explaining that he'd come by taxi, placed his own offering on the table.

'This makes me feel like being part of a family again,' he said, flashing his white smile round the table. 'Now fill me in on where we are with the case.'

Libby and Ben gave him as many details as they could before Flo and Lenny arrived and Hetty brought out a large pork joint.

Libby duly obeyed instructions, and the subject of Colin and the murders wasn't referred to again. However, after lunch and clearing up, Libby, Ben, and Edward made their way down the Manor drive to make the weekly call on Peter and Harry, and, inevitably, it was the subject under discussion once more. When they had been brought up to date, Peter said, 'So there really isn't any more you can do?'

'No…' said Libby.

'Except that she'll try,' said Ben.

'How about,' said Harry, from his usual seat on the sofa, feet on Peter's lap, 'you and I go and see Fiona?'

'Eh?' said Libby and Ben together, while Peter simply rolled his eyes and Edward looked amused.

'Well, you remember when we did a bit of prospecting together before?' said Harry. 'I can keep you under control.'

'And what will your excuse be?' asked Peter.

'That's up to Libby,' said Harry.

'I can't think,' said Libby. 'I wanted to go and ask her about Ossie's dad, but I can't think why I should. I mean, I know why I want to know, but I don't know of a reasonable excuse to give Fiona.'

'There isn't one,' said Ben. 'I think you should just leave it alone. We've given the police – well, Ian, anyway – all the information we have, and I really can't see any little nook or cranny you can start prising open.'

'Pity,' said Harry. 'I quite enjoy getting involved when I can.'

'You tell me to leave things alone as much as the others,' said Libby.

'When I see the need, yes,' said Harry, 'but to be honest, I like Colin and I think he's getting a raw deal.'

'And there's the homophobic element in the past,' said Peter thoughtfully. 'But Fiona didn't have anything to do with that.'

'You've all got more experience in these things than I

have,' said Edward, 'but I can't see that anyone involved now had anything to do with the case in the past. The only people who might are your friends John and Emma, and Ted Sachs, of course.'

'None of which have any reason to bump off either the singer or young Ossie,' said Peter. 'I'd leave it alone, if I were you.'

'All we've done,' Libby said to Ben as they walked home, 'is go over and over the same ground. I think I'll have to give it up.'

Ben laughed. 'If I've heard that once…'

'I know. You've heard it a dozen times.' Libby sighed. 'So what else can I get interested in?'

'Me,' said Ben.

Monday morning saw Libby in the conservatory eyeing her newly stretched paper and several pieces of driftwood which Guy had tried to persuade her to use for some "quirky" sea studies. 'The sort of thing the tourists love,' he had said. 'Give it a go.'

The phone provided a welcome reason to abandon both paper and driftwood.

'It's me,' said Fran. 'I've just had Fred Barrett on the phone.'

Libby experienced a jolt in her solar plexus. 'What did he want?'

'He's blaming us for, as he put it, setting the police on to him.'

'I suppose that was inevitable. They were bound to talk to him after what we told them.'

'Yes, but what was worse was that apparently, they've
250

also been on to Nigel Preece.'

'Why worse?'

'Because he didn't mention Preece to us, but Preece thinks he did.'

'But Preece came up in the original investigation. They were bound to get to him eventually in this one. They'll talk to all the witnesses from that time. And we know they'd spoken to him because Ian told us the police had been warned off.'

'He doesn't see it that way, seemingly. So Barrett told him about us.'

'Oh. That doesn't sound good.'

'No. I got the feeling that Barrett had somehow been got at by Preece to keep quiet about him.'

'During Barrett's private investigation, perhaps?'

'Must have been. Remember what Guy said? He isn't above using dirty methods to get his own way.'

'Oh, golly!' said Libby. 'Does this mean he's going to try using dirty methods on us?'

'Actually, I don't see why he should,' said Fran. 'The damage has been done now. Why bother?'

'Yes, but why did he bother to try and blacken Guy's name? Simply revenge. He might take revenge on us.'

They were both silent for a moment.

'Do you think -' they both began.

'You first,' said Libby.

'I was going to say, should we tell the police.'

'So was I,' said Libby. 'All we've done over the last week or so is say "Shall we tell the police?" They'll be fed up to the back teeth.'

251

'Leave it, then? After all, what can he do?'

'I don't know.' Libby shivered. 'And I don't want to find out.'

After thinking long and hard, Libby picked up her basket and headed off up the back track towards the brewery, Sidney accompanying part of the way. This part of the Manor Estate had been left to become a wildflower meadow, and Sidney regarded it as his own personal playground. Further along, where the restored Hoppers' Huts stood, now let out as holiday accommodation, was the boundary of the brand new hop garden, the first year bines having now reached the top of their supporting wires. The sun shone, and Libby felt that all should be right with the world, if only she could get rid of her nagging feeling that something was very wrong.

Ben wasn't at the brewery, so Libby went on to the Estate office in the Manor. Ben was sitting behind the desk, looking solemn.

'What's up?' she said, stopping just inside the door.

'Look at this.' Ben handed over a piece of paper.

In computer printed capitals, it read:

For the sake of your brewery, stop your old bitch from interfering.

Chapter Twenty Nine

'Nigel Preece!' gasped Libby.

'What?' Ben looked startled.

Libby explained about Fran's phone call. 'It's got to be him,' she finished. 'Just the same as when he threatened Guy.'

'But why?' Ben's brow wrinkled. 'The police were bound to talk to him anyway.'

'That's what Fran said. But he seems to be like that. Revenge.'

'It seems to me,' said Ben, 'that whoever wrote this thinks there's something else to find out. Not simply revenge.'

'And they think I'll find it out?' Libby shook her head. 'I'm not that good.'

Ben frowned and took the paper back. 'Whoever wrote it knows something about you – and me, come to that. Does Sir Nigel Preece know us?'

'I don't know. He might. Barrett will have told him.'

'There is that.' Ben sat up straight and picked up the phone. 'I'm phoning the police.'

Ben reported the anonymous letter to the incident room and ended the call.

'Someone will be in touch,' he told Libby.

'They'll be so fed up with us,' she said. 'I'm surprised they haven't asked us to move away.'

It wasn't long before a surprised Hetty opened the door and announced Inspector Maiden.

'Mr Wilde,' he said 'Mrs Sarjeant.'

'Oh, Ben and Libby, please,' said Libby. 'Sit down, Inspector.'

He smiled. 'It's Rob, then, remember?'

'Yes, thank you Rob.' Libby smiled back.

'Now,' he said, turning to Ben. 'Where's the letter?'

Ben handed it over. Rob took it with a pair of tweezers and laid it on the desk in front of him.

'Who's handled it?'

'Only Libby and me.'

'When did it come? Have you kept the envelope?'

Ben placed an envelope next to the letter. Rob took out a pair of thin gloves and an evidence bag.

'Came by post then?' He studied the envelope. 'You can't tell anything by postmarks these days.'

'How do you find out anything about these things? One printer's much the same as another. And nearly everybody's got one nowadays,' said Libby.

Rob nodded. 'I'll get it over to forensics straightaway. Meanwhile, have you any idea who might have sent it?'

'Libby has. I'm not so sure,' said Ben.

'Libby?' Rob turned to her.

Libby fidgeted. 'This is only guesswork.'

Rob smiled. 'Let's have it anyway.'

Once more, Libby launched into her story.

'It doesn't sound very likely said out loud, does it?' she said. 'I feel a bit silly, now.'

'Silly or not, someone sent it. Someone who knows about you.'

'Barrett will have told Preece about us,' said Ben. 'Preece got on to him after he was questioned. When would that have been? Yesterday?'

'Last week, I think. You remember we were warned off.'

'But,' said Libby, 'Barrett only called Fran this morning. Presumably that means Preece didn't get on to him until today. No time to post a letter. I've just destroyed my own theory, haven't I?'

'Unless Preece already knew about you. How could he?' asked Rob.

'Anyone could,' said Libby with a shrug. 'We haven't exactly kept our lights under bushels over the past few years.'

'That's all very well, but how would he know you were looking into this case?' asked Ben.

'He knew the singer's body had been found,' said Rob.

'And the news reports said you'd found it!' said Libby, enlightened. 'On the TV news, remember? Local brewery owner Ben Wilde, it called you.'

'I didn't actually find it,' said Ben, 'but yes – it did mention me. And Colin, of course.'

'Well, Colin didn't send it,' said Libby. 'He wants the truth to be found.'

'And you're saying Sir Nigel doesn't?' asked Rob.

'Somebody doesn't,' said Ben.

Rob went back to the incident room with the letter and envelope in separate evidence bags. 'Not that I think we'll find any prints except yours and the postman's,' he said.

'What now, then?' asked Libby when he'd gone.

Ben heaved a sigh. 'Let's go and ask Hetty for lunch.'

Hetty provided cold pork sandwiches and coffee while being brought up to date.

'What comes of interferin',' she said.

Libby felt herself going red.

'That's not really fair, Mum,' said Ben. 'It wasn't Libby's fault she was with Fiona at the Garden, or with me at the bat and trap pitch.'

Hetty shook her head. 'Better leave it alone, gal,' she said. 'We don't want no more accidents.'

With this Libby could heartily agree.

After lunch, Ben went off to the brewery and Libby strolled down to call on Harry and Peter.

'Oh, if it isn't the old trout!' said Harry, opening the front door. 'Decided you want my company after all?'

'Yes,' said Libby. 'Pete here?'

'London. I'm here all alone!' Harry waggled his eyebrows at her.

'So I can have my wicked way?' Libby smiled in a half hearted manner.

'OK, petal, what is it?' Harry ushered inside. 'Tea?'

'I've just had Hetty's coffee,' said Libby. 'I think I just want to have a moan.'

'OK.' Harry threw himself down on the sofa. 'Moan away.'

'Well,' he said, when she'd finished. 'You have got

yourselves into a pickle, haven't you?'

'I feel guilty because of Ben.'

'Look.' Harry swung his feet off the sofa and leant forward. 'Although it pains me to say it, this isn't your fault. Pure accident that you happened to be on the spot when both bodies were found.'

'That's what Ben said, but I needn't have gone poking around.'

'Where have you actually poked?' said Harry. 'Felling to see John whatsit – and that was because of the pub. Felling again to see the reporter bloke – that was actual poking. What else?'

Libby thought. 'I've been to see Fiona Darling.'

'Natural enough.'

'And talked to Colin.'

'Oh, come on!'

'What else have I done?'

'Just worried away at it. Nothing to frighten the horses. Who would have told this Nigel about it?'

'Only Barrett, the reporter.' Libby frowned. 'And this letter had to have been posted before Preece spoke to him.'

'Ah,' said Harry, 'but the police had spoken to him. And been warned off.'

'Why should they have mentioned me or Ben?'

'You said yourself, Ben made the headlines when he found the singer's body.'

'Not exactly the headlines, and he didn't exactly find it, either.'

'But his name was known,' said Harry. 'Personally, I don't think it is this Preece. Perhaps it's someone who

257

doesn't want the brewery to succeed?'

'Why would they say I had to be stopped in that case? I don't have anything to do with the brewery.'

Harry frowned. 'Ah, hadn't thought of that. It's a possibility, though. Ready for some tea, yet?'

Libby said she was and followed him into the tiny kitchen. 'I wonder if someone does resent Ben, though,' she said. 'I mean, there's the Hop Pocket as well. Someone might not want that to go ahead.'

'The only person I can think of there would be Tim,' said Harry, pouring boiling water into mugs. 'And he says he's pleased about it. Who else?'

'Someone who wanted to re-open the Garden?' suggested Libby. 'But it hadn't even been put up for sale, so that can't be right.'

'Someone might have had an eye on it, though,' said Harry, handing Libby her usual chipped flowery mug. 'It's an idea.'

'Well, at least we've got a bit more of the puzzle to worry about,' said Libby, going back to the sitting room. 'Although there's still nothing we can do.'

'Look after Colin?' said Harry. 'He'll be going through it, won't he?'

'Yes, and he doesn't know about all this business with Preece,' said Libby. 'Perhaps I should tell him.'

'And make him worry more? I shouldn't.'

Libby went home and called Fran.

'I agree it sounds like Preece,' said Fran, 'but as you've said, how could he know before speaking to Barrett?'

'Oh, I don't know,' said Libby. 'The whole thing's

258

barmy.'

'There must be someone else who knew you were investigating.'

'But, as Harry said, we haven't done much actual investigating.'

'Who knew you were asking questions, then. Or knew *we* were.'

'Colin, John and Emma, Fiona. None of them are likely,' said Libby.

'Ted Sachs?'

'Yes, I suppose so, but apart from the fact that he was at that original party, I don't see how he comes into it.'

'We could ask John and Emma and Sachs if they remember anyone else at the party,' said Fran. 'We said that before.'

'The police will have done that,' said Libby.

'They might not see the significance of the names,' sais Fran. 'One of them might leap out at you.'

'I doubt it. I didn't come from this area, I wouldn't know any of the names.'

'No, but maybe a name you know now would leap out.'

'We can't ask Sachs. We don't know him well enough,' said Libby. 'I suppose we could follow up our original idea of seeing John and Emma, though.'

'Why not? Although we still don't know where they live or work.'

'Ben's got John's number. I'll phone him.'

'Ben won't like it,' said Fran. 'I'd ask Colin.'

'I'll call him now,' said Libby. 'Do I tell him about Preece and the anonymous letter, though? Harry says not.'

259

'I think he's right,' said Fran. 'Call me back.'

Colin answered straight away.

'I'll just get the number,' he said. 'What do you want it for?'

'Just to ask if they remember anyone at that party,' said Libby. 'It might ring a bell. You know. You thought we should do that before.'

'Ring a bell with you? But you wouldn't know any of them.'

'I know, but Fran said it might be a name we know now.'

Colin was quiet for a moment. 'All right,' he said, 'but how about we go and talk to them together? The police haven't said I have to stay in the village.'

Libby thought about this. 'Might make things easier,' she said. 'When would you want to go?'

'Evening would be best,' said Colin. 'Tonight?'

Libby called Fran and between them they arranged to go and see the Newmans that evening, Colin reporting that John had seemed perfectly agreeable, if puzzled. Ben wasn't enthusiastic, but agreed it might help Colin.

Once again they met in the town square car park, Fran got in to Libby's car and Colin directed them back out through the Sand Gate to a small residential estate built on the Aldeburgh Road. The Newmans lived in a modern semi-detached house in a cul-de-sac with an extremely neat front garden.

'Not wildlife enthusiasts,' Libby muttered, as they got out of the car.

John opened the front door with a welcoming smile,

Emma hovering behind him. They were ushered into what Libby was sure was called a through lounge, where tea things were assembled on a coffee table in front of a large corner seating unit.

'So, what did you want to talk about?' asked John.

'Well,' Colin looked at Libby and Fran in turn. 'We just wondered if you could remember anything about anyone who was at that awful party. I've told the police everything I remember, but I didn't really know anyone, and certainly not their names.'

Emma looked frightened. 'We don't know anything!'

John smiled at her. 'Sorry, we've already had the police asking questions about it. It quite upset Emma.'

'We're sorry, Emma,' said Fran. 'But it'll help to clear Colin of suspicion.'

'They can't think it was you,' said John. 'I brought you home. And you'd had a miserable time.'

'They don't necessarily think the girl's body was left in Colin's hotel at the time,' said Libby. 'They think it might have been kept somewhere first.'

Emma went white. 'No!' she whispered.

'Well, you see why we thought it might help if we knew who else had been there,' said Colin. 'Can you remember?'

John frowned. 'We couldn't remember many when the police asked,' he said. 'But I'll try.'

He began to reel off a list of names, all of which were unfamiliar to his three listeners. Emma appeared to recover, and occasionally put in a name.

'And there were a couple who were with Nigel,' said John, and all his listeners sat up a little straighter. 'Nigel

261

Preece – you know? You knew he was there, of course. He was talking to you at one point, Colin.'

Now it was Colin who was turning pale. 'Is that the one who tried to take me aside?'

'Yes, that's him. I thought you knew him.'

Colin shook his head.

'So who was with him?' asked Libby quickly.

'Oh, some of his entourage,' said John.

'They always hung round,' said Emma. 'There was that black guy, wasn't there, John?'

'Oh, yes. I'd forgotten him. White-something. I've got it. Whitelaw.'

Chapter Thirty

Into the silence, Libby said brightly 'Oh, yes. He worked for Preece in his campaign, didn't he?'

Colin cleared his throat.

'Anyone else, can you think of?' asked Fran.

'Who else hung around with him at that time, Em? You knew them, I didn't,' said John.

'Well, I remember a Steve – who was always called Steven – and a David.' Emma frowned. 'That's about all I can remember. He wasn't exactly popular, Nigel.'

'Still isn't,' said John.

'Did you give the police those names?' asked Colin.

'Not Whitelaw, but I think we mentioned Steven and David. Not much help, is it?'

'You never know,' said Colin, with a weak smile. 'Well, we won't take up any more of your time, will we, Libby?'

'No,' said Libby. 'Unless you can think of anything else, Fran?'

Fran shook her head and they all stood up to leave, the tea things remaining unused.

'I hope we've helped,' said John, as he saw them to the door. 'I don't think we have, really.'

Libby smiled. 'As Colin said, you never know.'

'Well, that was a shock,' she said as they got into the car.

'Whitelaw? Yes,' Fran agreed.

'Tell me about Whitelaw.' Colin swivelled to look at Fran in the back seat. 'I don't think I've really followed that side of the story.'

Libby and Fran explained Whitelaw's involvement.

'But I don't think we've come across any of the other names they mentioned,' Libby finished. 'They were all so ordinary.'

'Even the ones where Emma remembered the surnames,' said Fran. 'And names like Steven and David – there must be hundreds of them'

'I suppose we could look up Preece's campaign team on the internet,' said Libby. 'Although again, I suppose the police will have done that.'

'Well, you tried.' Colin tried another smile. 'It might help.'

They dropped Fran at the car park and set off for Steeple Martin.

'Do you honestly think that will help?' Colin asked after a while.

'I don't know,' said Libby. 'Maybe we're clutching at straws.'

Colin nodded moodily, and stared out into the blackness. 'That's what I thought.'

'So that's where we are at the moment,' Libby reported to Ben when she got home. 'Nowhere, really.'

'Except for Whitelaw,' said Ben. 'It looks as though

he's more involved than you thought.'

'I still don't see how, though.' Libby sat down on the sofa and accepted a drink. 'He's the father of the boy whose body was found, but he couldn't have murdered him, he sold his house to the Darlings, and he knew Ted Sachs. Well, that's explained because they were obviously around Felling all at the same time. Except the Darlings. But where's the link?'

'No idea. Didn't Fiona say her husband knew Whitelaw through business, or something?'

'Yes – but it still doesn't seem to have any relevance. Whitelaw is a link, though. Perhaps I shall do a little digging.'

'Be careful,' said Ben. 'We don't want more anonymous letters.'

'Or people attacking me or the brewery,' agreed Libby darkly.

Libby's phone rang.

'It's me.' Fran sounded excited. 'I just thought of something.'

'What? Are you all right?'

'I'm fine. Listen – those names. We *do* know a David!'

'We do?'

'Yes! We've actually talked about him. David Darling.'

'Bloody hell!' exploded Libby.

'Exactly. There's the link.'

'But – hang on – link to what?'

'They knew one another. Preece, Whitelaw, and Darling. And probably Sachs, too.'

'So they were all involved in baiting Colin? Or all

involved in the girl's murder?'

'I don't know, but they've all got a link to the present day, too.'

'Oh, Lord!' said Libby. 'Now what?'

'I had another idea, too.'

'Oh? What?' said Libby suspiciously.

'Didn't John tell you at some point he was a member of a local bat and trap team?'

'I think so, why?'

'It must be attached to a pub, then. In Felling. Isn't the local where most gossip's exchanged?'

'Yes...'

'Couldn't you and Ben pay it a sort of official visit? To set up a match?'

Libby shot a look at Ben, who was obviously trying to follow the conversation and looking worried. 'I don't know. We won't be allowed to use the pitch for ages yet.'

'Ask him.' Fran was peremptory.

'Ben.' Libby lowered the phone. 'Fran wants to know if there's a chance we could visit the pub in Felling to arrange a bat and trap match.'

'What pub?' Ben was frowning.

'There must be one. John said -'

'I know. But why?'

'Tell you in a minute.' She raised the phone to her ear again. 'He hasn't actually said no.'

'Don't you think it would help?'

'I'm not sure,' said Libby. 'I mean, we've got all the information we need from John and Emma – and from Colin. And I don't know what we're going to do with it,

266

anyway. After all, everyone keeps saying leave it alone. I've lost count of the times, I've been told that this time, including by you.'

'I've just got a feeling…'

'What, a moment?'

'No, no, nothing like that. But if we could prove -'

'Prove what? That Colin didn't kill the singer? Well, yes, but linking those people together is hardly going to do that, is it?'

Fran clicked her tongue impatiently. 'It's not like you to be so – so *negative*!'

'I'm sorry.' Libby was genuinely penitent. 'I just can't see where we go with it. Or why.'

'All right.' Fran sighed. 'Just think about it. Talk to Ben.'

Libby ended the call and sat staring at her phone.

'Well?' said Ben. 'Are you going to tell me what that was all about?'

Libby told him.

'Actually,' he said, looking thoughtful, 'it's not a bad idea.'

'Eh?'

'Oh, not for the reasons Fran wanted us to go. But to see if they would like to have a match. And perhaps see if they've got any fixtures I could go and watch. You could come if you like.'

Libby stared at him. 'Really?'

'Yes. Nothing to do with the case.' He grinned. 'Just a jolly. I'll ring John in the morning.'

By the time Libby got downstairs in the morning, Ben
267

was already preparing to leave for the brewery.

'All set up,' he said, beaming. 'Not only have they got a pub, called The Gate Inn, by the way, right next to the Sand Gate – don't know why we didn't notice it – there's a bat and trap fixture on Saturday afternoon. John said we'd be very welcome. I might even get a chance to have a go!'

After he'd gone, Libby poured herself a cup of tea and sat down to update interested parties, starting with Fran.

'I won't be able to come,' said Fran. 'Saturday's a busy day. Pity. I'd love to see a match. Will you have a chance to chat to the locals?'

'I don't think Ben would like that. He made a point of saying it would be nothing to do with the case.'

'Oh.' Fran was silent. 'I'll carry on thinking about it, anyway.'

Next on Libby's list was Colin.

'Well, that's something to look forward to,' he said. 'I must admit I'm getting bored sitting round here twiddling my thumbs.'

'Wouldn't the police let you go into London to your office?'

'It's only the registered office, Libby,' said Colin. 'I do most of my work at home in Spain.'

'Oh! I thought John said you had a woman working for you who went in to collect your post – stuff like that.'

'Carina? Yes. She collects anything the solicitors can't deal with and tells me if there's anything that needs my attention. It's mostly done online these days – even signatures.'

'What – even on contracts?'

Colin laughed. 'Yes. Oh, there are some things we have to do by hand, of course, but I come over regularly to deal with those, or Carina posts them to me.'

'Who is she?' asked Libby. 'Sorry, I shouldn't be nosy.'

'Oh, just a friend.'

Libby felt snubbed. 'Can't you do anything online while you're here, though? You've got your laptop.'

'And a lot of the paperwork's back in the office in Spain' said Colin. 'I didn't expect to be here so long, did I?'

Libby had barely ended the call when the landline rang.

'Libby? Abby here.'

Dame Amanda. Libby mentally reviewed her diary and realised that she'd nearly missed the royal visit.

'Abby! Where are you?'

'Running late, dear. Coolidge is just fetching the car round, so we'll be another half an hour or so. Is that all right? So sorry.'

'No trouble at all,' said Libby. 'I'll see you at the theatre.'

Pausing only to call Ben to remind him, she rushed upstairs to have a very quick shower and throw on some clothes, grabbed her basket, and left the house. She arrived outside the theatre a bare five minutes before Coolidge drove up in an impressive black saloon. Even though Libby now knew he had been Dame Amanda's husband for years, he still gave the impression of being a very correct butler.

However, on the conducted tour round the Oast Theatre, he proved to be a knowledgeable and shrewd theatre professional.

'He knows a lot more about how things work than I do,' confided Dame Amanda, as she and Libby watched Ben and Coolidge poking about in the scenery dock.

'Ben knows more than I do,' said Libby. 'And he's a great set builder.'

'I don't suppose he'd – no, of course he wouldn't,' said Dame Amanda wistfully.

Libby smiled. 'Actually, he'll probably come butting in anyway, but he is rather busy at the moment.'

'Oh, yes, you told me about the brewery. How's that going? Coolidge wants to see it.'

'Oh, it isn't just the brewery now,' said Libby with a sigh. 'He's now started his own hop garden. And he's going to renovate and re-open a little pub in the village.'

'Goodness me!' Dame Amanda was round eyed. 'When does he get any time off? And that reminds me, I wonder if any of your regulars would be interested in auditioning for me? I thought it would be a good thing if there were old favourites as well as the people I bring in. Equity rates, of course.'

Libby was surprised. 'I'm sure they would. When would that be?'

'Fairly soon, I think. We want the publicity shots out, don't we? Would you give me a list of those you think I might be interested in and let them know, too?'

Libby, still rather surprised, said she would.

When the inspection was over, the visitors were taken into the Manor to see Hetty, who was gruffly gracious and offered coffee and homemade biscuits.

'So now tell us all about these murders you've had

here,' said Dame Amanda comfortably, settling herself at the kitchen table.

'Abby!' warned Coolidge.

Ben laughed. 'Don't worry about it. She'll tell you anyway.'

Libby gave him a look.

'Sorry.' Dame Amanda smiled at him. 'Remember, I've actually known her longer than you have!'

'But I've grown up since then,' said Libby. 'Mind you, some would say I hadn't. Anyway, these murders aren't really anything to do with us.'

Hetty made a scornful noise from beside the Aga.

'Except,' said Ben, 'that we nearly found *both* the bodies.'

Dame Amanda and Coolidge expressed astonishment, and Libby went on to explain.

'So it really isn't anything to do with us, except that we've provided background information and rather taken poor Colin under our wing.'

'Colin?' said Coolidge. 'That's the young man who owns the hotel? Who lives in Spain?'

Libby nodded. 'It's all a bit of a muddle really, and we can't see how the two murders link up. They're twenty years apart.'

'What about young Fran?' asked Amanda. 'Hasn't she had any insights?'

'No, but she's keen to carry on to try and clear Colin's name.'

'Felling,' pondered Coolidge. 'You know, that rings a bell. The vanishing singer. I remember that.'

271

'Do you, dear?' Amanda raised her eyebrows. 'Why?'

'Because I knew someone who was involved. Peripherally, I'm sure, but… You did, too, Abby.'

'I did?'

'Yes, dear. Nigel Preece.'

Chapter Thirty One

'Oh, no!' said Libby.

'Why, dear?' Amanda looked surprised.

'He just keeps popping up,' said Libby. 'I can't believe you knew him, too.'

'Not to say knew, exactly,' said Coolidge. 'You remember, Abby? Not a very nice person.'

No, that's what we've heard,' said Ben. 'How did you come across him?'

'Years ago. He introduced himself at an after show party, and thereafter tried to claim intimate friendship with Abby. He became a nuisance.'

'Oh, yes, I remember. Always surrounded with a little entourage. Thought himself no end of a personage,' said Amanda. 'How did we get rid of him?'

'We ignored him,' said Coolidge, with a wry smile. 'And then he started mouthing off about Abby in public.'

'Whatever did he say?' asked Libby.

'Oh, the usual things – you know. A has been who still thought we were still in the fifties. Thought she was better than she actually was. In fact, just the sort of person he was himself.'

'What happened in the end?' asked Ben.

'It all tailed off. Better to ignore that sort of thing. It happens a lot in our business, as I'm sure you know.' Abby smiled at Libby. 'But something happened, didn't it, dear?' she said to her husband.

'That was why I remember the singer affair. It was said he was involved in her disappearance. I wouldn't have taken any notice if it hadn't been for the fact that we always kept an eye out for his name in the papers.' Coolidge shook his head. 'He didn't say anything more about us. But then he became an MP and there was some other scandal, if I remember rightly. So how did you come across him?'

'Apparently he hosted the party where the singer disappeared,' said Libby. 'And the police have been warned off him in this investigation.'

'I don't know how he's got that much influence,' said Amanda. 'Is it family?'

'It must be,' said Ben. 'But Libby thinks he's taking a hand again. I'm not so sure.'

'Why is that, dear?' Amanda and Coolidge both looked at Libby.

'Well…' Libby looked at Ben. 'You tell it.'

Ben sighed. 'I received an anonymous letter. Threatening the brewery – and Libby.'

Amanda and Coolidge both expressed horror.

'And you think it was Preece?' said Coolidge.

'I can't think who else,' said Libby.

'He wouldn't have done it himself,' said Coolidge thoughtfully. 'He wouldn't get his hands dirty.'

'Well, we do know that several people who were part of

his – *entourage* – back then are still around now. One of them, perhaps?' said Libby.

'What I don't get, though,' said Ben, 'is how he's kept them around for so long.'

'He's got something on them,' said Coolidge, looking interested. 'What do they all do?'

'Two of them are businessmen of some sort,' said Libby. 'Pharmaceuticals, I think one of them is.'

'And one is a self-employed builder,' said Ben.

'They were all involved in the disappearance of that girl, then,' said Amanda brightly. 'And the guilt has bound them together!'

Coolidge smiled indulgently. 'But they've got a modern body, too, my darling.'

Amanda looked fazed for a moment. 'Well, obviously, they're all involved in that, too!'

'Except that one of them is the modern body's father,' said Ben.

'Ah.' Amanda looked crestfallen.

By this time they had finished their coffee.

'We must go,' said Coolidge. 'Thank you so much for the coffee.' He stood and gave Hetty a little bow. Libby was delighted to see Hetty's cheeks glow a faint pink. 'And thank you for the theatre tour, Ben and Libby. It's a delightful space.'

'Yes, it is,' said Amanda, gathering herself together and collecting her handbag. 'I do envy you, Libby. I tell you what,' she leant forward, 'I've got a project in mind that perhaps we could do together.' She looked at Coolidge. 'What do you think, dear?'

275

'If you mean what I think you do,' he said, looking resigned, 'I think you ought to speak to Clemency.'

Libby looked from Coolidge to Amanda. 'Very mysterious,' she said.

'Oh, well, you'll see her soon enough. She's coming back to do *Puss* too,' said Amanda. She kissed Hetty's cheek and made a regal exit.

'She doesn't change,' said Coolidge, as he handed her into their car. Libby kissed him.

'It's lovely to see you,' she said. 'I'm so glad you'll be here soon.'

Libby walked back to the brewery with Ben.

'You know,' he said, 'there's something in what they said. It does look as though Preece has something on Whitelaw, Darling, and Sachs.'

'I'm not sure,' said Libby. 'The fact that they're all connected to Ossie's murder – in an odd sort of way – looks a bit like coincidence. I know It's not like me to admit that, and I've spent a lot of time trying to link everything up, but when you think about it...'

'All right. I'll admit it, too. And now I'm going to have a walk round the garden -'

'Too many gardens,' grinned Libby. 'I presume you mean the hop garden?'

'Yes, sorry. The hop garden – to check on the bines. They're doing well for their first year, don't you think?'

Libby gave him an impulsive hug. 'When I think of you when I first came here – all smart suits and city, and now look at you! The typical countryman. All hops and bat and trap.'

276

'And look at you! Giving your beloved panto over to someone else. Never were there such times.'

'Actually,' said Libby, 'Abby's asked me - '

Ben groaned. 'Not to be in it, surely!'

'No, but to see if any of our regulars would like to audition.'

'Really? But you said the other day, when you'd been to see Bob, they were all grateful for the year off.'

'I bet some of them will love it,' said Libby.

'And what about this "project" Dame Amanda has in mind?'

'We'll have to see!' Libby gave him a mischievous smile. 'And now I'm going home. See you later.'

She walked on past the fledgling hop garden, past the hoppers' huts and through the meadow. Approaching the top end of Allhallow's Lane, she was surprised to see a small white van parked sideways across it. She stopped and peered through the side window. Empty. She looked round but could see no one.

'Workman,' she thought, and wondered who was having what done. There was no name on the van. She glanced at the wood which pressed up to the backs of the cottages and on along the edge of the Manor estate boundary, but could see no sign of anyone in there, either.

Stepping carefully, she rounded the front of the van and jogged towards number seventeen. As she did so, Mrs Mardle's door flew open.

'Oh, Libby!' she called. 'Quick! There's someone trying to get over your back fence!'

Visions of the fire that had once threatened to destroy

her cottage immediately came to mind.

'Did you call the police?' she gasped, struggling with her key.

'No – shall I do that?' Jinny Mardle looked frightened.

'Yes, please.' Libby shot through her door and right through to the conservatory, impeded along the way by a furiously growling Sidney, whose tail was standing out like a brush.

There was nothing to be seen, but opening the back door, she could hear something or someone crashing through the woodland. Turning back, she flew out to the front again and ran towards the white van, which was already in motion. She had to leap out of the way, conscious of Mrs Mardle screaming in the background. She just had the wit to try and note the registration number before the van disappeared in the direction of the Canterbury Road, almost crashing into another vehicle as it did so.

By this time, other residents had also made an appearance, and when a police car complete with flashing blue lights screeched round the corner, the speed of its arrival meaning the 999 call had obviously been diverted to the incident room, Mrs Mardle and Libby were surrounded by a small but concerned crowd.

Rachel Trent and two uniformed PCs got out and quietly dispersed the onlookers.

'Can you tell us what happened?' Rachel asked Mrs Mardle, who looked s if she was about to collapse.

'I think she ought to sit down,' said Libby, who felt that perhaps she should, too.

Mrs Mardle was ushered back inside her own cottage by one of the PCs, and Rachel turned to Libby.

'Do you want to sit down, too?'

'Yes, but should I come into Mrs Mardle's cottage? I ought to thank her.'

'Yes, just for a moment, then.'

'I'll just check on the cat,' said Libby.

Sidney was, by this time, unconcernedly having a wash in front of the empty fireplace. Libby left him to it and went back to Rachel.

Inside number 16, one of the PCs was in the kitchen, obviously making tea, while the other stood solicitously at Mrs Mardle's elbow. She held out a tremulous hand to Libby.

'Oh, dear, Libby! Is this all to do with this dreadful murder?'

Libby took her hand and knelt on the floor beside her. 'I don't know,' she said. 'DS Trent?'

Rachel sat opposite Mrs Mardle and asked her what she'd seen.

'I was just getting my bit of lunch, dear,' she said. 'And I looked out of my window. I can't see much of Libby's garden, but I can see the back fence. And there was this – this man. He had one leg over the fence and he seemed to slip…'

'The back gate is locked these days,' said Libby. 'After we had a fire…'

'Oh?' Rachel raised her eyebrows.

'Not relevant now,' said Libby. 'Go on, Nanny.'

'Anyway, dear, your Sidney suddenly jumped off the

279

fence and raced for the house, and this person seemed – well – surprised. Then he saw me looking. And then I came through to the front – I don't know why I did that, but there you were, and – well, you know the rest.'

'Tea, Sarge?' asked the PC from the kitchen.

'No, thanks,' said Rachel. 'Mrs Sarjeant and I will go next door. Look after Mrs Mardle, please.' She turned to the now recovering Mrs Mardle. 'Can we call anyone for you?'

'Shall I call Hetty?' Libby asked. 'Or Flo?'

'Would Hetty mind, dear?'

'Of course not.' Libby pulled out her phone and wondered what Ben was going to say to all this.

Assured that Hetty would come straight away, Rachel and Libby retired to number seventeen.

'You do get yourself into some messes, don't you?' said Rachel. 'So tell me what happened?'

'First of all, I want a cup of tea, even if you don't,' said Libby. 'Talk to me in the kitchen.'

'Go on, then,' said Rachel, seating herself at the kitchen table. 'What happened?'

Libby recounted the events since she had left Ben at the hop garden.

'And he drove straight at you?' said Rachel.

'Well, it seemed like that, but he was all over the place.'

'I don't suppose,' began Rachel doubtfully.

'Yes, I did.' Libby closed her eyes and thought. Then dictated the number plate. Rachel put in a call to request information.

'If we'd had that in the first place, we might have

caught him,' she said.

'What did you expect me to do?' asked Libby indignantly. 'Call you with a number plate just because there was a van parked across Allhallow's Lane?'

'No, of course not,' soothed Rachel. 'Now, did anyone know you would be out this morning?'

'No. I'd forgotten myself. The only people were Ben, Hetty, and the people we were meeting at the theatre.'

'And they are?'

Libby told her.

'Oh,' said Rachel. 'No connection, then.'

'None at all,' said Libby. 'A different side of my life entirely.'

The front door crashed open and Ben erupted into the room.

'Right,' he said. 'That's it. You're not going anywhere near this business from now on. Do you hear me?

Chapter Thirty Two

Rachel gaped. Libby, who had expected this reaction, sighed.

'Look, darling – it doesn't have to have any connection to – er – this business. Does it, Rachel? More probably just a sneak thief.'

'Oh, don't be ridiculous! You were specifically threatened in that letter!' Ben positively vibrated with anger.

'Insulted more than threatened,' said Libby, trying to lighten the atmosphere. 'And it was a little man in a little van. Not a criminal mastermind.'

'She could be right, Mr Wilde,' said Rachel, recovering her official manner. 'It certainly doesn't smack of any kind of professional criminal.'

'I can't believe it was a coincidence,' said Ben, calming down a little. 'Not with everything that's been happening.'

'Did you bring Hetty down?' asked Libby.

'Of course! She assumed I knew. Why didn't you call me?'

'I didn't have time!' said Libby. 'I didn't even call the police. That was Mrs Mardle.'

'The 999 call was put straight through to us as one of

the patrols recognised the location,' said Rachel. 'That was why we were here so quickly. Not in time to get on to the van, sadly, But we've put out a call. Libby was clever enough to note the reg number.'

'That's my girl,' said Ben, with a faint smile. He came and sat down beside Rachel at the table. 'Sorry. But to think what could have happened...'

'I'm a bit puzzled, actually,' said Libby. 'Did he know I was out, and if so what was he intending to do? And if he thought I was in – again, what? Murder in broad daylight?'

'Opportunist, don't you think?' said Rachel. 'Who was he? Doesn't sound like anyone we've come across during the course of this investigation.'

'Doesn't Ted Sachs have a van?' said Libby. 'He's a builder.'

'A large silver Transit,' said Rachel. 'So not him in this case.'

'Someone who thinks that the new investigation is shining a light on them and isn't too pleased about it?' said Libby.

'So why target you?' said Ben.

'I don't know.'

'Could someone have seen you leave the house this morning?' asked Rachel.

'Only the neighbours,' said Libby. 'I went up the back way and across the estate, so no one in the village saw me. And I came back the same way.'

'So did I, earlier,' said Ben. 'So for all anyone knew, we could both have been there. And it was a stupidly risky thing to do anyhow. We all overlook each others' back gardens, and many of the residents are retired and would be at home.'

Rachel finished her tea and stood up. 'Well, I think that's all. Nothing else you've got to tell me?'

'Oh...' Libby looked at Ben. 'There is something Fran remembered.'

'What?' Rachel sat down again.

'I don't suppose it means anything, but you know Ossie Whitelaw's father was connected to Sir Nigel back in the day? He was at that party. And Fiona Darling's husband, David was, too. At least, we think it was him.'

'We don't know that, Lib,' said Ben.

'Worth looking into, though,' said Rachel, and stood up again.

'Can we go next door and see how Mrs Mardle is?' Libby asked.

'Of course.' Rachel smiled. 'She's a heroine, isn't she?'

Mrs Mardle was certainly looking more cheerful when Hetty let them in to number 16.

'Are you all right, dear?' she asked Libby.

'I'm fine,' said Libby, bending down to kiss her cheek. 'And DS Trent says you're a heroine.'

Mrs Mardle went pink. 'Oh, I wouldn't say that, dear. Just trying to be a good neighbour.'

'Tea?' asked Hetty.

'No, thanks, just had some,' said Libby. 'I must have some lunch, though. Just wanted to make sure Nanny Mardle was OK.'

Outside again, Ben suggested a quick sandwich at the pub. 'Harry would want to know all about it, and we want a
284

bit of a rest, don't we?' he said, tucking Libby's arm into his. 'Come on, my intrepid warrior.'

'I was thinking,' said Libby, as they made their way to the pub.

'Oh, Lord,' said Ben.

'No, listen. How about growing something nice and prickly along the back fence? As a deterrent.'

'Shutting the stable door? I suppose it might help, but spikes would be better. And quicker.'

'But Sidney comes over the fence. He'd know how to avoid holly, but not spikes or broken glass.'

'All right – it's your fence.' Ben held open the pub door.

'I'll go and see Cassandra and Mike this afternoon,' said Libby, and went inside.

Libby's cousin Cassandra lived with Mike Farthing, of Mike Farthing Plants, at a house attached to his nursery just outside Shott, and after lunch, when Ben went back to the brewery, Libby set out.

The weather wasn't quite as summery as it had been, which Libby tried hard not to see as a bad omen. The drive to Shott was pleasant, however, and it occurred to her as she drove past The Poacher, the pub on the green, that perhaps she could call on Edward on the way home.

When she arrived at the nursery, she found Cassandra in the nursery poring over a catalogue.

'Libby! This is a surprise. What can we do for you? Or,' said Cassandra, suddenly suspicious, 'is this something to do with your murder?'

'No, and what do you know about "my murder"? It isn't

285

mine, anyway.'

'You have been mentioned in the press, though,' said Cassandra, and waved one of the remaining free newspapers under her nose. 'And Ben.'

Libby sighed. 'On the periphery,' she said. 'And what I wanted was to know if there was something quick growing we could use as a deterrent on the back fence.'

'A deterrent for what? Cats?'

'People.'

Cassandra opened her mouth and stopped.

'Yes, I know,' said Libby, sighing again. 'Someone tried this morning.'

'And this has nothing to do with the murder?'

'We don't know.'

Cassandra slid from her stool. 'Come into the greenhouse and we'll ask Mike. After all, you don't want to have to tell your story twice, do you?'

They found Mike, tall and rangy, grey hair flopping untidily over his brow, doing something clever over a bench in the first long tunnel. Somewhere further down, two of his assistants could be seen moving slowly between the ranks of plants.

'Now,' said Cassandra. 'Tell us all about it, and who tried to get into your garden.'

Libby gave them a much abbreviated version of the Murders at the Garden Hotel and surrounding events, finishing up with this morning's unwanted visitor.

'How do you do it, Libby?' asked Cassandra, shaking her head. 'You got bashed on the head that time we had all the bother with the ukulele band. And then there was that time -'

'All right, Cass,' said Mike, laughing. 'We know. So what is it you want, Libby? Only unless you buy fully mature shrubs, which will be expensive, nothing's going to be immediate.'

'What are we talking? Fifty? Sixty?' Libby looked nervous.

'Hundreds,' said Mike gently. 'Sorry.'

'Oh.' Libby was deflated. 'Perhaps Ben was right. He said spikes.'

You could,' said Mike thoughtfully, 'plant a thickish hedge up against the fence. Then they'd fall into it.'

'Oh!' Libby brightened. 'Would that be cheaper?'

'Cheaper, yes, but not that cheap,' said Mike. 'Now, let me think.' He thrust his hands in the large front pocket of his overall and pondered.

'So you said there were people at this party who were still around now,' said Cassandra. 'Who were they?'

'Oh, no one you'd know,' said Libby. 'A chap called Darling and another called Whitelaw. Oh and a builder called Sachs.'

'Sachs?' said Mike, coming out of his reverie. 'Didn't he leave us a leaflet, Cass?'

'Yes.' Cassandra looked surprised. 'He did. I expect I've still got it – in case we ever needed it.'

'I remember because it was an unusual name,' said Mike. 'I think Ron used him for something...'

'Ron Stewart?' asked Libby. Ron 'Screwball' Stewart had been the leader of the seventies rock band Jonah Fludde and lived a little way away in Bishop's Bottom.

'Yes. Shall I ask him?'

'Would he mind?' Libby looked doubtful.

'Of course not. You know he's always keen to help. I'll give him a ring.' Mike pulled out his mobile, and a hank of garden twine, from his pocket and wandered away.

'So have things been going for you, Cass?' asked Libby brightly.

Cassandra gave her an old fashioned look. 'Changing the subject, coz?'

'No!'

'Actually, then, very well. The business is expanding, due mostly to people becoming aware of the need for re-wilding...'

'What, in gardens?'

'Of course! And attracting pollinators, and encouraging hedgehogs.'

'Oh, yes. There's quite a lot about it on TV, isn't there?'

'And so there should be!' said Cassandra. 'What did he say, Mike?'

Mike came back to them grinning. 'I knew it! Said would Libby like to pop round for tea.'

'What, today?'

'Yes, when you leave here. Which means he thinks he's got something to tell you.'

'Right.' Libby took a deep breath. 'Although I don't know that I can take any more stuff about this bloody case! Still, it would be nice to see Ron again. Now, what about these plants?'

Mike said he would rather do a little research before recommending anything, so why didn't she pop off to

Ron's place and he would email her the results.

Libby drove away from the nursery wondering exactly what she was about to hear. Perhaps just gossip. Perhaps Ted Sachs had done a terrible job for Ron? But Ron had, as Mike said, been very helpful in the past, not only with information, but proper material help.

Five minutes brought her to Ron Stewart's house, neo-Georgian, now almost disappearing into lavish planting - Mike and Cassandra's re-wilding schemes, Libby guessed. The big iron gates already stood open, so either Ron had opened them especially for her, or he was no longer as much of a recluse as he had once been. As she drew to a halt in front of the house, the man himself appeared at the top of the short flight of stone steps, the very picture of the ageing rock star.

'Libby.' He held out a hand as she climbed the steps. 'Maria's looking forward to seeing you. Kitchen this time – we won't bother with the studio.' He gave her a grin and ushered her towards the back of the panelled hall. Upstairs, in the attic space, reached by a lift, was the purpose-built recording studio, although Libby wasn't quite sure what he recorded these days.

The kitchen was a modern take on a traditional farmhouse kitchen, more to Libby's taste than had been Fiona Darling's sleek space. Maria Stewart, much the same age as Libby, and quite definitely *not* an ageing rock star, came forward smiling.

'Libby! Lovely to see you again. You and Ben really ought to come over for dinner sometime.'

'Lovely to see you, too,' said Libby, receiving a kiss on

the cheek. 'How are you?'

'Oh, fine, fine. Now, tea? And I've got some cake I made yesterday, too.'

Settled at the big island unit a few minutes later, Ron stretched out long legs, clad, as always in ripped jeans, and put his head on one side.

'Sachs,' he said. 'I've come across him.'

'So Mike said. Did he mention…?'

'How his name came up? Of course.' Mike grinned. 'You've got involved in a murder again.'

Libby sighed. 'Well…'

'And now she'll say she hasn't,' said Maria. 'Not on purpose, anyway.'

'That's it exactly,' said Libby gratefully. 'Anyway, have you heard about - '

'The skeletons in the closet? Course we have,' said Ron. 'Can't avoid it if you watch local telly news. And we pick up the free paper – or Maria does. You were mentioned.'

'So Cass tells me,' said Libby. 'What do you know about the case?'

'Mostly, just what was in the paper and on the news, but we do know the second body was that young singer.' Maria looked at her husband. 'Go on – tell her.'

'Tell her what?' said Libby.

'We know quite a lot about that party,' said Ron.

Chapter Thirty Three

Libby felt that she couldn't take any more shocks.

'How?' she said.

Ron and Maria laughed.

'It's quite logical if you think about it,' said Ron. 'I'm a member of a rock band.'

'A famous rock band,' put in Maria.

'And the bloke who held that party thought it would be a feather in his cap if I went. Well, what he really wanted was the band. Course, by that time we weren't performing much, except for festivals.'

'Do you mean Nigel Preece?' Libby hadn't been prepared for this. 'But no one we've spoken to said you were there.'

'We weren't,' said Maria.

'Then how...?'

'Local singer goes missing. Local rocker gets asked a) if he knew her and b) what he thinks about it – and her.' said Ron. 'So I got told quite a lot about that party. And Sir bleedin' Nigel gets on to me. Wants me to speak up for him.'

'What? But you didn't know him, did you?'

'Oh, yes. We're both local, you see,' said Maria.

'I didn't know that!' Libby gasped.

'No reason why you should.' Maria smiled. 'I was Felling, yer man here was Itching. And if you were Felling you knew the Preeces. The old man was a tartar. Thought we were still living in the last century.' She stopped. 'Oh, century before last, I mean.'

'And Sir bleedin' Nigel still does,' said Ron. 'Anyway, I said how could I speak up for him – I hadn't been at his party, and he had the gall to threaten me!'.

'Ah.' Libby nodded. 'Running true to form.'

'Oh?'

'Yes. Two friends of mine have had similar experiences. One was Dame Amanda Knight and the other was Guy Wolfe.'

'Your mate Fran's husband? The artist?'

'That's the one.'

'And Dame Amanda Knight? That's going for the big guns, isn't it? Why was he upset with her?'

'Same as you, reading between the lines. He was trying to get on intimate terms – not *that* sort of intimate – and with Guy…' she paused.

'He tried it on,' said Maria shrewdly.

'Oh – you knew?'

'Swings both ways,' said Ron. 'We all knew.'

'Who's all?'

'The locals.' Ron shrugged. 'Thing is, this sort of thing had happened before.'

'What sort of thing?' Libby was feeling out of her depth.

'The party,' said Maria. 'There'd been others. And other

girls.'

Libby sat in stupefied silence.

'Give her another cuppa,' Ron said to his wife with a grin. 'I think she needs it.'

'Sorry,' said Libby. 'I just can't understand it. If you know that, why didn't the police know it? Didn't the locals say anything?'

'Any word against Nigel and his cronies and his bully boys'd be on to you. And the girls didn't say anything.'

Maria sniffed. 'Silly cows were flattered half the time. And he paid up.'

'Paid up?' Libby faltered.

'He'd send one of the boys round with a nice little wad,' said Ron. 'Never a cheque. Notes.'

'I can't believe this!' Libby looked from one to the other in horror. 'How come we haven't heard a whisper of this? And how come the police haven't? He can't have silenced everybody?'

'They haven't asked the right people,' said Ron. 'Now, if they'd come to me...'

'Why didn't you come forward?'

'And say what? I wasn't there? And Preece's name hadn't come out, so there wasn't anything to say. You can tell them now, if you like.' Ron smiled. 'You still mates with that DCI?'

'Ian Connell, yes. I'll tell him, if you're sure you don't mind.'

'No – anything to help.'

'I've lost track now,' said Libby. 'Originally I came here to talk about Ted Sachs. Was he one of Preece's cronies? The people we know were at the party said he was there.'

'He was one of the bully boys,' said Maria. 'The cronies were all much posher than Ted. They'd all been to school together.'

'Eton?' said Libby.

'Oh, no. One of the smaller ones. I don't think Eton or Harrow would have taken Preece. His father didn't have *quite* enough money.' Ron pulled a face. 'It was in Kent – what was it called?'

'Not Foxgrove?' said Libby.

'That's it! That's what he called his gang, too – his little Foxes.'

'That is *very* unfair on foxes,' said Libby. 'It's all beginning to make sense, now. So Ted Sachs was one of the people who went round cleaning up after him – them.'

'We think so,' said Maria. 'Mind, nothing was said outright. But when we had Sachs in to fix the panelling in the hall – he's a carpenter, did you know? – we recognised him.'

'You didn't recognise the name?' asked Libby.

'We didn't have it.' Ron shrugged. 'We got hold of the old bloke who did it in the first place, and he'd retired, but said this guy had been apprenticed to him and worked with him for years, so he sent him along. And there he was – Sachs in person.'

'And he couldn't get out of here fast enough!' said Maria, laughing. 'So what's he been up to?'

'Well, nothing, really. He's just there. He was the one who gave the keys to the woman who found the first body.

He'd been asked to do the renovations on the building by the landlord. Again, on recommendation.'

'Is that all?' said Ron.

'He just keeps cropping up,' said Libby. 'I wondered if it was him who tried to break in to my house today.'

'What?' Maria and Ron looked startled.

'You never said anything about that,' said Maria.

Libby told them. 'But it wasn't,' she said eventually. 'Wrong sort of van.'

'Have you met him?' asked Ron.

'Briefly.'

'Beefy bloke. Nervous type, though.'

They all sat silent for a minute.

'Well, I'd better go,' said Libby. 'Are you sure about telling the police what you know?'

'Oh, yes,' said Ron. 'Keep on the right side of the law.'

He and Maria saw Libby to the door.

'Keep in touch,' said Maria. 'We want to know how it goes. And come over to dinner.'

Libby had so much to think about as she drove home she completely forgot about going to see Edward. Which was just as well as she was much later than she had intended to be. In fact, Ben was already at home when she let herself in. He offered tea, and made it while she regaled him with the information she'd gathered.

'Actually,' she said, accepting the mug he held out, 'I've had a lot of tea. I should have asked for a scotch.'

'Too early,' said Ben. 'Make do with that. Now, what are you going to do?'

'I can't keep this to myself, can I? Besides, Ron's asked
295

me to pass it on. And, Gawd 'elp us, it'll have to be Ian, not Rachel or Rob Maiden.'

'Text,' said Ben promptly. 'Then he can't shout at you.'

So Libby sent the text. She had barely pressed send when the phone began to ring. She sent Ben a significant look and answered.

'What's this about, Libby? Why does Ron Stewart want to see me?'

'Or talk to you,' said Libby. 'It's about the case. The girl singer and the party. He'll explain.'

'He'd better!' said Ian. 'Why hasn't he come forward?'

'Because Sir Nigel's name hadn't come out in the media.'

'Bloody hell!' Ian's reply was explosive.

'I'm sure the police must have known a lot of what he told me,' said Libby. 'I can't see why they wouldn't have.'

'Right, I'm ringing him now.' Ian ended the call.

'Not even a thank you,' said Libby with a sigh. 'Can I have that scotch now?'

Ben volunteered to cook his speciality prawn curry, and Libby called Fran to update her on what had been a rather busy day.

'What was Ian going to do?' asked Fran.

'Ring Ron. I don't know what else, and I don't feel I can ask. But it's fantastic, isn't it? Why has all this stuff stayed hidden?'

'Ron told you. The locals were scared of Preece and his boys.'

'But neither John nor Emma said anything about it. Emma, at least, must have known.'

296

'Come to that, so must Barrett,' said Fran. 'No wonder he didn't want to say anything. So what's happening about your white van man?'

'I don't know. Rachel put out a call for the van, but I haven't heard anything.'

'It can't have gone out to the media,' said Fran, 'or you'd have had Jane on the phone asking for details.'

'That's true,' said Libby. 'Oh, well, I shall have to contain my soul in patience until someone sees fit to tell me something.'

No one disturbed the evening, and apart from checking on Mrs Mardle to see if she had quite recovered from the morning's adventure, it was spent quietly watching more old movies on television.

Wednesday morning brought Libby an email from Mike Farthing with details of intruder-proof hedging, suggesting pyracantha, holly, and berberis, and finishing up with a question about her visit to Ron Stewart. Feeling guilty that she hadn't told him yesterday, Libby rang.

'Hello, Libby,' said Cassandra. 'We were wondering...'

'Yes, I know, and I should have rung yesterday. But yes, Ron had a little bit of news about Ted Sachs.' She didn't feel she could share everything she'd been told. 'I've passed it on to the police. It was just that he had known him vaguely about twenty years ago.'

'And any news on your intruder?'

'No, nothing. I like the sound of the hedging, though. Will Mike order it in for me?

'I expect he'll even come and plant it for you,' said Cassandra with a laugh. 'He's dying to know more about your murders.'

I wish people wouldn't keep saying *my* murders, Libby thought, as she ended the call. Deciding that she really ought to get on with Guy's paintings, which remained two pieces of blank stretched paper in the conservatory, she left the kitchen.

Half way through the charcoal outline of the first, her phone rang.

'Van's been found,' Rachel told her. 'Burnt out. Reported stolen yesterday morning.'

'Ah.' Libby sighed. 'I did wonder.'

'The guy who reported it said he thought it was rather funny, as it wasn't worth anything.'

'Where was it taken from?'

'Ashford way. He said it wasn't even worth part exchange, and when he'd bought his new one, he kept it as a spare, intending to run it into the ground, more or less.'

'No link, then?'

'None.'

'Oh. Did DCI Connell say anything about going to see Ron Stewart yesterday?'

'I believe so.' Rachel was guarded.

'I know, you can't tell me. But I passed on some information – I wondered if he'd acted on it.'

'You were right – I can't tell you. I'm sorry.'

'Oh, that's all right,' sighed Libby. 'I know the drill by now. Thanks for letting me know about the van.'

The charcoal sketch had lost its appeal, and on impulse, Libby decided to pay Fiona Darling another visit. She wasn't quite sure why, but Fiona was a link to both her husband, Whitelaw senior, and Ted Sachs.

'You'll be stepping on people's toes,' said Fran's voice in her head, but she ignored it.

The converted barn was quiet. Libby could hear a bell ringing somewhere inside when she pressed the ornate bell push, but no one came. After a moment, wondering whether to use the heavy iron knocker, she turned away.

'Hello?' said a voice.

She turned back to see a fair, stocky man coming round the side of the house. She forced herself to smile. Well, she thought, they didn't *know* their David was Mr Darling.

'Hello,' she said, stepping forward. 'I'm Libby Sarjeant. I just popped in to see Fiona.'

His face darkened. 'She's not here.'

'Oh.' Libby bit her lip. 'Could I leave a message? Is it Mr Darling?'

'Yes, it is. And no, you can't leave a message. I don't expect her back.'

Chapter Thirty Four

'Oh.' Libby was nonplussed. Now what? 'Oh, well, thank you,' she said, and once more turned away.

'Why did you want to see her?' David Darling's voice was close behind her. She jumped.

'I just wanted to check on her,' she said. 'She was lonely, and my friend Donna -'

'You were interfering.' He stood glowering at her, hands on hips.

'Interfering? How?'

He apparently had no answer to this, but simply stood there, a threatening presence.

'I'll go, then,' said Libby, hoping her suddenly shaky legs would carry her back to the car. She managed to get there, open the door and climb in before a second man came round the side of the house, stopped dead and retreated. She started the car, crashed the gears, and reversed to the lane. The second man had been Ted Sachs.

Again, she drove to Cattlegreen Nurseries, parked the car and took out her phone.

'Rachel! I don't know if this means anything, but I've just been to see Fiona Darling and her husband said she's not there and isn't coming back. And Ted Sachs was there and didn't want me to see him.' She let out a breath she didn't know she'd been holding.

'Are you all right?' Rachel sounded concerned.

'He was threatening – Darling. He said I was interfering.'

'Where are you now?'

'Outside Cattlegreen Nurseries.'

'Stay there.' Rachel was brisk. 'Someone will be along.'

Libby ended the call and realised someone was staring through the side window. She stifled a scream.

'Libby!' Joe and Nella's son, Owen, looked worried. 'Dad said he saw you and sent me out.'

Libby opened the door and got out.

'Oh, Owen, I'm sorry.' She leant against the car.

'Shall I make you some hot chocolate?' Winter or summer, Owen's cure for everything was hot chocolate. Libby patted him on the arm.

'That would be lovely,' she said. Can I come inside?'

Owen beamed and took Libby's arm.

Inside, Joe was just finishing with a customer, who looked at Libby curiously as she went out.

'Here,' said Joe, pulling out a battered chair. 'Sit down.'

'Chocolate,' Owen told his father and disappeared into the back of the building.

'Do you really want chocolate?' Joe asked.

'Do you know, I think I do,' said Libby. 'Comforting.'

'So what's up?'

'I just had an awkward encounter and the police told me to wait for them here. Sorry, Joe.'

'You getting up to your tricks again?' Joe shook his

head at her. 'What shall we do with you?'

Libby gave him a half-hearted smile. 'Wasn't my fault, honestly.'

'These murders at the old Garden, is it?'

'Yes – well, connected, I think. Really, Joe, I wasn't involved.'

'You went with that Mrs Darling, though, didn't you?' Joe jerked his head in the direction of Steeple Well. 'She comes in here.'

'Well, said Libby with a sigh, 'I don't think she'll be coming again.'

'Oh?'

'Her husband said she's gone.'

'Gone? They've only just come!'

'I think she's left him,' said Libby.

Owen came back with a large steaming mug. Libby smiled gratefully.

'You all right?' He asked her.

'Yes, I'm fine, thank you, Owen. How's Tessa?'

Owen and Tessa, an unlikely couple, had been married only a couple of years. Owen was stepfather to Davey and Kayley, Tessa's children. He smiled broadly.

'Fine, Libby, fine! We all are.'

The sound of a car on the gravelled forecourt caught the attention of all of them. Libby turned her head to see Rachel and the silent PC Robinson get out.

'Mrs Sarjeant,' said Rachel formally. 'Are you all right?'

Owen drew closer protectively.

'Yes thank you, DS Trent.' Libby smiled up at Owen.

302

'Owen's made me some hot chocolate.'

Owen smiled proudly back. Rachel looked slightly bewildered.

'Perhaps we could have a word?' she said.

'Of course.' Libby stood up and handed her mug to Owen. 'I'll be back in a minute,' she assured him. She followed Rachel outside.

'So tell me what happened,' Rachel said.

Libby described her encounter with Darling.

'I wasn't even sure that he was the David who had been with Preece and Whitelaw at that party, but when Sachs appeared… And he was so belligerent.' Libby frowned. 'You don't think he's done anything to Fiona, do you?'

'DI Maiden's gone over there to speak to him now. Although I don't suppose he'll get much out of him,' said Rachel. She moved a little nearer to Libby. 'It's all a bit confusing, isn't it?' she said confidentially.

'Yes.' Libby sighed. 'I'm glad it's your pigeon, not mine!'

'Yes, thanks!' said Rachel, with a wry smile. 'So there's nothing else you can tell us, then?'

'No, sorry.'

'We'll get on, then. You go back to your hot chocolate.'

Libby went back inside and retrieved her mug.

'Everything all right?' asked Joe.

'Yes, thanks, and thank you for providing shelter,' said Libby. 'I'll go home and get some lunch.'

She finished her hot chocolate, gave Owen a kiss, and went back to the car. Before she started it, she rang Fran to give her an update.

'Just don't do anything else, Lib,' said Fran. 'You've obviously got a bit close and they're getting rattled.'

'That presupposes they actually are involved with all this, then,' said Libby. 'And be fair, David Darling didn't come looking for me, I rather thrust myself on him.'

'Well, it proves that he is the David we'd heard about, doesn't it?'

'Yes, I think so. I wonder what he'll say to Rob Maiden.'

'Not much, I would imagine.'

'Yes, that's what Rachel said. Oh, well, I'll go home then. I might actually go and touch Harry up for lunch. I don't fancy being on my own yet.'

She parked the car in Allhallow's Lane and set off for the high street. As she passed the vicarage, Beth hailed her from the front door.

'What's been happening?' she asked. 'Police cars yesterday?'

Libby told her about the intruder. 'And I'm buying intruder proof hedging for the back fence,' she said. 'I'm a liability as a neighbour, aren't I?'

'You provide local interest, certainly,' said Beth. 'Wednesday, isn't it? All right if we come for a drink tonight? I think John'll be home.'

'Lovely,' said Libby. 'Shall we call for you on the way past?'

'No, we'll pop round after John's eaten. See you later, then.'

Libby went on her way to the Pink Geranium, resisting going in to Bob the butcher to ask him what he thought

304

about auditioning for Dame Amanda. She would think about that when the current problem had been resolved, or at least moved away from her vicinity.

To her surprise and slight annoyance, the Pink Geranium was almost full.

'Always room for a small one,' said Harry, coming forward to open the door. 'I'm a bit busy, as you can see, but you look as though you could do with a bit of pampering. Come through to the garden.'

The garden was actually a small courtyard which opened off the kitchen, and which Harry had intended to open to customers, but as there was also a staircase leading to the upstairs flat, currently let to Adam Sarjeant, he decided to keep it private. In the past it had been space for Libby to have a cigarette and today awoke a nostalgic longing which she attributed to delayed shock.

'Wine?' asked Harry. She nodded.

'So what's up?' he said, after delivering it.

'Scary encounter,' she said. 'Tell you when you've got a minute.'

He frowned, nodded, and went back to the kitchen.

'Do you want me to call Ben?' he called from inside.

'God, no!' Libby shuddered. Harry laughed.

One of Harry's floating population of waiting staff brought her a bowl of soup and a basket of bread, and she ate mechanically. Finally, Harry slid into the seat opposite and leant his elbows on the table.

'OK, come on, then.'

Libby sat back in her chair and picked up her wine glass. 'I went to see Fiona Darling.'

'Ah.' Harry nodded. 'And she wasn't there.'

'What? You knew?'

'Donna. She'd given Fiona her phone number in case she wanted anything. So she phoned yesterday. Said thank you for the help – which Donna hadn't really given her – but she was leaving her husband and going back to London.'

'Well, that's a relief,' said Libby. 'Rachel and I were wondering if... well, if something had happened to her.'

'If he'd bumped her off, you mean?'

'Yes. I think Donna had better tell the police.'

'You tell them, flower. Be more natural, wouldn't it?'

'I suppose so. I'll call later.'

'So that's who the encounter was with? Fiona's husband?'

'Yes, and he was threatening. And Ted Sachs was there. And I've sicked the police on to them. Oh, Lord,' Libby groaned.

'So does this prove any of your theories?'

'I don't know! Most of it was speculation, wasn't it?'

'The police seemed to take it seriously enough,' said Harry. 'And then there's white van man from yesterday – which, you naughty person, you didn't tell us about.'

'Sorry,' said Libby automatically.

'Any more news on that little episode?'

'No. Rachel says the van was stolen and found burnt out. And to be honest, it could have just been an opportunist burglar. It needn't have been anything to do with this – stuff.'

'Be a bit odd if it wasn't, petal.' Harry frowned at her.

'I'd watch myself, if I were you.'

'Oh, not you as well,' said Libby. 'Everyone's telling me to be careful.'

'Just shows how much we all love you,' said Harry, patting her hand. 'Now I've got to get back to my kitchen. A woman's work is never done.'

Libby finished her wine and stood up. 'How much...?' she began.

'Don't be a wazzock. Go on, go home.'

Libby sidled out through the kitchen and started for home. At the corner of Allhallow's Lane she remembered she was supposed to be telling the police about Donna's information, and fished her phone out of her basket. She called the incident room number, where she was immediately put through to Rachel.

'What's happened?'

'Nothing, don't worry. I just had to tell you something.' She relayed what Harry had told her. 'So nothing's happened to Fiona. Did DI Maiden get anything out of Darling?'

'Well, not a lot,' said Rachel.

'Hang on,' said Libby. 'I'm at my front door. I'll just put you down for a minute and let myself in.' She dropped the phone into her basket and found her keys.

'Well,' said a voice, as she stepped inside. 'If it isn't the indefatigable Mrs Sarjeant.'

She stopped dead. Sitting at ease on the sofa, legs neatly crossed, was Sir Nigel Preece.

Chapter Thirty Five

Libby dropped her basket.

'Do you know who I am?' he said. 'I don't believe we've ever met.'

Libby cleared her throat. 'I – I've seen pictures.'

'Of course you have. You'll have done quite a lot of research, won't you? I know a lot about you.' He smiled. 'And you know several of my friends, I believe.'

'D-do I?'

'You saw my friend David – Dave the Rave, we used to call him – only this morning. Forgotten already? And dear Ted. You saw him, too, although you had met him before.'

'Er – yes.' Libby prayed Rachel hadn't rung off and could hear all this clearly. At least Sir Nigel hadn't decided to go through her basket.

'And now, my dear Mrs Sarjeant, or may I call you Libby? Do tell me why you and your friend have been so assiduously looking into things that don't concern you?'

'I haven't! When you've got two bodies in a house belonging to a friend, you're naturally interested.'

'Unnaturally, I should say. I don't appreciate the interest.'

'Why not?' asked Libby bravely. 'If you didn't have

anything to do with the bodies? And,' she went on, 'how did you get in here?'

Unconcerned, Sir Nigel gestured towards the kitchen, and Libby turned her head to see a scared-looking Ted Sachs holding a struggling Sidney.

'Put my cat down!' Libby screeched. Sidney and Sachs both jumped, and Sidney lashed out, catching Sachs on the cheek and jumping free.

'Dear me,' said Sir Nigel. 'Never mind, Ted. I'm sure it won't kill you. As we were saying, Libby. Our associate yesterday managed to cut the padlock chain on your back gate. Quite successful, we thought. You were never in danger. So, we just let ourselves in. Luckily, we didn't encounter your nosy neighbour.'

No, thought Libby, because Mrs Mardle would be at Carpenter's Hall with Flo and Hetty.

'Come along then, my dear. Tell us what you've found out?'

'Nothing,' said Libby bravely. 'I don't know anything.'

'I wonder why the police were being – let's say, a tad intrusive, then? All off their own bat, was it? And your – what? Partner? Boyfriend? Why was he so interested in the Garden Hotel?'

'Nothing to do with you!' Come along, Rachel, prayed Libby. 'Get me out of this.'

'Such a shame if he lost his lovely new hop garden – and his brewery.' Sir Nigel narrowed his eyes. 'And his dear old mother. Now, what about her?'

This time Libby couldn't speak. She discovered that she was shaking from head to foot.

Sir Nigel gestured to Ted, who came forward and grabbed Libby's arms. She struggled, but Ted held on. Sir Nigel stood up.

'Now, let's go,' he said. 'The front way, I think. Just like proper guests. Turn her round, Ted.'

Ted manhandled her in front of him and reached past to open the door. Libby could barely put one foot in front of the other as he pushed her outside.

And suddenly there was Ian.

Behind him, Rachel, Rob Maiden and a positive bevy of uniformed officers, some of them, Libby noticed, armed, came forward. Sir Nigel, close behind Libby, tried to turn back, but Ian was too quick for him. Pushing Libby aside and into the arms of Rob Maiden, he grabbed an elegantly clothed sleeve and pulled. Sir Nigel staggered and fell backwards. Libby hardly heard the words of the formal arrest. She was too busy collapsing onto the pavement.

Rachel came forward and helped her to sit up. 'Well done,' she whispered. 'Brilliant in fact. Where was it?'

'Where -?'

'Your phone. We put it on a speaker. We recorded everything.'

'In my basket. I kept hoping you hadn't switched off.' Libby sat up straight. 'What's happening?'

'Ian's arrested Preece and Sachs. DCI Connell, I mean. Can you stand up?'

Libby was helped to her feet, and ushered gently back into her own house. There was no sign of Sidney. Ian and PC Robinson, smiling broadly, followed, with, surprisingly, Mrs Mardle.

'I just came home in the middle of it, dear,' she said, her eyes bright with interest. 'Now that nice policeman's gong to let me make you a lovely cup of tea.'

Libby, mouth agape, looked at Ian, who nodded. 'Perhaps Mrs Mardle could make us all one?' he said.

'Oh, yes, dear!' said Mrs Mardle. 'I'll find everything. Proper tea, isn't it?'

Libby lay back on the sofa and wondered when she would wake up.

'We won't know the details yet,' said Ian, 'but Sachs is in the mood to crack, and so's David Darling. I don't know about Nicholas Whitelaw, yet. We don't know where he went after he left here. It certainly wasn't home.'

'But they're definitely guilty?' asked Libby. 'Of both murders?'

'We think so, but which one of them we don't know.'

'Did you know about their group from school?'

'The Little Foxes? Yes. And quite a lot more besides. There was rather an unpleasant club at that school. We think it might still be in existence.'

Mrs Mardle appeared with a tray Libby couldn't ever remember using before and placed it on the table in the window.

'We'll just let it draw a bit,' she said. 'How are you now, dear? Does Colin know? And your Ben?'

'Ben's on his way,' said Rachel. 'Accompanied. He was in a bit of a state.'

'Oh, hell,' said Libby.

'And Mr Hardcastle has been informed,' said Ian. 'He wanted to come, too, but we persuaded him not to. I think

311

your sitting room's quite crowded enough already.'

Mrs Mardle poured out tea, Ian asked everyone to sit down, and Libby looked round at the most unlikely tea party she had ever hosted.

'You haven't told me off yet,' she said to Ian, and heard both Rachel's and PC Robinson's in-drawn breath.

He grinned at her. 'I really can't think why I should. You didn't let Sir Nigel in, did you? And you were in the middle of giving DS Trent important information. Not to mention your quick thinking about your mobile.'

'Actually, it wasn't,' confessed Libby. 'I'd already dropped it into my basket to let myself in. I just left it there. I didn't want them finding it.'

There were murmurs of approval all round, just as the door opened and Ben walked in. He looked round the room, went straight to Libby and enfolded her in a bear hug. She was a little surprised and disconcerted to find that he, too, was shaking.

'Bit too close for comfort, he said gruffly.

'We'll just finish our tea,' said Ian, 'and get out of your way. Libby can give us a formal statement tomorrow.'

Rachel and Robinson swallowed unhealthy amounts of tea, and Mrs Mardle made to clear the tray.

'Leave it,' said Ben, 'thank you all the same.' He gave Mrs Mardle an absentminded pat.

Ian shepherded them all outside, pausing in the doorway.

'Feel up to the pub tonight?'

Ben looked at Libby. 'Do you?'

'Yes,' she said firmly. 'I want to be normal.'

312

'Good,' said Ian. 'Assuming all the local suspects will be there, I'll try and get along to give you one of my famous round-ups.'

'Is that allowed?' asked Libby, with a mischievous grin.

'Oh, you're better!' said Ian, and left.

Ben spent the rest of the afternoon treating his beloved like a piece of fragile china, until she threw a cushion at him and he burst out laughing.

'Shall I phone Fran and Guy and ask them to come over?' he said. 'Fran will want to know.'

'Yes, please. Beth and John are coming, too.'

'I'd better ask Tim if we can book the bar as a private hire, then,' said Ben, pulling out his phone.

Fran and Guy arrived at number seventeen just after eight o'clock and were told the whole story.

'I don't want to go through it all tonight,' said Libby. 'I'll tell Harry and Peter another time. We just want to know about the arrests. And the murders.'

By the time they walked into the pub, Patti and Anne were already there with Beth and John Cole, all agog.

Ben grinned at them all. 'I can see you've heard something's been going on. But give us a chance to get the drinks and we'll tell you.'

Anne was obviously bursting with curiosity, and Patti had to keep shutting her up. Beth and John laughed at her. By the time Guy and Ben came back with drinks, there were enough chairs round the table, and Tim, grinning, had obligingly locked the door into the other bar.

'Where's Colin?' asked Libby. 'He should be here.'

313

'Oh, he popped his head round the door,' said Patti. 'He seemed embarrassed.'

'I'll go up and get him,' said Ben. 'I've already heard the story.'

'Tell us, then, Libby!' said Anne. 'Beth says there was a police raid on your house! And police there yesterday, too. What's going on?'

Libby gave them a brief outline of the events of the last thirty-six hours, finishing just as Ben reappeared with Colin.

'It's all right, he knows about what happened earlier,' said Ben.

Colin came quickly round the table, and Libby was enfolded in another bear hug. 'I'm so sorry, Libby,' he muttered.

'Why?' Libby kissed his cheek. 'You didn't do anything.'

'But you've been trying to help me. It's my fault...'

'Don't be daft,' said Ben.

'Really, Colin, please don't blame yourself,' said Fran. 'She's quite capable of getting into trouble all by herself.'

'Oi!' said Libby, indignant at the laughter which broke out all round the table.

'What's the joke?' asked Peter, coming through from the front door. 'And I almost had to bribe Tim to let me in.'

'We're having one of Ian's round-ups,' said Libby, 'so not open to the public.'

'Ah, case solved then? I heard there'd been some shenanigans this afternoon.'

'Actually, we've got Harry to thank,' said Libby. 'If he

hadn't told me about Fiona and persuaded me to tell the police, I could have been – well, I don't know. Kidnapped at the very least.'

'OK – explain,' said Peter. 'And I don't think we'll tell him. You know how he'd crow about it.'

'Are you talking about me?' Harry came in, still in his chef's whites.

'What are you doing here?' asked Ben.

'Oh, charming!' Harry tossed his head. 'Persuaded my girls and boys they could manage without me. We hadn't got any more bookings, so we put the closed sign up. I didn't want to miss anything.'

Libby had just finished explaining once again what had happened that afternoon, when the door opened again and Edward and Ian came in.

'I had to be in at the kill, so to speak,' said Edward. 'Anyone want a drink?'

Eventually, the expanded circle was settled and they all looked to Ian to begin.

'How about if I just tell the story as it happened from the start?' he said. 'Beginning with the infamous party you attended, Colin.' There was unanimous assent, although Colin looked a bit apprehensive.

'Nigel Preece hosted a party held in the rather ramshackle barn on his father's property. There had been illegal parties held there in the past, but these seem to have tailed off. Nigel and his group of friends, three of whom you know about -'

'Who?' said Anne.

'Oscar Whitelaw's father, Nicholas-'

'The boy who was found first,' nodded Beth.

'David Darling, husband of Fiona Darling who found his body,' Ian went on, 'and Ted Sachs who gave Mrs Darling the keys to the Garden Hotel. There were more of them, but we needn't worry about them now. They were an unsavoury group, who had all been to school together.'

'Foxgrove?' asked Beth.

'Yes, Foxgrove. There is still a rather nasty club at the school, which has traditions of its own, as many of these places do, including what they call blooding rites.'

The women expressed disgust.

'No wonder Ossie was unhappy,' said Beth, looking rather unhappy herself.

'He wasn't old enough to become a member of the Little Foxes,' said Ian.

'I do object to that name,' muttered Libby.

'Well, you needn't any more. We've now got enough evidence to have it shut down – and possibly, the school, too.'

'No!'

'It turns out that Sir Nigel was using the club as a recruitment centre. And funding the school into the bargain. Anyway, to go on with the story, this rather unpleasant group were in the habit of attending parties, preferably where they weren't known, and, while they were there, indulging in a little bit of gang rape.'

This time there were expressions of outrage.

'However, this became known, as far as we can tell, and parties, including the ones held in the barn, faded out. So Nigel decided to hold his own party, and invite all the locals who hadn't been regulars at the previous events.'

'I was going to ask about that,' said Guy. 'Why did all those people go to that party if it was known about Preece's activities.'

'The previous events were attended by a rather different crowd, mostly out of the area. And the girls who were attacked – and some men – were paid off. Someone – often Ted, he tells us – would go and see them with cash. Never, of course, a cheque. So they kept their mouths shut.'

'How did Ted get in with them?' asked Fran. 'He was hardly public school material.'

'He'd had a run-in with Preece, involving drugs, we believe, and was thereafter kept on a leash.'

'Even now?' asked Patti.

'I'm coming to that,' said Ian. 'As you know, our singer, Shareen Wallis, made a play for Colin here. Then a group of them, we believe the Little Foxes, also started plaguing him. Finally, Preece himself – sorry, Colin.'

Colin, looking miserable, shook his head. 'No, go on. I want to know.'

'So that was when Colin asked his friend John to take him home. That's right, isn't it?' He turned to Colin, who nodded. 'And then, Preece went to keep the assignation he'd made – with Shareen.'

'It *was* Preece, then,' said Libby.

'Yes – with, and we haven't had this confirmed yet, Whitelaw and Darling. Unfortunately for them, they were a little too rough.'

'Oh, God,' said Patti. The others looked shocked. 'I'm allowed,' she said.

317

'And Ted was commissioned with getting rid of the body?' said Ben.

Ian nodded.

'Why did he choose the Garden?' asked Colin. 'I didn't know him.'

'He played bat and trap.'

There was a satisfied 'Ah!' from the whole group.

'Again, as far as we can tell, he knew about the cellar door, even though neither of you remember it,' he said to Colin and Ben, 'and he knew the cellar wasn't in use. He didn't bring her there that night, but a couple of days later. We don't know where she was kept in between.

'And so,' he went on, 'we come to poor Ossie Whitelaw. We know he'd run away from home, and came back to the place he had felt safe with his so-called mates. His father had bought the house in Steeple Well to be near enough to keep an eye on the old Garden, and employed Ted to do some work for old times' sake. When he had to sell up –'

'He sold it to the Darlings so *David* could keep an eye on it!' said Libby triumphantly.

'And he also employed Ted Sachs, partly to keep an eye on his wife.'

'But what about Ossie?' asked Beth.

'Ted used to pay surreptitious visits to the Garden to see that nothing was amiss. He knew about the boys who used to meet there, and he was worried they might find the body. One night he went there. And there was Ossie.' Ian stopped. 'I'm afraid he got rather hysterical at this point, but it seems that Ossie was coming out of the cellar door in

318

the kitchen. Ted didn't stop to ask what he was doing, but simply lashed out.'

They were all silent for a moment.

'And then,' said Ian, 'they all had a shock. Colin sent Ted the keys. As far as they knew, this meant the place was going to be sold. So Ted came up with his plan.'

'Plan?' said Harry. 'I don't see -'

'Oh, I do,' said Fran. 'Give Fiona the idea of the community centre, so she would give him the opportunity to perhaps do maintenance? And David Darling would be there to make sure she toed the line.'

'Exactly. And they all did what they were told because Preece had them over a barrel.'

'Couldn't they deny what he said about them, though?' asked Anne.

'I gather he has proof,' said Ian wryly. 'Not, of course, that he has said anything yet, simply surrounding himself with as many solicitors as he can. Not to mention one of the best criminal barristers in England. I've never met a more thoroughly nasty piece of work. I almost feel sorry for Ted Sachs.'

'And Fiona Darling really is all right?' asked Libby.

'Yes, we got hold of her at her mother's. She'd apparently been suspecting something for a long time, and when the investigation began hotting up she got scared. She doesn't seem to be worried about either her husband or Mr Sachs.'

'A heartless floozie, in fact,' said Edward, and made them all laugh.

'So that's it, then,' said Peter. 'Clever Connell does it
319

again.'

'I think Libby deserves a good deal of the praise in this one,' said Ian, 'not least because of her performance today. Oh, hell.' He thumped his head. 'I wish I hadn't said that!'

MURDER BY THE BARREL
Lesley Cookman

When the sleepy village of Steeple Martin announces its very first beer festival, the locals are excited. Beer, sun and music, what could possibly go wrong?

But when an unexpected death shakes the village, it's up to Libby Sarjeant to solve the puzzle.

MURDER AND THE GLOVEMAKER'S SON
Lesley Cookman

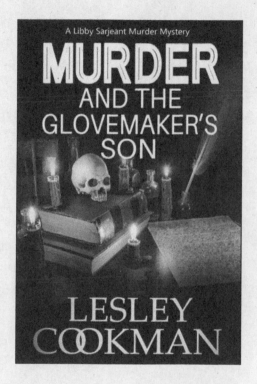

The Oast Theatre in Steeple Martin is hosting a touring production of *Twelfth Night*, but when a document goes missing along with its owner, it seems that the play may not go ahead at all.

When a body turns up, Libby Sarjeant and Fran Wolfe become involved with the investigation with the help, naturally, of their friends and relatives.